CW00862802

Titles by P. L. Byers

Divine Intervention
A Life Worth Living

Sisters of My Heart Trilogy
A Reason to Dream
(Book One)
A Reason to Hope
(Book Two)
A Reason to Trust
(Book Three)

Out of the Darkness Series
Love's True Destiny
Always You
The Unexpected Truth
My Only Chance
A Single Night
My Every Thought

Who's Laughing Now
Purposeful Betrayal

PURPOSEFUL BETRAYAL

P. L. BYERS

authorHOUSE®

AuthorHouse™
1663 Liberty Drive
Bloomington, IN 47403
www.authorhouse.com
Phone: 833-262-8899

Published by AuthorHouse 08/27/2021

ISBN: 978-1-6655-3579-3 (sc)
ISBN: 978-1-6655-3577-9 (hc)
ISBN: 978-1-6655-3578-6 (e)

Library of Congress Control Number: 2021917172

Print information available on the last page.

Author photo taken by Karen Moriarty Photography at www.kemphoto.com
P. L. Byers' website created and maintained by www.bigpresenceagency.com

Contents

Dedication

Who would ever have thought we would see a worldwide Pandemic? You read about these things in novels and hear of people predicting them. But to experience it ourselves has been, and continues to feel, unreal.

I dedicate this book to all the first responders who have put themselves in harm's way to care for others during these unprecedented times. From the doctors and nurses in the hospitals who took care of the sick and dying, to the police officers and paramedics and fire fighters who responded when called upon, to the grocery store workers who kept our stores open so we could buy food. Thank you from the bottom of my heart!

There are so many more who stepped up without any recognition or kudos for their efforts. Neighbors looking out for neighbors, simple positive messages written on a sidewalks or on rocks strategically placed around to uplift people as they walk, to name only a few. In this stressful environment any small act of kindness goes a long way. Thank you to those (and you know who you are) for every little thing you thought to do that may have impacted someone in need. Your deeds may not have made the news, but you can be sure that your kindness changed someone's life.

Acknowledgment

I am so blessed to have a kind, supportive husband encouraging me in my writing endeavors. Thank you, Mark, for always caring about my dreams and for being there when I need you.

I heavily rely on my beta reader when it comes to reviewing my manuscripts. Lisa, you are my first line of defense in catching things that I miss when I'm writing, and you do such a terrific job. It means everything to me that you always jump on board when I need your advice, thoughts and opinions. You are simply the very best!!

Thank you to my editor, Noel. No matter how busy you are, you always willingly take on my manuscripts and it means the world to me that I can count on you. I appreciate all the time and effort you put into them. You do amazing work, and my manuscripts are always better with your critiques and revisions!

Chapter One

BRINLEY CREW PACED the small cabin wringing her hands in frustration. Last night had been a horrible night. For two years she had worked hard at keeping the memories at bay. For two years she had worked through the pain, compartmentalizing each moment into a metaphorical box and safely tucking them away, somewhere in the back of her mind. It did her no good to remember. It only brought excruciating agony and debilitating pain. No, memories were for those fortunate souls who had happy things to remember. Her life was a series of losses and better left to the murky recesses of her mind.

So why now? What had triggered the nightmares to come to her at this particular time after years of tenaciously working to keep them at bay?

Sighing in frustration, Brinley made herself a cup of tea. When it was ready, she grabbed a blanket from the back of the couch and made her way outside to the makeshift patio and sat in the only chair next to a picnic table and a small fire pit. Wrapping the blanket tightly around her, she settled in and took a sip of her tea.

Listening to the bubbling sound of the rain-laden stream, Brinley closed her eyes and let the sound lull her into a better mood.

She loved this place. The cabin was not much to speak of. To say it was rustic was being kind, but it suited her needs. And while she had a comfortable bed, electricity, and a working washer and dryer, its most redeeming quality was the seclusion. The nearest cabin to hers was at least a mile away with trees and rocky terrain separating them. The fact that it had been left empty the past year was an added bonus.

Brinley had hoped that living in Green River, Wyoming, for the past few years would give her the solitude to heal from the devastating loss of both her husband and young daughter. Her friends had tried to convince her that running away wouldn't help her recover from what had happened, but their concerns fell on deaf ears. The thought of returning to a normal life without her family was too much to bear. So, once husband and daughter were cremated and buried next to each other and she'd endured their memorial service, she searched online for a secluded cabin nearly four hours from Casper, Wyoming. She signed a three-year lease and walked away from everything that was familiar to her.

In the beginning, she never left the cabin. Her days consisted of lying on the mattress in her bedroom, curled in a fetal position, sobbing until her head pounded, then moving to the couch where she would sit and stare blankly at the knotted wood of the log cabin. Day and night ceased to exist. She moved robotically, eating only when she felt like she needed to, relying on cups of tea and stale crackers to keep the hunger pangs at bay.

Eventually the tears finally stopped, leaving in their place an emptiness that nothing could fill. Brinley tried reading a few of the books that she had brought with her but when the third chapter came and went and she couldn't remember a single thing she had read, she finally gave up. Instead, she started taking walks. At first, she started with a few laps outside around the cabin. When she could do that without becoming breathless, she increased how many times she went around. Before she knew it, Brinley started venturing out further, across the small bridge that spanned the width of the stream, down the gravel driveway and back. Within another month, her walks extended from beyond the driveway to a path she found nearly a hundred yards from the property she was renting. Gradually Brinley started jogging and before she knew it the exercise became a part of her daily routine.

The gaunt, hallow lines of her face were slowly disappearing and the bruised skin beneath her eyes was turning back to a healthy pink.

The one thing that remained was the desire to be left alone. The only time she left the cabin was when she needed to resupply her cabinets. Whereas before teas bags and crackers were her staples, she was now branching out to proteins and leafy vegetables. Cans of tuna were always on hand, helping her to delay the inevitable trip into town. The locals had gotten used to their reclusive neighbor, nodding politely when she made her trips into the small store, keeping conversation to a minimum, respecting the privacy she obviously sought.

Brinley adjusted to the climate of her secluded cabin. The first winter quickly taught her that she needed to keep her supply of wood at a certain level. While the cabin did have an oil-burning furnace, it was old, and she learned that she couldn't rely on it at all times. After one particular cold night spent wrapped in several blankets in an effort not to freeze, she set out the next morning to find a way to have wood delivered. There were some comforts she was willing to pay for and heat ranked up there with a working bathroom. Rustic was one thing; cold was something else entirely. And since she wasn't exactly a wood-chopping lumberjack, she needed to find an alternative.

After inquiring at the small store she frequented, Brinley made her way to the home of an older gentleman who seemed to like his solitude as much as she did. When the gruff man answered the door, she explained that the store owner had referred him and asked about wood deliveries. After a few minutes of bargaining back and forth, Brinley left with a smile on her face, satisfied with the deal she'd made. From that point on, she got regular deliveries of perfectly cut wood, dumped at the end of her driveway every other Sunday during the winter months. It didn't bother her to carry it to her cabin and stack it herself. She liked the exercise and she got to keep her privacy. As long as she put cash in an envelope and put it in the rusted tin that served as her mailbox for him to grab after the delivery, they were good. It was a system that worked for them both.

Draining the rest of the tea from her mug, Brinley pushed the blanket off her shoulders and stood. It was time to get dressed and start her run. While the current temperature was just a little above sixty, it wasn't going to stay cool for much longer. August tended to bring much warmer temperatures in the daytime hours and according to the weather report, today was going to be no different.

What started out as a quick three-mile run turned into a longer five-mile run in the hopes of clearing her mind from the dreams that had plagued her night. Brinley figured that if she went to bed exhausted, she would be able to close her eyes and not see the faces of her husband and daughter. The memories of what she had lost were just too painful, which was one of the main reasons she refused to put out framed pictures of them. The reminder of what she had lost was simply too much to bear.

Walking into the cabin, Brinley grabbed a bottle of water from her dilapidated but adequate refrigerator, leaned against the scarred linoleum counter and drained the bottle. Tossing it in the garbage, she went into the small bathroom and stood under the weak stream of cool water, washing the sweat of her exercise away.

After several minutes, she shut the taps off and grabbed a towel, drying off before stepping from the tub. When she was dressed, she went back into her living room and made herself a sandwich, listening to an old radio as she munched on her lunch.

This was the worst part of her day. Getting from lunchtime to when she could finally go to bed. There was no television to keep her mind busy. No Internet that allowed her to stream videos or surf the web. Her cell phone didn't even get reception from the cabin, so it was sitting in a drawer, its battery long dead from not being used. In fact, the only way she had to reach the outside world was if she went to the store where she bought her groceries and used their Internet. It wasn't a fancy Internet café like they had in Casper, just a small table near the front of the store, but it got the job done when she needed to pay any bills online. The old man who rented her the place had offered to bring someone out to investigate getting a few modern conveniences, especially when he learned how long she'd wanted to live there, but Brinley had refused. She no longer wanted anything to do with a world that had taken everything from her. It was best if she lived the rest of her life alone. You couldn't take anything from someone who already had lost everything.

Shaking her head to dispel the melancholy that was invading her thoughts, Brinley finally took out one of the puzzles that had been left behind by someone who had previously rented the cabin and sat down at the kitchen table. For the next hour she removed the pieces of the thousand-piece puzzle box and organized them into categories by color and the straight edge border pieces. When that task was complete, she started connecting the border before beginning to work on the interior. The only time she stepped away from her task was to make a quick salad for dinner.

By midnight she had most of the puzzle put together. Usually, she couldn't stop a project until it was completed but her eyes ached from the strain and her shoulders hurt from being hunched over the kitchen table. As much as she tried avoiding going to bed, she could no longer put it off.

Scooting her chair back, Brinley stood and rubbed her eyes. Sighing heavily, she made her way to the tiny bathroom to brush her teeth and put her nightgown on. When she was done, she crawled under the covers of her bed and laid with her head on the soft pillow, praying for pleasant dreams. As her eyes drifted closed, she thought of clear blue waters, crashing waves, and hot sandy beaches.

Chapter Two

Smoke filled her lungs. As hard as she tried to take in air, only the acrid stench of burning wood seeped in. She was going to die and there was nothing she could do about it.

Clawing at her throat, with tears streaming down her face, Brinley tried one last time to stand but something was holding her legs from being able to move. Thrashing around, her hand connected with something hard, the pain shooting up her arm, waking her from the nightmare gripping her mind.

Drawing in several shaky breaths, Brinley opened her eyes and looked around the room. No smoke, thank God. Just her mind forcing her to relive the worst moments of her life.

Frustrated, she kicked the blankets to loosen the grip they had around her legs and shakily stood and brushed her shoulder-length hair from her eyes. *Damnit,* she whispered, walking into the bathroom to splash cold water on her face.

Walking back to the bedroom, she glanced at the clock on the bedside table and groaned. Four o'clock in the morning. Knowing there was no way she would be able to go back to sleep, she threw on the tattered robe she kept on the chair in her room and drew it on. Once in the kitchen, she put water in the bent pan she kept on the stove and turned the burner on. Grabbing a mug, she stuck a tea bag in it, a teaspoonful of sugar and waited for the water to boil. When it was steeping, she carried the mug to the table and looked down at the puzzle. *Why not,* she grumbled out loud and sat down to finish her project from the night before.

By the time the sun was starting to rise, Brinley had completed the jigsaw puzzle, made her bed, brushed her teeth, and was dressed and ready to start her day. She did a few simple stretches to get warmed up, then went outside to start her run.

Inhaling the crisp morning air, she looked around in appreciation. The quietness of her surroundings had ceased to bother her. She took solace in the fact that there was no one around to interrupt her morning runs. She liked being out on the trails alone, left to her thoughts, not having to interact with anyone.

Brinley started out with a slow pace. She wasn't in a hurry to get back to the cabin. Especially after the nightmares of the past two nights. Instead, she slowly jogged along, taking in the beautiful view as the sun peeked through the trees, chasing away the last of the mist that hung in the early morning air. Dew dripped onto her heated skin as she brushed past the long hanging branches, causing a burst of goose bumps to cover her arms.

Several times Brinley had to slow her pace after slipping on the damp, leaf covered trail. She was an early riser by nature, but she wasn't typically running at this early hour. Usually by the time she got started the moisture had gone from the night before. This morning, however, she needed to go carefully because of the dampness.

By the second mile she hit her stride and was able to pick up the pace a bit. Sweat started to drip from her skin as the sun heated the day. Still, Brinley kept going, hoping the exhaustion from extending her run would help her to forget the nightmares.

Why now? Why after months of peaceful dreams was she being plagued? It wasn't as if she'd been thinking about the past. It was behind her. She'd worked very hard to make sure that it stayed there. So, what was it that was bringing everything back again? She'd done her time. She'd cried and raged at the world, then worked hard to move forward. So again…why now?

Heaving a deep breath, Brinley picked up her pace a little more. Unsure whether she was out to torture her body or try to outrun the nightmares, she kept going, ignoring the signs her body was trying to give her. In fact, Brinley was so distracted with her thoughts that she completely missed a root that was sticking up through a pile of leaves. Her foot caught on it, jolting her body to a stop as her foot stuck between it and the ground. She went down, her arms flailing about as she tried to break her fall. Her body hit the ground with a jarring bump, her head hitting something hard as she landed.

Lying on the ground motionless, Brinley could do nothing but try to breathe. Minutes went by before she could even consider trying to move. Her entire body was nothing but a lump of quivering flesh. The pain radiating from her ankle and head made her so nauseous that she thought she was going to throw up. Panic started to well as she began to realize her circumstance. She was in the middle of nowhere with no way to get help. In fact, she'd been so distracted with her thoughts that she'd veered onto a path that she'd never been on before. She didn't even know exactly where she was or how close civilization was to her.

"Calm down," she lectured herself aloud. Panicking was only going to make matters worse.

Rolling onto her back, she pushed herself up to a sitting position. Brinley gingerly touched her head where it had hit the ground. She'd just managed to turn her head as she fell forward but didn't protect it fast enough. She felt a large lump that had already begun to form on her right temple. When she pulled her hand away, she looked in horror at the red smear on her fingertips. Blood couldn't be a good sign. And by the amount on her hand, it was obvious that she had a good-sized gash at her temple.

Moving her leg to disentangle her foot from the root, Brinley inhaled sharply when pain shot up and through her knee. Placing her hands behind her back, she tried scooting backward to dislodge her ankle, being careful not to twist her knee in any direction. When she was finally free of the protruding limb, she reached down to pull the leg of her jogging pants up. When the material reached her calf, Brinley examined her ankle, groaning when she how swollen it was above her sneaker. She wasn't sure what was most concerning. The lump and gash at her temple, her swollen ankle, or the pain that screamed up her leg whenever she moved her knee. How on earth was she going to get out of this mess?

Brushing at the blood that had trailed down her cheek, Brinley looked around, hoping she would be able to see another jogger somewhere in her vicinity. When minutes had passed and her prayers went unanswered, she gave up and started to look around to see if there was a sturdy branch that had fallen near her that she could use as a crutch to help her walk. Finding nothing, she used her hands to scoot to the edge of the trail hoping to find something that could help. As her knee and ankle bumped the ground with her every movement, tears began to streak down her face.

She'd moved no more than five feet before she gave up and sat on the damp ground and gave in to the overwhelming emotions of helplessness that consumed her. When her pity party was over, Brinley tried screaming, hoping to get the attention of anyone who might be nearby. When her voice eventually became hoarse, she gave up, electing to conserve her energy for her next attempt at standing.

Gritting her teeth, she forced herself to scoot to the left, stopping to brush leaves aside in search of a branch, before moving again and repeating the process. Finally, on the third attempt, her hand hit something hard and she quickly pushed the leaves aside, squealing in delight when she unearthed a thick, four-foot branch that was just what she'd been looking for.

After resting for a few minutes, Brinley braced herself against the pain she knew would come and brought her body up on her one good knee, using the newly found branch to stabilize her. When she'd stopped shaking, she took a deep breath to ready herself for the final move to standing on her good foot. With jerky movements, she slowly raised up, putting all her body weight on her good leg while holding tightly to the stick for balance. She'd nearly accomplished her goal when she heard a crack that echoed through the dense wooded area. As the branch broke in half, she fell backwards, slamming onto the hard dirt, hitting the back of her head as she landed.

Brinley laid there, breathing through the pain and cursing at the gods that seemed to thwart her every move. Her personal life, her family life, this damn morning run, nothing was easy for her. Every time she thought she was going to find a sliver of something close to contentment, it was ripped from her grasp. Even the happiness she was finally beginning to feel in her running had now become a nightmare. If she made it out of this predicament and healed enough to get back on her feet, she'd be damned if she ever went out jogging again. Exercise sucked anyway!

As the sun topped the trees, Brinley lay on the ground feeling sorry for herself. She'd lost track of time but by the heat that was beginning to bake her through the shade of the leaves, she knew it was well past noon. She was exhausted, in pain, and her stomach was growling from lack of food. The cup of tea she'd had that morning hadn't gone very far and now she was cursing that she hadn't taken a few minutes to eat at least something, much less grab a bottle of water to take with her. Talk about stupidity!

Sweat formed on Brinley's skin and rolled down her face and neck, dripping onto the ground below her. It wasn't until she felt something crawling up her body that she realized it was a bug and not the moisture rolling off her. Shrieking in disgust, she frantically rubbed at her skin, trying to push off any creatures trying to invade her space.

She couldn't just lie here! Lecturing herself to block out the pain, she spent the next hour or so crawling along the path, scraping her hands and elbows in the rough dirt as she went. At certain intervals she stopped to yell for help, listening briefly for anyone calling back before she crawled some more. She rested only when she was out of breath and forced herself to keep going when she thought of how cold the night would get and what little protection she had on. Food ceased to be a concern as did the dirt that was getting caked into the cuts on her hands and elbows. Pain had long since become a dull ache, the fear of being attacked by animals that came out at night a larger concern than her comfort.

Dusk was just about on her when sheer exhaustion overcame her to the point that she finally gave up. She couldn't move another inch. Pain and tiredness were so overwhelming that she didn't care what would happen to her. She was done.

"You win," she screamed into the woods, flopping onto her back and looking up at the waning sun through the trees. "I can't go any more. You win," she finished on a whisper. "I quit."

Dropping her arm over her eyes to block out the trees, she wept into her sleeve. When she had no more tears to cry, and her head ached violently, she let her arm fall back to the ground and closed her eyes. She thought of Annie's beautiful face. She recalled the smell of her sweet little body after a bath as they snuggled together before bedtime. She remembered her infectious little laugh that made any bad day so much better just by hearing it. Her daughter who had been her entire world… right up until the day she died.

As Brinley laid there, thinking of her daughter, she felt a surge of anger. Who would remember her daughter if she just gave up? She was all that was left of their family. Who would make sure that the house that was left standing was taken care of? Her daughter's things were still in that house!

With a renewed surge of determination, Brinley rolled back to her stomach. She'd crawl all the damn way back to Casper if she had to! It was not going to end like this if she had anything to say about it.

"Give up my ass," she mumbled out loud, as she began the arduous task of moving forward.

Several minutes later she heard the suspicious snap of a twig somewhere ahead of her. Stopping, she rolled over to sit up and braced her back against the stump of a tree that was near her. She sat still, listening for any movement. If it was an animal, she needed to find something to defend herself with—and quickly! It took a few seconds, but she found several large rocks and placed them at her side. Reaching behind her, she found a small branch that was about three feet long and four inches in diameter. It wasn't much but at least it was something.

Another snap sounded as Brinley picked up the first rock and held it above her head, ready to launch it at whatever was coming her way. About a second before she threw it, her eyes focused enough for her to realize it wasn't an animal heading toward her, but a man.

At about the same time Brinley realized it was a human form and started to lower the rock, her eyes connected with a set of the clearest blue eyes she had ever seen. She watched as he stopped short and stared at her for a few seconds.

"Well, what do we have here?" he asked with a grin.

Chapter Three

Wells Kennedy was completely taken aback at finding a woman sitting on the trail he was jogging on. The last thing he expected, especially since it was getting late, was running across another person in this particular area. Known for the rocky terrain and wild animals that scavenged the area at night, most people had enough common sense to steer clear this late in the day.

It wasn't until he really looked at her that he gasped. "Oh, God. You're hurt," he said in concern as he dropped to his knees in front of her. "What the hell happened to you?"

Brinley frowned at the tone of his voice. "I had an accident," she informed him tartly. Seriously, what did he think happened to her?

"I'm sorry," he apologized. "That didn't come out right." Hearing her stomach growl, he looked at her in concern. "How long have you been out here?"

"A long time," she said wearily. "I started my run around six this morning. I fell a few hours after I began."

"Good lord," he exclaimed. "Where's your running pack?" he asked looking around. Seeing none, he looked back at her, beginning to suspect that she was a newbie to running and hadn't started her morning prepared at all for what could happen. Like a damn fall!

"I didn't carry one," she answered, confirming his suspicions.

"Water? Cell phone?"

When she shook her head indicating she had none of those things, he huffed in disgust. "You're reckless," he lectured as he reached for the strap on his shoulder and pulled down the backpack that she hadn't seen hidden behind him.

Wells quickly uncapped a bottle of water he'd taken from the pack and handed it to her. He watched as she chugged the entire bottle, stopping only when the last drop hit her tongue. Sighing in pleasure, she handed the empty container back to him.

"Thank you," she murmured, embarrassed that she'd guzzled the water without considering that he might have wanted some. It's just that when the refreshing, cool liquid first hit her tongue it tasted so good that she couldn't seem to stop until the last of it was gone. Brinley hadn't realized how dehydrated she was.

"So, what happened," he asked, storing the empty bottle back in his pack. Then taking out another bottle along with a cloth, he saturated it in some of the water. Handing the remaining water to her, he started to dab at the blood on her face.

"My foot caught on a root. I was distracted and didn't see it. When I went down, I twisted my knee, my ankle, and hit my head on something."

"Did you lose consciousness?" he asked brusquely, feeling her head for lumps.

"I don't think so. I stayed on the ground for a while trying to get my bearings."

"You have a lump on your right temple near the hairline as well as a bad gash and another lump in the back of your head."

"I could have told you that," she replied sarcastically.

"Fine. Sounds like you've got things covered here, I'll just leave you to your own devices," he said, standing to go.

Realizing she was antagonizing the one person who could help her out of this mess, she whispered softly, "I'm sorry. Please, I need help. I've been crawling for hours trying to find someone. Don't leave me here."

"Christ," he muttered, kneeling back down. Picking up her hands, he examined the dirt, cuts, and scrapes on them before lifting her arms and seeing the damage to her elbows. "You weren't kidding. We need to get you to a hospital."

"No hospital. I just need help getting back to my cabin. I'm staying at the McKinley place. Do you know where it is?"

"I do," he answered, "but my cabin is closer."

"Please, can you just take me to my place?" she implored.

Realizing that she was awfully close to breaking down, he relented. "Fine. I'm assuming that since you were crawling that your knee and ankle are too injured to walk on. That means I'm going to have to carry you. You okay with that?"

"Of course. If you are," she answered.

"Good thing I ate my Wheaties this morning," he joked. When she didn't respond to his humor, Wells merely stood and hooked his running pack through his arms and onto his back. "This might hurt," he warned as he leaned down and lifted Brinley into his arms.

Hearing her sharp intake of breath, he carefully stood and adjusted her in his arms. "Okay?" he asked when he had her settled against him.

"Fine," she gritted.

"When you need a break, just let me know and I'll stop for a few. We're about a half mile from your cabin."

"That close?" she asked in surprise.

"You don't know where you are?" he asked in horror.

"I took a trail I hadn't been on before," she defended. "How was I supposed to know where it led?"

"You shouldn't take any trail if you don't know where it leads. For this very reason," he lectured.

"I made a mistake," she pouted. "And paid a pretty severe price for it. Lesson learned."

Wells decided it was better not to comment on her stupidity. It would only make matters worse, and they were going to be in extremely close proximity of each other at least for the next forty-five minutes or so.

"I'm Wells, by the way," he said after a few minutes of silence. "Wells Kennedy."

"Brinley Crew," she responded. "Thanks for rescuing me, Wells."

"I have to admit, when I started my run, finding you was the last thing I expected. So, Brinley Crew, tell me, wouldn't your husband or boyfriend have missed you long before now?"

Brinley hesitated to answer his question. It seemed irresponsible to tell a complete stranger that she was entirely alone. For all she knew, he could be a rapist. Or worse, a murderer. Better that she keep that little tidbit to herself. "My boyfriend had an errand to run," she lied. "He won't be back until later this evening."

For some reason Wells couldn't explain, he knew she was lying. Probably from the way she tensed up when he asked the question. For what purpose he couldn't fathom but he left the lie alone.

As Wells trudged through the forest, weariness came over Brinley, so much so that she couldn't seem to keep her head up. The third time she jerked in his arms, trying to keep her head off his shoulder, Wells sighed. "Put your head on my shoulder and rest, Brinley. It's okay," he soothed.

Giving in to his offer, Brinley put her head down. The motion of Wells walking rocked her into a dreamlike state. She could barely keep her eyes open, completely unaware of anything except for the muscles that her body rested against. She could feel the soft rippling as he held her against his chest, the scent of his body soothing her in a way that surprised her.

She must have fallen asleep because the next thing she knew the sound of his footsteps changed from the crunching of leaves to a harder thud as he stepped on the wooden boards of her front steps. "We're here," he said, his breath close to her ear causing wisps of her hair to move and tickle her cheek when he spoke. "Key?" he asked.

"It's open," Brinley answered, reaching down as he held her and turned the knob.

"Figures," he frowned. The woman did nothing to protect herself.

"What's that supposed to mean?" Brinley demanded.

"Nothing," Wells snapped, walking over to the couch and gently placing her on the cushions. He didn't miss the cringe as he released her leg or the way she reached up and touched the knot on her temple, scrunching her eyes in pain as she felt the spot.

"I really think I should take you to the emergency room to get checked out. You could have a concussion; your ankle could be broken.

Hell, you could have even torn something in your knee. You need to be looked at by a professional."

"I'm fine," she protested. "Nothing a few days of rest won't cure."

"Be serious," he chided. "Let me take you in just to be sure."

"I said I'm fine," she snapped.

Ignoring her protestations, Wells turned and headed for the only other room in the cabin, certain it was the bedroom and bathroom. Grabbing a hand towel from the rack, he wet one end and walked back to where Brinley was sitting. Without saying anything, he knelt beside her and started to dab at the dirt around the cut on her face.

"I can do that," she snapped, taking the cloth from his hand.

"Do you have any ace bandages around? I can at least wrap your ankle."

"Look, Wells, I appreciate your help, but now that I'm back in my own cabin I can manage on my own. You can finish your run. I'm all set."

Wells stared down at Brinley for a few long seconds before shaking his head. "You're a stubborn woman, Brinley Crew. To your own detriment," he added before turning and walking out of the cabin, slamming the door as he exited.

Brinley sat on the couch staring at the closed door. What on earth was she thinking? The poor man was only trying to help her, and she had acted like an angry shrew. Sure, she kept her distance from people in general but rudely pushing him away when he was only trying to help was not right. She hadn't even taken a minute to find out exactly where he was staying.

Embarrassed at the way she acted, Brinley decided then and there that when she was back on her feet she would find out where he was and try to do something nice for him. Maybe cook a meal or take a small gift. The reality was that if he hadn't come along when he had, she'd still be out on that trail, maybe even fighting off a wild animal who considered her its next meal.

Tossing the towel aside, Brinley rested her head gently on the back of the couch. She was exhausted. Her body felt like it weighed a ton. It was only after a few minutes when her stomach started protesting that she knew she was going to have to try to get up. There were some crackers in her cupboard that would have to do for her dinner. She needed something fast to help get rid of the nauseating feeling she had from not eating any solid food.

Her first attempt to stand on her good leg kept her upright for all of two seconds before it gave out and she landed on the floor in front of the couch. Brinley sat there with tears in her eyes, her head pounding from the jolt when she landed on the hard wood. Eventually she was able to raise herself enough to sit on the couch. The second attempt went pretty much as before so when she finally was able to get herself back on the couch, she laid down, tossed her arm over her eyes and let the tears come. The only difference in being here as opposed to being on the trail was that at least she was safe from animals. Other than that, she was still thirsty, extremely hungry, and unable to get to anything she needed. It hurt to move, her head was killing her, and she swore she could feel bugs still crawling on her skin.

Brinley had just started to silently curse when she heard her door open. Removing her arm from her eyes, she looked up to see Wells standing just inside her cabin, his arms full of brown grocery bags and what looked like a bag with CVS Pharmacy written in red letters.

"You came back," she sniffled.

Wells saw that her cheeks were wet from tears she had obviously been shedding. His heart nearly broke at the sight. She looked incredibly sad with her torn, dirty clothes hanging off her slight frame and her face streaked with lines where her tears had run through the dirt on her cheeks. As much as he cursed himself for gathering things to help her when she obviously hadn't wanted him around, seeing her like this suddenly made him glad that he had persisted. She may not want to admit that she needed him, but she was in such a vulnerable spot there was no doubt that she did.

"You seriously didn't think I'd just leave you like this, did you? What kind of a man do you think I am?" he smiled, trying to ease the tension in the room.

Chapter Four

WELLS WATCHED AS first gratitude, then discomfort flashed across Brinley's face. It was obvious that asking for help was something she was not particularly good at. Knowing the only way to get around her was to charge forward, he went to her kitchen counter and set the bags down. Filling a bowl with warm, soapy water he went over to the couch and set it on the coffee table. Retrieving the cloth from earlier, he handed it to her.

"Why don't you clean your hands and face while I plate some food for you. After you've eaten, we'll see about getting you cleaner. I think right now it's more important that you eat so you can take some of the meds I brought."

Silently Brinley did as he suggested as he rummaged around her kitchen. It didn't take long before he joined her, placing a plate on her lap as he sat in the chair to her right. Looking at the dish of meatloaf, mashed potatoes, and green beans, she could have wept. The smells alone were starting to make her drool. Cutting a piece of the meatloaf, she looked dubiously over at Wells before putting it in her mouth.

"Relax, I didn't make it," he laughed. "I bought it at the general store yesterday. The owner's wife makes the food and packages them up to sell. Her pot roast was pretty good, so I imagine this meatloaf won't disappoint either."

"I didn't mean to insult you by questioning your ability to cook," she smiled tentatively.

"Not insulted," he said around a bite of mashed potatoes. "I can't cook for shit."

Brinley took a bite of the meatloaf and sighed in pleasure. It tasted wonderful but if she were being honest, it could have tasted like sawdust and she would have enjoyed it. Having something to eat, after starving all day, was like nirvana.

After the first bite, Brinley couldn't seem to make herself stop until every morsel was gone. Without asking, Wells grabbed her empty plate and went to her kitchen and added another small slice of the delicious meat as well as another scoop of mashed potatoes. "Eat," he said when she hesitated as he handed it to her.

Acquiescing to his suggestion, she finished her second helping and washed it down with the bottle of water he'd put on the coffee table. "That was delicious," she admitted. "Thank you so much. I was starved."

Frowning at the reminder of her carelessness, Wells stood and took her plate. "There's more."

"Thanks, but I really am full now." Scratching at her arms, she watched Wells as he cleaned the kitchen, putting the leftover food in her refrigerator.

When he turned around and saw her nails raking over her skin, he walked over and put his hand on hers to stop her. "You're going to leave marks," he admonished. "Come on, I think it's time for a shower."

"I can't…I mean…"

"Now's not the time for modesty. You need to get that dirt off so I can take a better look at those scratches. Trust me, you don't want them to get infected on top of whatever's going on with your knee and ankle."

"What are you? A doctor?"

"Not hardly. I was the medic for my Seal team. It was up to me to keep the guys on my team in the best possible condition while we were deployed. Ran in to some crazy shit overseas, trust me. And while I haven't had the training doctors do, I know enough to keep your limbs from falling off. So, are we going to get you cleaned off or you going to go all prissy on me and refuse my help? And don't give me that bullshit about your boyfriend coming back because you and I both know he doesn't exist."

"What makes you so sure..." she started.

"When I went into your bathroom earlier to get that washcloth, everything in there was feminine and girly. You don't have a closet in the bedroom, just the rack your clothes are hanging on. There wasn't one manly piece of clothing there. No boots, no work shirts, no nothing."

"How did you get all that in the minute you were in there?"

"Lady, I was trained to be observant. Not picking up on things like that could have gotten me or my guys killed."

"You say that in the past tense," she observed.

"Retired."

"You're too young to retire."

"Injury forced me out," he answered back. "Stop procrastinating. Time to get you cleaned up."

Not waiting for her objection, Wells picked her up and carried her through the bedroom and into the bathroom. "I'm going to lean you against the sink. Can you stand on the good leg while I start the shower?"

"Yes."

Brinley watched as Wells leaned in and turned the water on, the muscles in his back rippling as he leaned over. She couldn't take her eyes off him, the way his T-shirt stretched against his skin and his jeans molded against his backside. The sight was entrancing, making her feel like the schoolgirl she hadn't been in a number of years.

When he stood back to his full height, Brinley averted her eyes as he turned. "So, here's the plan," he informed her. "I'm going to help you undress, then I'm going to set you in the shower. You can lean against the wall and wash up. If you need help washing your hair or anything, just call out. Sound good?" he asked efficiently.

"Ummm...fine," she answered, realizing there was no other way. She desperately needed to get clean and the only way that was going to happen was with his help.

Setting any embarrassment aside, Brinley raised her arms as Wells lifted her top up and off. Grabbing the waistband of her leggings, he pulled them down her legs along with her underwear. When he got them to her ankles, he pulled them first over her bad leg that she was holding up. Without asking, he stood and picked her up off the floor, using his foot to maneuver them off her good leg. When she was completely naked, he stepped to the shower and placed her under the water, waiting long enough to make sure she was steady on her working leg.

"Okay?" he asked, watching to make sure she remained upright.

"Yeah," she answered shyly.

When Wells left her alone, she let out a sigh. Letting a stranger see her naked was very unnerving. She wasn't the type of woman who liked attention, in any form. In fact, she tended to keep in the background whenever possible. It was one of the things she and her husband used to constantly argue about before he died. He always encouraged her to dress more sexily, but Brinley simply wasn't comfortable showing off her body. Not that she didn't have a great shape—because she did—but she wasn't the type to flaunt it.

"You okay in there?" Wells yelled out, shaking Brinley from his thoughts. She was an incredibly beautiful woman. He tried very hard not to ogle her as he helped her undress, but he was after all, a normal red-blooded male…not a saint.

"I'm good," she answered back, grabbing her loofah and bottle of body wash and scrubbing her skin.

It was a wonderful feeling as the water poured from her limbs. Brinley glanced down and cringed when she saw the dirt and a few bugs that had hitched a ride on her body wash down the drain. Grabbing the shampoo bottle, she lathered her hair and used her nails to scratch her scalp clean, being careful around the lumps. When she was done and had the suds rinsed out, she turned the now cold water off. She was about to call out to Wells when a hand reached in, a towel hanging off his fingers.

"Dry off as much as you can, then I'll carry you into the bedroom."

Brinley did as he asked, pushing the shower curtain aside when she was through. Wells was right there, picking her up and walking toward the bed. He set her down gently and asked what she wanted to sleep in. Brinley directed him toward her dresser and watched as he pulled out a clean pair of underwear and the requested oversized nightshirt. Without saying a word or commenting on anything, he helped her get dressed.

When he had her settled under the covers, her injured knee and ankle propped up on pillows he'd taken from the couch, he told her not to move, then went back out to the kitchen. When he returned, he had two freezer bags with ice in them in his hands. Without a word he lifted the covers, placed a kitchen towel over her knee and ankle before placing the ice on top. He reached for a bottle of water that he must have placed on her nightstand while she was in the shower along with four white pills.

"Take these," he insisted.

"What are they?" Brinley asked curiously as she reached for them.

"Two are extra-strength Tylenol to help with the pain and swelling. The other two are over-the-counter sleep aids that should relax you enough to get some rest. Can I get you anything else?" he asked after she swallowed the tablets and handed the water back to him.

"I'm good but thank you. I don't know what I would have done if you hadn't rescued me."

"You're welcome. Call if you need anything. I'll be on the couch."

"Wait," Brinley said in a strained voice. He couldn't seriously be thinking of staying here in her cabin. With her. It was small. There wasn't much room. She didn't like people in her space! What if another nightmare came? The last thing she wanted was a witness. Then she'd feel like she had to explain what had happened and her life was hers and hers alone to deal with.

Wells turned and stared at her without saying a word. Did she really think he'd just leave her when she could barely get out of bed? Her ridiculousness was truly starting to annoy the hell out of him.

"Fine," she acquiesced, giving in to his decision. "Thank you," she added as an afterthought. He really was being exceedingly kind to her and acting like a petulant child was not very flattering. Besides, if the nightmares came, she could just explain it away by the trauma of what happened that afternoon. Certainly that would be believable... she honestly was starting to think her life was going to end on that trail!

"Good night, Brinley," Wells said with finality as he turned and made his way out to the couch.

Brinley listened as he moved about her cabin. She heard him open the small closet next to the front door where she kept her boots and coat as well as extra blankets and a pillow on the top shelf. At first, she was discomfited by how easily he made himself at home, but when he extinguished the lights and the cabin was engulfed in darkness, she found that knowing he was close gave her comfort. Something she hadn't allowed herself to feel in nearly two years.

When the subtle squeak of the old couch finally silenced, indicating Wells was settled for the night, Brinley closed her eyes and for the first time in a while, instantly fell asleep.

As for Wells, sleep didn't come as easily. He laid on the lumpy couch cushions thinking back to the sight of Brinley lying on the trail, blood on her face, scratches up and down her arms, and dirt caked on her skin. The desperation in her eyes was something that would stay with him for a while. He knew what terror felt like; he'd felt it many times when he was on a mission in some godforsaken country with enemies surrounding him. The difference was, he was trained for things like that; Brinley was not. The ditzy woman hadn't even been prepared to go jogging. Who went into a wooded area with God knows what kind of animals on the trail and not bring the basics like water with her? Much less any way to reach out for help.

She was reckless. And stubborn. And beautiful. And the last thing he needed was to care. Especially for this woman. Having feelings for her would not serve his purpose!

Chapter Five

PAIN SEARED UP Brinley's leg when she tried to roll over, bringing her instantly awake. *Damn,* she muttered under her breath, turning to glance at the small clock on her bedside table. Surprise registered when she saw that it was seven o'clock in the morning. The last thing she remembered was drifting off to sleep listening as Wells settled on her couch.

Wells! How could she have slept so soundly knowing a strange man was a mere twenty feet from where she slept? She hadn't allowed anyone this close since the fire. She preferred her solitude, so why did having that man close comfort her?

Trauma, she concluded. It had to have been because of the scare she had yesterday. He'd saved her from a dire situation so of course it was natural that she would feel more comfortable with him than most people. Besides, he was relatively nice to her. And if he were going to rape or kill her, surely he would have done it by now.

Shaking her ridiculous thoughts away, she listened intently, trying to hear if her potential killer was awake or still asleep. After several moments, Brinley came to the conclusion that he was either a silent sleeper or he had disappeared altogether. Which didn't bode well for her because she suddenly realized how absolutely desperate she was to use the bathroom.

Contemplating her situation for a few seconds she decided there was no choice. She was going to have to hop to the bathroom and hope that the jarring didn't increase her headache or cause her bladder to let loose. How embarrassing would that be!

Coming to her one-legged standing pose—thank you very much to her former yoga instructor—she was about to do her first bunny impression when she heard the door in her living room open. Sitting back down, she looked to her door and watched as Wells came into her bedroom, a pair of crutches in his hand.

"I wasn't sure if you were still sleeping or if you had left," she said lamely.

"Sorry," Wells smiled. "I ran out for these," he said, holding the crutches up and waving them. "I ran down to the general store to see what they might have and. lo and behold, the old guy there happened to have a pair from a while back when he broke his ankle. He was nice enough to let me borrow them for you."

"Oh, thank God," Brinley said, waving her hand indicating she wanted them.

"Desperate, are you?" Wells chuckled as he walked over and put the two sticks in her hands. "How long have you been awake trying not to have an accident?"

"Long enough," she snapped as she placed the armrests under her arms and started toward the bathroom.

"Take it easy," Wells admonished as she wobbled precariously for the first few steps.

When she finally made it into the bathroom and slammed the door shut, Wells grinned and made his way back out to her kitchen. She really was adorable just waking from her sleep. Grouchy…but adorable.

Grabbing the bags he brought in with the crutches and had dropped by the front door, Wells placed them on her counter and started to unpack. He was just about finished when Brinley hobbled in to join him.

"Feel better?" he asked, turning to look at her.

"You have no idea," she grinned, making her way to the small kitchen table and awkwardly sitting down. Leaning the crutches against her legs, she looked over to Wells. "What are you doing?"

"Making us breakfast. Are you hungry?"

Torn between wanting to prove her independence and the need to quiet her grumbling stomach, Brinley took a few seconds before answering. "I'm starved but you really don't have to go to any trouble."

"It's no trouble. I have to eat anyway. It's just as easy cooking eggs for two people. I grabbed a can of corned beef hash and some bread to go with it. I hope that's okay," he said, turning toward the stove and grabbing the skillet hanging from a hook next to it.

"It's fine," Brinley said, watching as Wells started to fix their breakfast.

He really was quite handsome, she observed, watching as he moved about her kitchen with ease. His short, military-cut brown hair was neatly groomed. He must have been up a while because she could almost detect the scent of his aftershave. He was clean-shaven and had changed his clothes. He was tall, well over six feet, and muscularly built, as proven when he carried her from the woods the day before. As far as she could see there wasn't an ounce of fat anywhere on his lean body. Damn him!

"Would you like some coffee?" Wells asked, shaking Brinley from her appraisal of everything Wells.

Embarrassed at having been caught, she shook her head. By the grin on his face, it was obvious he knew exactly what she had been doing. "No thanks," she stammered. "I prefer tea."

"Tea it is," he agreed, grabbing the pan and filling it with water.

"So, what are you doing here, Wells?" she asked, grasping for something to fill the quietness. "This area is pretty remote for a guy like you."

"A guy like me. What do you men…a guy like me?"

"It wasn't an insult," she defended. "I just mean that you're young, handsome. Shouldn't you be out partying? Breaking girls' hearts? Oh…" she stopped short. "I'm sorry. I didn't even think to ask. Maybe you aren't here alone. Please tell me that I'm not keeping you away from your…wife…girlfriend?"

"Not married…never have been, and no girlfriend so relax. I'm not that big of a jerk that I would abandon someone I came with." Seeing the question in her eyes, he sighed heavily. "Look, there's no mystery here. I'm a retired Navy Seal. Not by choice. I was injured on my last mission and going back wasn't an option. I came here to heal, get my head together, and figure out what's next for me. End of story."

"I'm sorry," Brinley offered.

"Not your fault," he answered back. "And for your information, the bar scene isn't my thing. I'm thirty-one and hooking up with random women holds no appeal for me. But thanks for thinking I'm a young stud. How old are you, by the way, and why exactly are you here alone?"

"First off, I didn't call you a stud. Secondly, I'm twenty-seven and my reasons for being here are not up for discussion."

Wells watched as Brinley closed herself off to any further conversation concerning her life. Knowing he wouldn't get anywhere with her, he quietly turned back to the stove and plated their food. Placing it and her cup of tea in front of her, he joined her at the table, and they sat in relative silence as they ate the food he prepared. When they were finished, he stood and cleared the table.

"You need to stop doing so much, Wells. I appreciate it but you've gone to so much trouble."

"I don't mind, Brinley. I'm glad I could do it."

Brinley wasn't sure what to make of the man doing her dishes or the fact that he so easily jumped in to take care of her. The fact that she liked it unnerved her.

When Wells finished, he joined her at the table again. "I really think you should let me take you to the hospital today. Just to get checked out to make sure that nothing is broken. I'm a pretty good field medic," he quickly continued when she started to interrupt, "but I don't have x-ray eyes. You don't want to do more damage by trying to walk on an ankle that's broken. Besides, knocks on the head should be taken seriously. They're nothing to mess with."

"I appreciate the offer but I'm fine. If, after a few days, things aren't any better, I promise that I'll go. Right now, I just want to relax and give my body time to heal on its own."

"You're a stubborn woman," he admonished.

"So you've said before," she reminded him.

"Fine," he grumbled, getting up from the table and retrieving a bag she hadn't seen before. She watched as he pulled out a heating pad and two rubber ice bags. Going into the kitchen, he filled both bags with ice, then carried them into the living room and set them on the coffee table. "Go have a seat," he told her as he went into her bedroom.

By the time Brinley made it to the couch, Wells was there with one of the pillows from her bed. "Take these," he said handing her two pills, then going into the kitchen to retrieve a bottle of water. He stood over her and watched as she dutifully swallowed them both. "Lie back," he encouraged, placing one ice bag on her knee and one on her ankle when she was settled.

"Wells…"

"I have some errands to run this afternoon. Use the ice bags, twenty minutes on then twenty off for the next few hours to help with swelling. After that, you should use heat to help the muscles. I made a couple of sandwiches and put them in baggies as well as some grapes in your fridge for lunch. Easy to get and carry using the crutches. There are a couple bottles of ginger ale in there too if you're thirsty. I'll be back around six tonight and I'll bring dinner with me."

"Wells, you don't have to do that."

"I still can't believe you don't have a phone out here. Having no way to contact anyone is just irresponsible," he groused.

"I'll be fine," she insisted.

"Like you were yesterday?' he argued.

"That was…"

"Do you need anything before I head out?" he interrupted.

"No, thank you, though."

Wells stared at her for a few seconds like he had something else he wanted to say. Finally, he merely shook his head. "I'll be back by six," he repeated, then walked out the door, leaving her to her own devices.

Brinley sighed in relief when she heard his car drive off. Strange that she had no idea when he had left her this morning or heard him drive his car back to her cabin. He must have gotten up pretty early to jog back to his own place to get his car, then drive into town to get the things he'd brought back with him and still make it back right when she woke up. Did he get any sleep at all?

As Brinley rested on the couch, she thought about the kind things he had done for her since he had found her on the trail. There was no way she would ever be able to repay his thoughtfulness. Seriously, who thought about things like finding crutches and ice packs and heating pads? Food was a no-brainer, but he thought of everything that would help to ease her pain. How do you thank someone for that?

As her unconscious thoughts screamed *be nicer to the man*, her real thoughts immediately went to suspicion. What did he want from her? Was there some ulterior motive to his being so kind?

"Stop it, Brinley," she lectured herself out loud.

Eventually her thoughts became muddled and Brinley drifted off to sleep. She woke from her nap a few hours later, the ice bags having fallen off at some point. Grabbing the crutches, she made her way into her bedroom to get changed and wash up. On the way back to the couch, she refilled the ice bags then took the book she was reading from the counter and went back and settled on the couch.

The pain, while still there, was subsiding a little. It no longer felt like someone was clubbing her right leg when she moved. If she was very careful, she could move around with only a slight throbbing pain present. The knot on the back of her head and at her temple were receding, but the black and blue bruises weren't going away any time soon. The scratches on her arms and legs were at least clean and only hurt when she brushed against them. Improvement from where she had been the day before.

A little after noon Brinley made her way into the kitchen, grateful that Wells had thought ahead enough to make her lunch. While she could have managed something on her own, she was glad to be able to just grab the baggie with her sandwich and the grapes and a soda.

When she was back on the couch and took out the sandwich he'd prepared for her, she was in heaven. It had been a long time since she had lunchmeat of any type so the turkey breast with cheese and fresh tomato tasted incredibly good to her. The grapes were sweet when she bit into them and the cold, refreshing ginger ale soothed her throat like nothing she could remember from before. It had been a long time since she'd enjoyed such a simple meal.

Lying back on the pillow, Brinley found herself looking forward to Wells's return.

"Not good," she murmured as she closed her eyes.

Chapter Six

Wells paced around the small living room like a caged animal. He kept glancing at the timer on his oven then back to the clock on the wall waiting for six o'clock to come.

Brinley was going to be pissed at him! When she found out what his errand was today, there would be hell to pay, and it would all rain down on his head and his alone. But it had to be done and no matter how angry she became, he didn't regret his decision.

It was fortunate that the man who owned Brinley's cabin also owned the one he was renting. Knowing Wells was former military, the man seemed to trust him. Otherwise, Wells was certain the old coot wouldn't have given him any information on Brinley. It did come as a bit of a surprise when the gruff old man told him that she had been on her own in the dilapidated cabin for as long as she had been. Why on earth would a woman choose to live alone, without any contact with the outside world for so long? What surprised him even more was when Mr. McKinley explained that he had offered to have cable and Internet installed for Brinley when he learned how long she wanted to rent the cabin. And the crazy, stubborn woman declined the offer. What exactly was she hiding from that made her cut all ties to everything and everyone she knew?

Wells knew full well that her decisions and how she lived her life were absolutely none of his business but in his opinion, it was stupid to take such a chance. It made him angry to think of what could have happened to her just because she was unprepared. It went against all his training to take risks that were unnecessary. Life was difficult enough, so not to try and mitigate possible disasters was plain idiotic. It shocked him to see how she was living; he hadn't expected that. But then, there was a lot about her that was unexpected.

Something else that Wells found unexpected was the fact that he himself was enjoying being alone. Normally he was constantly surrounded by others. As a Navy Seal he ate, slept, and trained with the members of his team. They were always together when they were out on a mission and found that even with time off, they socialized together. But now, having solitude and being content with it surprised him. It was his injury that threw him more than anything.

At first the guys from his team were constantly with him. They made sure that he was never left alone, not while he was in the hospital and not when he was released and back at his condo. Someone was always at his doorstep with some type of food and a willingness to sit with him whether they were watching a sporting event on television or a movie. Wells appreciated the company but eventually the guys were called back to active duty and he was left on his own. It hurt to watch them go out without him, but it hurt worse when they eventually brought in his replacement. Watching the new guy train with *his* team hurt like a son of a bitch!

The words his superior officer spoke that day had nearly crushed him. *Unfit for duty…honorably discharged…*words that literally left him reeling from shock. Just like that. He'd lost his job…his income…his identity. Being a Seal wasn't just what he did. It was who he was.

Wells barely survived the last mission they were on in Syria. The bomb that went off while he and his team were clearing one of the small villages nearly killed him. The shrapnel embedded in his legs was painful, but it was the larger pieces that landed in his chest close to his heart, causing a pericardial effusion, that came close to ending his life. He barely grasped the significance of the buildup of excess fluid of his pericardium, but he clearly understood it when he was life-flighted to the nearest base with a good hospital. He heard right before he was going under anesthesia that the pressure on the heart due to the fluid was affecting his heart function. If they didn't do something fast, he was headed for heart failure or quite possibly his death. Great thing to have in your head as you slipped into unconsciousness. Wells clearly remembered praying that the doctor was good at his job.

Fortunately, the doctor *was* good, but the damage was significant. To most people suffering the same condition—who led normal lives—it wouldn't have been a big deal. But the stress put on a Navy Seal is quite different. And because the Navy had no desire to take a chance on sending him back out with his team, he was relieved of duty. The desk job they offered didn't sit well with him, so he was done—a Seal set adrift with no clue how to live a normal life.

Wells walked over to the rocking chair that sat in the corner of his cabin and lovingly stroked the wood. This was the only thing that was saving him from going stark raving mad. Taking a piece of wood and shaping it to become something beautiful. There was still a lot more work to be done before the chair was finished but the smooth, sleek curves of the wood with the intricate etched designs gave him pleasure. He had done this. Woodworking wasn't just a hobby; it was something that he was good at and enjoyed doing. He'd lost hours in forming the solid oak pieces into what now was a stunning rocking chair that would sell for quite a bit of change. He had been shocked at how much some people were willing to pay for his handcrafted furniture.

Not that he needed the cash. Between the money from his military benefits and what he inherited from his father's estate when he passed away, finances were not a concern for Wells. It was feeling useful that mattered the most. Money was a necessity but not something he placed a whole lot of value in.

Hearing the timer on his oven go off, Wells went over and took out the casserole he made and placed it on the cooling rack. It was time to start packing up to head back over to Brinley's place. It was nearly six o'clock…right when he said he would return.

It worried him how much he looked forward to seeing her again. It had only been nine hours since he'd last seen her, so it surprised him how much he wanted to get back there. Mentally kicking himself for feeling that way, he moved around the kitchen to gather everything he needed.

It really was ridiculous, this need he had to check on her. It was dangerous, too, and didn't fit into what he needed to accomplish. But there was something about her wide, electric-blue eyes that called to him. She couldn't be any taller than a little over five feet and her slim, athletic body wasn't the usual type of woman he went after but there was just something that called out to him. Even her wavy brown hair wasn't his preferred choice. Give him a blonde any day of the week and he was in…but on Brin…the chestnut curls suited her.

The one thing that didn't fit was the sadness that seemed to permeate her entire body, from the devastation in her eyes to the way she carried herself. It was obvious that she was a woman who felt she had the world on her shoulders. And as much as he liked her, getting too close would be a mistake. A dangerous mistake. He'd been observing her for several weeks now and while the chance meeting on the trail surprised him, their meeting was inevitable and had been since he started his search for the truth.

Shaking his head at his own thoughts, Wells gathered what he needed to take over to Brin's place. Once his vehicle was loaded, he made the short drove over to her cabin.

Chapter Seven

Brinley found herself sitting on the couch, watching the front door, waiting for Wells to return. It was ten minutes until six o'clock and here she sat like a young girl waiting for her date. "Embarrassing!" she muttered, grabbing an old magazine from the coffee table in an attempt to appear as if she hadn't a care in the world, much less that she was anticipating his arrival.

Her day was rather boring, she reasoned in her mind, which was why she was looking forward to company. Her afternoon nap, which lasted for several hours, left her feeling groggy when she first woke. When the cobwebs in her head finally lifted, she desperately searched for something to do. At first, she tried reading the book she'd started the week before but that held no interest for her. For her next attempt at amusing herself, Brinley grabbed the stack of magazines from the coffee table and leafed through them. Unfortunately, they were left from previous guests of the cottage and dated back to 1983. The articles weren't remotely interesting and probably hadn't been when they were relevant.

Tossing them aside she then stood to practice getting better with the crutches. She even tried to stand on her bad leg and while it wasn't as excruciating as before, it wasn't long when the pain let her know it was time to sit back down and elevate it, using the ice bags as Wells had suggested.

Eventually she hobbled into her small bathroom and took a quick shower, managing to only slip once as she stood on her good leg to wash her hair. By the time she wiped the moisture from her skin, dressed in comfy clothes and dried her hair, she was flat-out exhausted. The fact that, no matter how drained she felt, she took the time to apply a little make-up, made her feel frustrated. Seriously…who was she trying to impress?

Hearing a car door shut, Brinley tossed the magazine back onto the coffee table and grabbed the can of soda she'd been sipping on. When Wells walked through the door, she met his eyes and said quietly, "You're back already."

Wells took in her perfectly coifed hair, the rose-pink tint to her lips, and the slightly floral scent in the air and realized that she had gone to some trouble with her appearance. While on one hand it made him nervous—he was not looking for a relationship—on the other hand it pleased him that she was getting around.

"Right when I said I would be. How was your day?" he asked, carrying a casserole dish into her kitchen."

"Uneventful," she answered.

"Are you hungry?" he asked, nonchalantly opening a bottle of wine. After searching but not finding wine glasses, he found two clean cups and poured some wine in them. Walking over he handed her one, making sure to give her the cup with just a little in it. She was, after all, still nursing a head injury.

"What's this for?' she asked, feeling stupid and a little ungrateful the minute it was out of her mouth. "I'm sorry," Brinley apologized. "That was a little rude."

"Don't worry about it," Wells replied going back into the kitchen and setting out plates and silverware for their dinner. As he placed the hot dish on the table, Brinley joined him, placing her crutches on the floor beside her.

"I'm just feeling out of sorts," she tried to explain as she sat down. "I'm not used to relying on anyone for anything. And here you are, doing everything. I don't know what I would have done if you hadn't found me yesterday, much less taken care of me. I'm not sure how I feel about that."

"You needed help; I was there. Don't make too big a deal out of it."

"But you've been so kind, and I've been…well…a bit ungrateful about the whole thing."

"I get it," he answered brusquely. "How are you feeling? How's the pain level?"

"Not bad," she said, going with his quick change of topic. He didn't seem to respond to her gratitude any more than he did her bitchiness. "I tried standing on my own for a little. It hurt but I was able to do it. In another day or so I should be able to walk without the crutches."

"That's good," Wells chimed in, dishing out the delicious-smelling food.

Brinley sniffed appreciatively before picking up her fork and taking a bite. "Wow," she exclaimed. "This is really good. What is it?" she inquired, taking another mouthful.

"It's my mom's recipe. Chicken Poppy Seed Casserole. Used to be a favorite of mine when I was growing up."

"Where do your parents live?"

"It's just my mom and me. Dad died when I was a teenager. It was hard but Ruby Kennedy has always been a force to be reckoned with. She always made sure I had what I needed. She was the best mother and father I could have asked for. She lives in a small house back in Casper. I tried to get her to move in with me but she's pretty independent, prefers to be on her own. What about you? Where's your family from?"

"So, if you live back in Casper, what brings you here to Green River? Why are you here and not back with your mom?"

For distracting techniques Brinley seemed like a pro. It was obvious that she had no desire to talk about herself in any way. Wells pondered his approach for a few seconds before deciding to let it go. As much as he wanted more in-depth details about her life—he already knew the general basics—pushing her too soon would not serve his purpose. So, he let it go.

"As you know, I'm here recovering from being injured on my last mission. It was hard being close to the base and the guys, watching them go out on missions while I stayed behind. I needed to get my head on straight, so I did a little research and came across an ad for the cabin down the road from you. Rented it sight unseen."

"What do you do to fill your time?" Brinley asked. "Other than rescuing strange women on a trail."

Wells' laugh was deep and rich. "That is a sideline, but what I really love to do is work with my hands. Right now, I'm making a rocking chair out of oak. It's almost done, which makes me a little sad. There's something about taking a piece of rough wood and shaping it into something beautiful with my own hands. It's gratifying to see."

"That's impressive," Brinley said in awe. "I'd like to see it some time. How did you learn to do that type of thing?"

"My dad had a workshop in our house. When I was little, I used to watch him. He'd pull up this old bar stool next to where he was working, and I would sit on it watching everything he did. He taught me what all the tools and machines did, how to use them, how to be safe while working on pieces of wood. Even when I screwed something up, he never got mad at me. He'd just show me what I did wrong so I wouldn't make the same mistake again. It was my favorite time with him."

"It must have been hard on you when your dad died. Sounds like you two were very close."

"When I was younger," he corrected. "When I became a teenager we grew apart. I was hanging out with a group of guys that made spending time with my dad sound uncool. I wanted to fit in, so I stopped doing things with him. I became a surly pain in the ass, staying out late, breaking my curfew. Got into trouble breaking into a house with my friends and got caught. I thought Dad would beat the shit out of me, but he just came to the police station and got me. The disappointment I felt from him was worse than anything I could have imagined. I sometimes wished he'd have just hit me and gotten it over with. I felt so awful I stopped hanging with those guys. Changed my group of friends, worked harder at school. I never wanted to disappoint him like that again. I never really apologized for what I put him through. Six months after the incident he died, and I've regretted not saying those words ever since."

"I'm sure he knew," Brinley comforted.

"Mom said he did, but I don't know. I hope so. I have dessert," Wells said, standing up and moving toward the counter. The subject was obviously closed.

"Whatcha got?" Brinley asked eagerly.

Wells carried over a small cake and set it between them, handing Brinley a fork as he sat back down and took the cover off. "Three Layer Chocolate Ganache Cake," he said proudly. "The lady at the little store made it herself. Said it was an old family recipe."

"No plates?" she asked.

"Nope. We're just going to dig in and eat until we're disgustingly full," he laughed.

Brinley watched as Wells did just that. He dug in with gusto, not waiting for her to do the same. She watched as he took several bites, then grabbed her fork and followed suit. It was obvious that he was not going to wait for her and if she didn't join him, she would likely not get a single bite.

When the small cake was nearly gone, Brinley put her fork down and wiped her mouth. "That was delicious but if I eat another bite I'm going to bust. Literally!"

Wells quickly finished the last of the cake and pushed back from the table. "Perfect end to a great meal. Coffee…tea?" he asked.

"Lord, no. Help yourself though."

"I'm just going to have a glass of milk," he said getting up.

"I don't have any, sorry."

"Yes, you do," he corrected. "I brought some over this morning. Didn't you see it in your fridge when you grabbed your lunch?"

"I did not. You're quite the shopper."

Wells got his milk and sat back down at the table. After a few seconds, he looked over at Brinley. "I did something today that might make you angry."

"What?" Brinley asked, her hackles instantly going up.

"I spoke to your landlord."

"You did what?" she asked calmly even though she felt her anger rising.

"I spoke to Mr. McKinley about having Internet hooked up so you would have a way to make a call. Send an e-mail, maybe watch television. Now don't go getting all upset," he urged as she grabbed her crutches and awkwardly stood up.

"You had no right," she practically yelled as she wobbled a few feet away. "If I wanted contact of any kind, I would have asked for it myself. I specifically told Mr. McKinley that I wasn't interested. Why would you do that? Why would you go against my wishes? He must have told you I already declined when he originally offered."

"He did," Wells said following her into the living room. "But when I explained what had happened to you…"

"What happened to me happened out in the woods. There's no reception there anyway, you idiot. Having Internet in the cabin wouldn't have changed that."

"You shouldn't be so secluded, Brin. It's dangerous and unnecessary. What would you have done if something happened here in the cabin? You have no way of getting help. Thank God you fell in the woods. At least there you were out in the open where I could find you. Please think about it. You don't have to use the damn Internet if you don't want to but at least it's there in case of an emergency."

"I need you to leave," Brinley said quietly, her back turned to him.

"Brinley, be reasonable…"

"Please. Just leave me alone."

Wells hesitated for several seconds before taking a step closer. "Will you be okay? Can I do anything before I leave? Help you get ready for bed?"

"I can do it on my own," she answered stubbornly.

Wells watched her briefly, then realized that the best thing he could do was to leave her alone. Staying would only aggravate her more.

"I'll check in on you tomorrow," he said before turning to walk out the door. He would have said to call him if she needed anything, but the damn woman didn't have a working phone. Which only served to prove his point, something he knew pointing out would only anger her more than he'd already done. And so, he left.

Chapter Eight

BRIN TOSSED AND turned a good portion of the night. Finally, around six the next morning she got out of bed. Not bothering to attempt to make it on her own, she grabbed her crutches, took care of her morning rituals, and went out to the kitchen to make herself a cup of tea. Leaning against the counter, she sipped the hot brew as she thought about the night before.

Her reaction to Wells's interference was perhaps a bit over the top. On one hand, it angered her that he had gone behind her back. Granted, her response would have been just as negative if he had approached her before he spoke to her landlord, but it made it worse knowing he took it upon himself to decide what he thought she needed. She hated it when men got all superior, thinking they knew what was best. Her husband had been like that, and it was one of the things that they argued most about during their marriage.

On the other hand, in an emergency maybe it wouldn't be so bad having a way to reach out to someone. Although she had been fine the past two years without it.

"Such confusion," she mumbled to herself as she left the crutches leaning against the counter and took a few steps, unaided by the pine sticks. She made it a good fifteen feet before she felt her knee and ankle start to give.

Feeling relief that it was better than the day before, Brinley hobbled back to the kitchen counter and made herself some toast. Sitting at the table she thoughtfully chewed the buttery bread as she mulled over her plan of action for the day. Not that she would be able to do much, but the idea of getting out of the cabin appealed to her.

Finishing her breakfast, Brinley made her way into the bedroom, getting her things together before heading into the bathroom to take a long, lukewarm shower. When she was dressed and her hair was blown dry, she made her way out to the living room, grabbed her book and went out to the small patio and sat in the cozy outdoor resin rocking chair—her one splurge when she first moved into the cabin—and settled down to enjoy the morning.

She'd only been reading for about an hour when a work truck pulled into the driveway, the Verizon emblem boldly displayed on the side. Brinley watched as a middle-aged man got out of the truck, a clipboard in hand, and walked to where she was sitting.

"Good morning, ma'am. I'm here to install some lines for your cable and Internet," he informed her.

Brinley started to answer when an old pick-up truck came screeching into the drive, rocks spewing from the back tires as it came to an abrupt halt.

"Sorry…sorry," Mr. McKinley huffed as he came to stand next to the cable guy. "I wanted to get here before he did," he informed Brinley. "I wanted to talk to you about this before the installer arrived. Your man wanted a rush put on this. I just didn't think when I placed the request with Verizon, they'd be able to get here so fast."

"He's not my man," Brinley corrected him. "But it's fine," she agreed.

Mr. McKinley turned to the worker. "What do you need from me?"

"Nothing at all, sir. It shouldn't take me long to get the wires run in the house. After that I'll just be working on the poles at the end of the street getting everything connected. Is it okay if I go in and get started?" he asked Brinley.

"Of course."

Both Brinley and Mr. McKinley watched as the technician removed what he needed from his truck and entered the house.

"I'm sorry for what happened to you, Ms. Crew. I had no idea you'd gotten injured until your ma…I mean Wells, came to see me yesterday. If I'd known I would have been over to check on you."

"It was my own fault," Brinley answered gently. "And call me Brinley."

"So, other than your mishap, everything at the cabin going okay? Anything need my attention while I'm here?" he inquired.

"It's fine," she answered.

"You know, it's good that this gets done anyway," Mr. McKinley said as conversation lagged. "It'll be more appealing for other renters. You know…once you decide to leave. Not that I'm rushing you, mind you. You're a good tenant and don't cause me no problems. Stay as long as you like. I'm just saying that a woman as young as you might want to get back to the real world, you know?"

"I know," Brinley murmured.

There was a brief moment of awkward silence before the older man muttered something about going in to check on the installer and walked away. Brinley watched as the door closed and smiled to herself. It seemed Mr. McKinley had no idea what to make of her. He could join the club. She was starting to think she had no clue where her head was at herself.

It was lunchtime before she was informed by both Mr. McKinley and the Verizon installer that her Internet was up and running as well as the cable. When both men departed, she made her way back into the cabin and stopped at the small desk that sat in the corner of the living room. She stared at it for a few moments before opening the drawer and pulling out her cell phone and charging cable. Without questioning her actions, she plugged the cord in, inserted the other end into her phone and nearly jumped when it made a chirping sound indicating that it was in fact charging.

Laughing at her stupidity, Brinley continued into the kitchen and took out what she needed to make herself some lunch. Grateful that there was still some leftover lunchmeat that Wells had brought the day before, she made a sandwich, then hobbled into the living room, laid the crutches on the floor and sat down to eat.

Food was starting to taste better than it had in a long time, so she gobbled it down quickly, then stared at the small television that, up until this moment, had sat in silence. When she first arrived at the cabin she had been informed that there was no cable but with a little twisting of the rabbit ears hanging off the back of the box, she could possibly get one of the local channels that aired the town meetings when they had them. Mostly in the past, renters had used the set to watch the few VCR tapes that had been left behind by previous tenants. Brinley hadn't the desire for anything but silence when she arrived but the temptation to see if it now worked played in the back of her head. However, feeling overwhelmed by the available technology, she grabbed her book and decided to let it go for another day.

Once she was stretched out on the couch, making sure to elevate her injured leg, she read for a short time before her book eventually landed on her chest. She woke from her nap a short time later, made herself a light dinner, then headed out to her patio to enjoy the sunset and a hot cup of tea.

It was there that Wells found her, staring off into space. "It is okay if I join you?" he asked tentatively. He wouldn't be surprised if she was still angry enough to send him packing.

"Of course," she answered, nodding to the empty chair beside her.

"Still mad? he asked as he settled next to her.

"I think I'm over it," she smiled.

"Really? You were pretty pissed at me yesterday. I figured it would be some time before you were in the forgiving mood."

"And yet you still came over."

"I wanted to make sure you were doing okay. See if there was anything you needed."

Brinley stared at him for a few seconds, letting him stew for a bit before she finally answered. "While I didn't appreciate your going behind my back, I understand why you did it. It was actually quite thoughtful. Irritating, but thoughtful."

"I tend to irritate a lot of people," Wells laughed, swatting at the mosquito that landed on his arm.

Waving at the bug nearing her face, Brinley reached for her crutches and stood up. "Why don't we go inside," she offered. "In another few minutes we'll get eaten alive."

Wells followed her in, closing the screened door behind him. Looking at the desk as he turned to face her, he smiled. "Made any calls yet?" he asked curiously, indicating that he had seen her phone charging.

"None," she said brusquely. "And I don't intend to. I just thought that since I had a connection now, I would have the phone charged just in case I needed it."

It amazed him that Brinley could so easily shut herself off from the outside world. What kind of woman would do something like that? Not reach out to other people…no friends, family, former coworkers? There was so much more to her story than evidently even he knew. Curious!

"So, how's your leg?" he asked, changing the subject so she wouldn't completely shut down on him. "Have you been elevating it?"

Relieved that he wasn't pushing her into a discussion she had no intention of having, she leaned against the counter. "Better every day. I was able to walk on it more today than I did yesterday. I imagine in another couple of days I won't need the crutches at all," she said proudly.

"That's really good, Brinley. You're a quick healer. Is there anything I can pick up for you tomorrow? Do you need supplies of any kind?" he offered.

"I appreciate everything you've done for me, Wells, but I think I'm good now. I have enough for another four days or so and by then I'll be able to get out on my own. You were a godsend though. I owe you big time."

"You don't owe me anything, Brin. I was happy I could help. Look, I'd better get going. I just wanted to check on you, make sure you were okay. Here," he said, reaching into his jeans pocket and taking out a piece of paper and handing it to her. "That's my cell number. Now that you can," he said with a smirk, "call me if you need anything. I'm just a quick call away."

Brinley hesitated a second before taking the paper from his hand, jerking back in surprise when their skin touched. "Thank you," she said quietly, shocked at her reaction to their simple touch. "I appreciate it."

Wells stared at her for a short moment before turning to go. He felt the spark when they touched and knew damn well that she had too. It was best to beat a hasty retreat while he could. "Call if you need anything," he yelled back as he shut the door on his way out.

Brinley stared at the closed door, then back at her cell phone for a long while. Laughing at her own ridiculousness, she made her way back to her bedroom. Seriously! It was as if the charged cell phone and Wells's hand were the very devil. "Stop being stupid, Brin," she lectured herself as she got ready to head to bed early. The last thing she needed was to dwell on the beginnings of her schoolgirl crush on Wells. Sleep…restful sleep was what she needed.

Chapter Nine

BRINLEY SMILED TO herself as she walked around the outside perimeter of her cabin, completely unaided by the crutches. It had been ten days since her little mishap, and she was thrilled with her progress. The bumps on her head were completely gone and no longer hurt her whenever she brushed her hair. In fact, the purplish-green bruising at her temple could be covered with just a little make-up. The pain in her ankle and knee was nearly gone, only slight discomfort occurred and a little swelling when she pushed herself too hard or stood on it too long. She was feeling better than she had in a while, although her days of jogging were a thing of the past. For the foreseeable future the only exercise she had planned were long walks with bottles of water and a cell phone at her disposal. She'd learned a hard lesson and wasn't likely to forget it too soon.

Her visits over the last few days with Wells were the sole highlights of her days. He didn't stop by often, but she was beginning to enjoy his company when he did. He always kept their conversation light, and his sense of humor kept her smiling in his presence. He was perhaps the most nonthreatening male she'd ever encountered, which seemed strange given the fact that he was a former Navy Seal and a large muscular one to boot! He was easy to like and since he'd not been over for a few days, she was finding that she missed him.

Thinking of Wells, Brinley decided that it was time to take a little drive to the store to replenish her supplies. Might be a good time to stop by and visit him, maybe return the crutches he'd borrowed for her.

Besides, she was curious to see the place he was calling his temporary home. He'd been to her place plenty of times, but she'd never ventured to his cabin. Deciding that an impromptu visit was a good idea, Brinley went inside to grab her keys, the crutches, and her purse.

The drive took a few short minutes but when she pulled into his driveway, she lost her nerve. Maybe stopping in wasn't such a good idea. He could be busy working and not want to be interrupted. He could even have a woman inside, God forbid, which convinced her even more that she had made a huge mistake. The last thing she wanted to see was the guy she was secretly crushing on with someone else.

Wells watched through his living room window as Brinley's car pulled into his driveway. He was surprised—pleasantly so—to see that she took the initiative to come to him. But as she sat in her car, not making a move to get out, he knew she was second-guessing her decision. He could see her facial expressions change through the windshield of her car and knew the instant she had decided to cut bait and run. Before she could restart her car and drive away, he opened his front door and stepped out onto the landing and waved his hand in welcome.

Seeing the smile that came to her face, he watched as Brinley got out of the car, waving back at him. When she pulled the crutches from her backseat, she shut her door and made her way to where he was standing. "You're walking normally," he grinned as he took the crutches she held out to him.

"I'm feeling great," Brinley answered. "I don't need these anymore, so I thought I'd better return them."

"I'll make sure to get them to their rightful owner. Want to come in for a bit?" he asked, hoping she would take him up on his offer. While it really wasn't a good idea to get any closer to Brinley than he'd already become, he was finding it hard to resist the temptation.

"Uh...sure," she gave in, following him through the front door.

When Brinley came to a stop inside the cabin, she couldn't help but admire the cleanliness of the place. It was obvious that she was in the presence of a military man, with the precision of every single piece of furniture, magazine, and knickknack, down to the placement of his neatly ordered pillows in their rightful spot. Her scattered items around her own cabin must have driven him nuts when he visited!

The second thing that hit her was the faint smell of varnish. Turning, she saw a beautiful rocking chair sitting on an old drop cloth, the sun gleaming off its surface. "Oh my," she exclaimed, moving to get a closer look at the exquisitely crafted, intricately detailed rocking chair. "This is so beautiful," she praised. "So, this is what you've been working on?"

"Yep," he said, coming to stand next to her. "I finished it last night. Go ahead, sit on it," he offered.

Brinley grinned before moving onto the tarp and running her hand over the wood. The ivy leaves lovingly etched into the wood on the top part of the chair were so detailed that she couldn't help but admire it. "How on earth did you do this?"

"It's not hard. Once I stenciled the pattern on, I used a couple of different methods. For the deeper, recessed parts of the design I used a small chisel. For the lighter parts I used my Dremel. Once you know what you're doing it's not that hard."

Knowing he was most definitely understating the amount of work that went into this beautiful creation, Brinley cautiously sat on the smooth surface of the seat and leaned back. The chair gently rocked with a slight push of her feet, gliding back and forth smoothly on the floor. Her hands rested on the arms of the chair, admiring more of the etchings he'd created on the flat surface. Tears came to her eyes as she remembered a time not too far in the past when she had sat in a similar rocking chair in Annie's bedroom, holding her in her arms as she slept.

Wells saw the change that came over Brinley and quickly stepped in. "Not bad for a big ole Navy Seal…huh?" he interjected with a slight laugh.

Brinley stood up, brushing a tear from the corner of her eyes. "It's beautiful, Wells. Your father taught you well."

"I was just going to sit out back and have a glass of lemonade. Care to join me?"

"Sure."

"Great, head out through that door," he said pointing to the back wall of his cabin. "I'll be out in a few with our drinks."

Grateful to have a few seconds to herself, Brinley did as he directed and headed out to his patio. Lecturing herself to get a grip, she wiped the last trace of moisture from her cheek and sat at the small table, the only furniture Wells had on the patio, and looked around, admiring the view.

It wasn't long before Wells joined her, carrying a tray with the promised lemonade and a plate of cookies and some white napkins. "Can't have a drink without a snack to go with it, right? I learned this from my mother."

Brinley had to laugh at the store-bought Nutter Butter cookies he'd taken from a package and neatly placed on the plate, displaying them as if he'd slaved over their baking for hours. The funny thing was Brinley had always loved those cookies but stopped buying them when her skirts began to get a little tight and her husband, Dean, had commented on it.

Shaking the memory off, Brinley took one of the cookies and bit into it, sighing in pleasure. "I haven't had one of these in years," she mentioned, groaning in pleasure. "So good," she added, stuffing the last bite in her mouth.

"Girl after my own heart," Wells joked, grabbing one off the plate and stuffing it in his mouth whole. "So good," he agreed, laughing as he nearly choked on the delicious cookie.

"Serves you right," she admonished. "A treat such as this needs to be savored, not stuffed in your mouth like you're a starving man."

"Says you," he drawled, grabbing another cookie and shoving it in his mouth. "So," he continued after he finished his cookie and took a drink of lemonade. "Can I ask you a question?"

"Sure," Brinley responded cautiously.

"Why are you here in Green River and how come you've stayed so long? It's been like what…nearly two years?"

Brinley hated that this came up, but she wasn't that surprised. Over the past ten days or so, Wells had been more than forthcoming with information on his own life and had graciously accepted her swift conversation changes whenever he asked a question concerning her. If she had any intentions of remaining friends with this man, it only seemed fair that she share a bit of her own life. It wasn't like she was holding state secrets or anything. She wasn't hiding anything, other than a lot of pain and heartache that she didn't like dumping on others. It was so much easier to hear of other people's happy lives and not reveal her sad state. While she hadn't really interacted with many people since the death of her husband and daughter, she knew if she did she would be the recipient of pity and concern. Something she couldn't bear and avoided at all costs.

"Let's start with something simple," Wells encouraged. "Where are you from?"

Brinley giggled as he raised his eyebrows suggestively. "I've lived in Casper, Wyoming, all my life. My house is there. Sort of," she finished softly.

Wells moved his hands in a rolling motion, encouraging her to continue.

"There's really not much to tell. My parents died when I was fifteen years old in a car accident. They were hit by a drunk driver. I had no other relatives so a family friend took me in until I went away to college, then I was on my own. I graduated with a degree in business administration, got a job right out of college with McGill & Son Construction as their human resource director, met my husband there, got married and had a baby. And now I'm here."

"Without the husband and baby," Wells said evenly. "How come?"

Brinley sighed heavily. "One night there was a fire at our house. I was upstairs in the bedroom sound asleep. I'd been sick with the flu for several days. It was hard. Dean worked a lot of hours and I was exhausted taking care of a fifteen-month-old baby and battling the flu. I finally begged Dean to come home early to take care of Annie for a while so I could get some rest. I took some Nyquil and was completely dead to the world. I woke up to Annie's crying. Smoke had filled the bedroom and hallway. A fire started downstairs and by the time I woke up the flames were on the steps creeping closer to Annie's room. I started crawling toward her but passed out before I got to her. A neighbor must have called 9-1-1 because the next thing I know I'm in the back of an ambulance with an oxygen mask over my face."

"Oh God, Brin. I'm so sorry."

"Dean was dead, burned to death by the flames. Annie died of smoke inhalation the next day. It was too much for her little body," Brinley whispered as Wells reached across the table and grabbed her hand. "When they let me out of the hospital, I took care of the funeral arrangements, hired someone to repair the first-floor living room and stairway that was destroyed, then left Casper and didn't look back. Found the cabin I'm staying in now and the rest is history."

"You grieved alone," Wells concluded.

"Alone is better," Brinley stated matter-of-factly.

"You can't believe that," he said gently.

"I *know* it," she said adamantly. "If you're alone you can't get hurt. I'm done losing people from my life."

"Brin…"

"Enough…" she said firmly, wiping the tears from her eyes and removing her hand from his. "I need to head to the store before it gets too late. Can I pick anything up for you this time?" she said, standing up to leave. "It's my turn to do something nice for you."

"Why don't you stay here for dinner," Wells offered. He hated the thought of her going back to her place alone after reliving the death of her husband and child.

"I'm good, really I am. I plan on picking up what I need, then heading back home and getting lost in a good book. You sure I can't pick anything up for you?"

"I'm good," he said following her around the side of his cabin and out to her car. "I know that was hard," he said grabbing Brinley's hand before she got in her car. "Promise me you'll call if you need me."

"I promise," she laughed. "Thanks to you I can do that now."

Wells watched as Brinley started her car, waved briefly, then backed out of his driveway. He stood there for a while, long after she left, thinking about what she had told him. He'd known the gist of what had happened but hearing about her ordeal firsthand was jarring. Whereas before he believed she was involved, he was now convinced that she was completely innocent. This changed everything. He was going to have to tread very carefully.

Chapter Ten

BRINLEY TAPPED HER foot on the wooden floor as she leaned against her kitchen counter surveying the set table. Was it too much? Maybe the candles were a little too suggestive. Deciding they were, she went to the table and removed them, glanced back at the table, decided it was now too bare and put them right back. She didn't have to light them after all, did she? They could just be there for the look. Table symmetry was important after all, right? Satisfied with her decision, Brinley went back to the stove to stir the gravy she had made to go with her roast.

The past week had been very enlightening. She and Wells had spent a lot of time together, talking as they walked through the wooded areas near their cabins or sitting on one of their patios. She enjoyed her conversations with him. He was easy to talk to and she always came away surprised with how comfortable she had gotten with him. Through his gentle questioning she had opened up a lot about her relationship with her now-deceased husband. The more she spoke of Dean, the more it seemed she had questions.

Dean's dismissive attitude toward her and their daughter she had chalked up to the stresses of taking over his father's construction company. Now she realized he was simply being cold. His father's death had taken a toll on Dean but she was thinking with more clarity and realized he had always been like that with her, even before James McGill died and Dean had taken on the burden of McGill & Son Construction. In fact, Dean was very similar to his father. There were many times when Brinley sat in her office and could hear the old man yelling at one of his employees about some infraction or another. As their Human Resources director, she fielded many complaints concerning both James and Dean. She spent a great deal of her time calming ruffled feathers.

Early on it was easy to blame the stresses of the company for Dean's inadequacies as a husband and father. Memories of her precious daughter toddling in her awkward gait toward the front door, raising her little arms up as Dean walked through the front door wanting to be picked up and how he would brush her aside came rushing back. She hated those moments when Annie would turn toward her with her bottom lip quivering at the rejection by her own father. Dean always tried to cover it up with a pat on the top of her head and a quick "Daddy loves his little girl" comment as he walked toward the cupboard for a glass of his favorite scotch he always kept on hand. He seemed to prefer his nighttime cocktail to the moments he could have spent with his wife and daughter giving them the time and attention they needed and deserved.

It was a little eye-opening to realize after all this time that she hadn't been truly happy in her marriage. She'd settled for less than she deserved. The only reason she could think of as to why she allowed herself to be in that type of relationship was because she'd spent so much of her time alone. She was looking for someone to have as a partner and Dean came along at the right time. They worked well together; he was convenient and had paid attention to her. She'd set the bar extremely low and at the time had been happy just to not be alone. After the death of her parents, she'd always longed for a family and evidently had jumped at the opportunity when Dean asked for her hand in marriage.

After spending just weeks in Wells's company she was starting to see the difference between the two men. She liked the way it felt to have someone show an interest in her life. Wells was very good at drawing her out, getting her to talk about her parents, her life with Dean, what it had meant to her to be a mother, and how hard it had been to lose her only child. He was a good listener and was equally good at sharing about his own life.

A knock at the door made her jump and very nearly drop the spoon she was using to stir the gravy. Placing it on the spoon rest beside the pan, she turned just as Wells walked in, a smile on his face.

"Hey," he grinned, carrying a bottle of wine in and setting it on the table. "I wasn't sure what you were making so I bought a bottle of merlot. I hope that's okay."

"That's fine," Brinley answered, taking in the spectacular view of dark chest hair peeking out from the opened blue shirt lovingly molded to Wells's upper body. Swallowing deeply, she raised her eyes and smiled back at him. "Roast," she murmured quietly. "We're having roast so the merlot will go nicely with it."

"Perfect. I'll open it so it can breathe for a few."

The smirk on his face as he turned told Brinley that he knew exactly what she had been looking at. She had to get her thoughts under control. She was acting like a young adolescent having her first crush, for god's sake!

"So, what did you do today?" Brinley asked as she went over to open the oven to check on their dinner. The antiquated oven made it difficult to judge the timing of a perfectly medium-rare temperature of the meat.

"I sold my rocking chair," he answered proudly.

"Oh Wells, that's awesome," she said closing the oven door and turning toward him. "I'm so happy for you. It really was a beautiful work of art."

"Thanks. It's always so satisfying when I sell a piece that I've worked so hard on. I'm happy it's going to someone who loves it but after…well, then I feel that loss."

"Loss?"

"I put my heart and soul in my projects. When you think about it, every day for hours on end my only thought is developing that wood into something special. When that ends, I feel a little lost, empty almost."

"So, what will you do?" she asked curiously.

"Come up with a new project. And fast," he joked. "Me being idle is never a good thing."

"Do you have something in mind?" Brinley asked, and judging the roast to be done, started setting the food out on the table.

"Not sure yet. I was thinking of maybe doing something for my mom. If I start now I could have it done by Christmas, give it to her as a present."

"Why do I get the impression you're not completely sold on that idea? I think she'd love something made by you."

"Dad taught me everything I know. She has a ton of things around her place that he did for her. I'm not so sure anything I could come up with could compare to things he did," Wells said honestly.

"But you're her son," Brinley encouraged. "That's different. I'm sure it would mean the world to her to have something that you made with your own hands."

Brinley placed a bowl of mashed potatoes on the table, then went over to her purse hanging by the front door. Taking out a piece of paper, she turned, walked over to Wells, and handed it to him.

Admiring the colorful squiggles on the piece of paper, Wells smiled down at Brinley. "Annie do this?" he asked, understanding the importance of the unidentifiable artwork.

"Two days before the fire. You can't even tell what it is, but I remember her sitting in her highchair with the crayons in her little hand laughing as she streaked them across this paper. It means everything to me. Just like anything you do will mean something to your mom. Do it, Wells. Trust me, it will make your mother's entire Christmas because you made it for her."

"Maybe you're right," he said, handing the paper back to Brinley, then cupping her cheek with his hand, grateful that she had shared something that meant so much to her.

They stared at each other for several seconds before Wells awkwardly stepped back. The intimacy with that look was more than he should have allowed himself. "I guess I have a new project," he intoned.

"Good," Brinley encouraged, bereft of his touch. "Let's eat before it gets cold."

Wells poured them each a glass of wine as Brinley took the roast out of the oven. When they were seated at the table they dug into the food, each talking about their day and any plans they had about the next. That was one of the things Brinley loved about spending time with Wells. The conversation was always easy. She especially liked it when he told her funny stories about his mom and their nightly chats. It said a lot about him that he still spoke to her every day, checking in to make sure she was doing all right.

"What did you do when you were deployed outside of the country?" Brin asked. "She must have hated it when you couldn't call her all the time."

"It was hard on her, but she never made me feel guilty. I know she worried, especially since when I was able to call, she never really knew where I was, and I couldn't tell her. That's why I do it now. I don't want her to worry anymore."

"You're a good son."

"Some days Mom would agree with you, others not so much," he laughed finishing the last bite of roast beef from his plate. Taking the half-eaten roll he'd saved, he used it to sop up the remaining gravy and stuck it in his mouth, humming in pleasure. "So good," he said when he caught her smiling at him.

"I'm glad you liked it," Brinley said as she stood up and started to clear the dishes.

They worked in companionable silence to clean the table and had the dishes done in record time.

"Would you like some coffee, a couple of cookies?" Brinley asked as she hung the dishtowel on the handle of the stove.

Wells watched as a slight blush crept up Brinley's neck. There had been no mistaking the sexual attraction that radiated between them. But getting involved with her—no matter how attractive he found her—was a very bad idea.

"I really should go," he told her. "The dinner was delicious though," he said as he started to brush past her.

When his arm glanced off the side of her firm breast, he inhaled a deep breath and closed his eyes. There was something about her scent and the way her eyes looked at him with hope and longing that had him changing his mind. "Fuck it," he whispered as he cupped her cheeks in the palm of his hands and took her mouth in what could only be described as an all-consuming kiss.

Brinley had no idea how much time lapsed. She loved the feel of being in Wells's arms, the strength he exuded as he masterfully wrapped them around her. It was only when the sound of an animal howling outside her cabin reached her ears that she came to her senses and stepped back from Wells, touching her swollen lips in surprise. His appeal was devastating to her senses.

"Wells…I…" she stammered.

"I'd better go," he interrupted. There was no way he would apologize for kissing her—it was, after all, the best kiss of his life—but he should have known better. Had in fact lectured himself before coming over that he needed to keep his distance. He was on a search for the truth and while he felt she was not as involved as he originally thought, she wouldn't appreciate that he had orchestrated their meeting. She was not the woman for him.

Brinley watched as he grabbed his keys from the kitchen counter. When he started toward the door, something inside of her broke. She'd spent so much time alone, grieving alone, surviving alone, that she simply couldn't do it anymore. Throwing caution to the wind, she called out to Wells. "Don't go," she nearly pleaded.

Wells turned from the door and shook his head. "I really need to go, Brin. I shouldn't have kissed you."

"I'm asking you to stay," she stated quietly.

"I can't. You know what will happen if I do. I don't want you to have any regrets."

In answer Brinley walked up to him and placed her hands on his chest. "No regrets," she assured him before leaning up on her toes, wrapping her arms around his neck, and pressing her lips against his.

Wells remained stock-still, trying to resist the temptation that Brinley posed. It took all of one minute before he growled in frustration, picked her up and carried her through to her bedroom. He was going to burn in hell for this but there was no way he could resist her.

When he got to the side of her bed, Wells slowly released her legs to the floor. When she was steady enough, he reached for the buttons on her shirt and looked her in the eye as he started to undo them. "You have to be sure, Brin," he breathed heavily. "You think you know me, but you don't."

"I know what I need to know," Brin responded, pushing his hands aside and finishing the job. She might not know the nitty-gritty details of his life, but she knew his soul. She knew his kindness by the way he took care of her when she was vulnerable. She knew his integrity by the way he put his life on hold to serve his country at the risk of losing his own. Not many men were so selfless, but he had lived it and to her, that spoke volumes.

Grabbing the ends of her blouse, she pushed it off her shoulders and stood in front of him, waiting to see what he would do.

It didn't take long before she had her answer. He reached out and gently touched the fingertips of both hands to her cheeks. He slowly ran them down to her neck, pausing to kiss each area as he went. He worshipped the softness of her skin, grazing the delicate features with his lips. When he reached her breasts, he molded them in his hands and placed a kiss in the center of her chest. Releasing her, he reached around her back, and unclasped her bra. He drew the straps from her shoulders and tossed the filmy material aside.

"You're killing me," Brinley whispered as he placed kisses all over her skin, always coming close but not touching her nipples.

"Patience," he purred as he reached for the waistband of her slacks.

Kissing his way down her stomach, he knelt at her feet, drawing the material of her slacks and her panties down as he went. When he had her completely naked, he smiled up at her. "Beautiful," he praised.

Self-conscious, Brinley moved her hands to cover herself when Wells stopped her with a single word. "Don't," he said simply.

Obeying his command, she closed her eyes and gave in to the sensual torture he proceeded to engulf her in. He left no part of her body untouched, exploring each gentle curve and contour as he made his way back up her body. By the time his mouth closed over a nipple, Brinley's legs gave out. He caught her to him, lifting her to the bed and placing her in the center, his mouth never leaving her. After he gave a generous amount of attention to both breasts, he finally stood back and stared into Brinley's eyes as he started to undress.

The visual contact was more erotic than anything she had ever experienced before. It was as though he were looking directly into her soul and could read her very thoughts. The only time she even thought about looking away was when he bent to remove his jeans and boxers. When he stood back up, she nearly swallowed her tongue. The man was absolute perfection. His chest looked as if it was chiseled from clay, it was so beautifully muscular with just the right amount of hair. Not even the scars on his chest and arms could take away from his attractiveness. He had a flat stomach and thighs as thick as tree trunks. And although she didn't have much experience with the male anatomy other than her husband's, he was most definitely generously proportioned in that category.

No longer able to stand not touching him, she reached out her hand, beckoning him to the bed.

Reaching into his jeans he took out his wallet, removed a foil packet and joined her on the bed.

"Was I a foregone conclusion?" she teased.

"Nothing about you is a foregone conclusion," he answered, covering her body with his. "You are the most unpredictable, frustrating woman I've ever met. But I find I like that about you."

Humming in pleasure, Brinley gave in to the ardent kisses Wells was covering her body with. He kissed her taut nipples, rousing a melting sweetness within her. His expert touch sent her to higher levels of ecstasy than she had ever experienced before. His raw sensuousness carried her to greater heights, so much so that when he finally, carefully entered her, she thought her heart would explode.

"Stay with me," he urged breathlessly, finding a rhythm that soon had them both on edge.

Heat rippled under Brinley's skin as she recognized the flush of sexual desire that she knew signaled her imminent orgasm. Not wanting to disappoint Wells or herself, she hung on for as long as she could.

"Let go," he urged as with one final thrust, they both found their release in a kaleidoscope of sweaty limbs, rapid heartbeats, and erotic whisperings.

As Brinley fought to catch her breath, the turbulence of Wells's passion swirled around her. Nothing had prepared her for what it was like to be like to be with a man like him. He left her speechless and uncertain of herself.

"Are you okay?" Wells asked as he looked down and saw the confusion in Brinley's eyes. "What's wrong?"

Seeing the concern on his face, Brinley clasped his cheeks in her hands. "Absolutely nothing is wrong," she said, leaning up to place a kiss on his lips.

"What aren't you saying?" Wells asked curiously.

Brinley pushed until he rolled off her and was on his back. She snuggled into his side, placing her hand over the scar near his heart and her head on his shoulder. Feeling his hand on her hip she sighed. "It was…intense,' she tried to explain. "I haven't felt that before."

"With anyone?"

"I was only ever with my husband and I feel like I'm betraying our marriage but no, it was never like that with him."

"If it makes you feel any better, I've never felt it so strongly before either. I've been with other women but this…this was different. I can't explain it."

"Maybe we shouldn't. Explain it I mean." Leaning up she gazed down at Wells. "I'm not expecting anything," she started. "This is new to me and I just want to enjoy being with you. Is that okay? No explanations, no commitments."

"I agree," he said, pulling her down next to him. "No explanations, no commitments."

"But we can do it again, though, right?" she asked sleepily.

She felt his chest rumble with laughter. "Yeah, we can do it again," he said as her breath evened out indicating she had fallen asleep.

By morning they had done it several more times, with short naps in between. The sun was just coming up the last time they made love. Laughing, they both got in the tiny shower to conserve what little hot water her small tank produced. At first Brinley felt awkward having him in such close quarters with her but in his usual fashion, Wells made it easier with his quick sense of humor.

He made them a light breakfast of toast and scrambled eggs and cleaned the kitchen before declaring that he needed to get going. Brinley walked him to the door, sad that he was leaving.

"No regrets, right?" he asked as he kissed her goodbye.

"No regrets," she assured him as he stepped out the door.

Wells walked to his car and got in, resting his head on the steering wheel for several seconds, taking a deep breath to calm his uneasy conscience. He had no regrets for giving in and making love to her. She was the most amazing woman he'd been with in a long time.

"She's going to hate me," he whispered sadly as he started the car and backed out of her driveway.

Chapter Eleven

Brinley paced her small living room, frustrated at herself and with Wells. Mostly with herself for feeling so needy in wanting to see him again, a little at Wells for not being needy enough. Not that he wasn't being a perfect gentleman. In the two days since she'd last seen him—the morning after they made love—he'd called each day to check on her to make sure she was all right. Unfortunately, he always seemed to have something important to do that prevented them from seeing each other. She detested how excited she got when her phone rang and it was his voice. Then she felt let down when they hung up and hadn't made a plan to get together.

No commitments…what a stupid thing for her to say to him. He probably thought she was some cold, aloof woman and was only respecting what she had said to him. When in fact all she really wanted was to be with him. It served her right to stew like this. What an idiot!

It was all Dean's fault, she decided as she laid in bed the night before wanting, needing Wells to be with her. Dean had taught her in the early stages of their marriage not to rely on him. Once he had his ring on her finger, he rarely made it home for dinners, much less allowed time for them to simply spend time together doing small things. Each time she asked him to watch a movie with her, take a walk, plan a vacation, he always had an excuse. And always it was blamed on the job. Not even when their daughter was born did he take any time to be with them. The fact that he arrived at the hospital thirty minutes before she was born and left twenty minutes after meeting her showed Brinley a lot.

For years she tried to be an understanding wife but now looking back in hindsight, he was not a loving, caring man and never had been. Not with her and certainly not with their daughter. Now that the blinders were off, she wasn't very proud of what she had allowed her marriage to become. And certainly, she was as much at fault as he had been.

But he was gone now, and it was time for her to pick up the pieces. It wasn't until about three o'clock this morning that she decided that maybe it was time to go back to Casper to check on things. Not to stay, she wasn't ready for that yet, but going back for a brief visit seemed like a good idea. Wells had done that for her. Spending time with him had given her a little peace, enough that she was finding the courage to start living again.

Brinley stopped pacing and smiled to herself. It *was* time to start living again. And just maybe it was also time to strike out and be bold. Why sit around and wait for things to happen? She'd done that enough in the twenty-seven years that she'd been alive. So, what if she simply went for a walk and by some chance it *happened* to lead her by Wells's place? What would be the harm in that?

Wells finished cleaning the kitchen then made his way into the bedroom to pack a few things. It was time to make a visit back home. His mom had been relentless in asking him to come back for a visit so maybe it was time. He could check on his condo while he was there, make sure the bills were paid and maybe even check up on his friends if they weren't out on deployment. He hadn't bothered answering his phone in a while so it was well past time that he reached out to everyone in his circle.

Besides, he needed to get his head on straight. He hadn't been able to stop thinking about Brinley. She was a constant thought in his head, and it took everything he had not to go over to her place to spend time with her. It was strange how in just a short amount of time he missed her. He enjoyed being around women, but it was different with her. He loved just hanging out with her. He not only liked her, but he respected her. So much so that he was thinking it was time to have a conversation. He couldn't stand the thought of hurting her so when he got back, he would sit her down and tell her everything and hope like hell that she wouldn't hate him.

After tossing a few things into his overnight bag, Wells zipped it closed and walked out to his truck. His plan was to get an early start in the morning so he was loading his vehicle with everything he wanted to take so he wouldn't have to worry about it at five o'clock when it was still dark outside.

Closing the back door to the cab of his truck, he turned when he heard a noise and watched as Brinley stepped from the wooded path near his place.

"Hey," she said breathlessly.

"Hey yourself," he smiled back, happy to see her.

"I was out for a walk and just happened to be passing by. Where you heading?" she asked nodding to the door he'd just closed.

"I thought I'd head back to Casper in the morning, spend a few hours, check on some things, see my mom."

"So, you're coming right back?"

"I am. Want to come in for a drink?" he asked politely.

Brinley hesitated for a few seconds. She hated that after such an intense night together they were back to being awkward around each other.

Wells, seeing the hesitation and strain on her face, couldn't stand to see Brinley looking so unsure of herself. In two strides he was in front of her, weaving his fingers through her hair as he captured her lips in an intimate kiss. As he expected, she responded without reservation, wrapping her arms around his waist, pulling him closer.

When Wells drew back, Brinley smiled up at him. "Okay, to be honest, I purposely walked by your place. I missed you."

"Come inside," he said, wrapping an arm around her waist and guiding her to his front door. Her honesty unnerved him. He owed her the same.

When they were seated at the table with a glass of iced tea, Wells reached over to hold her hand. "How are you?"

"Wells," she laughed. "You asked me that last night when you called. And the night before. I'm good. Really good in fact."

"Really good? Do tell," he encouraged. He liked that she was smiling. He liked that some of the weight of her life she seemed to carry on her shoulders when he first met her was lifting. He could tell just by sitting next to her that she was finally letting go of some of her grief.

"I was actually thinking that it was time to head back to Casper myself. I really should check on the house, start facing the past."

"To stay?"

"No. I'm not ready for that. I thought that I could, like you, just go back for the day maybe. It's a first step, anyway."

"Do you want to come with me tomorrow?" he asked, surprised that those words came out of his mouth. This trip was about getting some distance from her, not putting him into closer contact.

"Really?' she asked. "I hadn't thought about doing it right away but maybe it's time. Besides, being with you might make it easier."

"I'm sure it would."

"Wait, how far apart do you live from where my house is? Maybe it wouldn't make sense to go together."

"It's not far," he told her. "Maybe about five miles." When she looked at him strangely, his face turned a shade of pink. "Okay, maybe I looked you up," he said trying to cover his tracks. He'd known for a long time exactly where she lived. "What can I say? I was curious."

"Hmmm," she whispered, thinking about actually going back to a place that held such awful memories.

"Brin, if you aren't sure about this that's fine. Don't push yourself to do something you're not ready for," he offered.

"No, I think I need to do this. If you're sure you don't mind the company. You could just drop me off at the house, go do whatever you need to and pick me up when you're ready to head back."

"Sounds like a plan. I was going to head out around five in the morning. Is that too early for you? The drive takes about three hours and forty-five minutes, so I wanted to get an early start."

"That's fine with me."

"You could stay here tonight," he offered with a smile.

"Are you trying to seduce me, Mr. Kennedy?"

"Maybe."

"I'd like that."

Standing up Wells grabbed her hand. "Come on, I'll drive you over to your place to grab what you need."

"I can walk, you know."

"Takes too long," he grinned, wiggling his eyebrows suggestively in that way he had.

Laughing, Brinley followed him out to his truck and let him help her in.

It didn't take long for her to pack what she needed. They weren't staying the night in Casper, so it was only the few things for the one night with Wells. Within twenty minutes they were back at his place in the kitchen together preparing a light dinner. They ate in front of the television—something she hadn't done in forever—watching a movie he had picked out. There was something very natural about sitting on the couch snuggled in Wells's arms watching television. Brinley loved the comfort he brought her simply by being near him. It was unlike anything she had experienced before, and she was finding that she liked it.

At one point during the movie Wells leaned over and started nibbling on the curve of Brinley's neck. She shivered and felt like a breathless girl of eighteen, not the seasoned woman she really was. When he pulled away, she looked over to him and found him watching her. There was a deeper significance to the visual interchange between them. It was hard to define but it drew her to him like nothing else could have.

Without reservation she raised up, swinging her left leg over his hips so that she was in his lap facing him. He made no attempt to hide the fact that he was watching her, waiting to see what she was up to. She was only marginally aware of his assessment as she started kissing the exposed part of his chest near his throat. Slowly she rained gentle pecks up his neck and chin until she finally reached his lips. She abandoned all pretense at tenderness and pushed her tongue into his mouth, thrilling in his immediate response.

When Wells took over there was no doubt about his desire. He pushed her back onto the couch, coming over her to deepen the kiss. While his mouth covered hers, Brinley was barely aware that his hand was between them, pushing her top up past her bra. With renewed impatience, Wells broke the kiss and roughly pushed her bra up and exposed her breasts. Cupping them in his hands, he lowered his head and feasted on them like a man starved.

Not wanting to be a passive participant, Brinley reached below and awkwardly unzipped his pants. It took several seconds but when she finally had them undone, she pushed them over his hips as far as she could get them, then tried to maneuver her foot enough to get inside the waistband to push.

"You could help," she panted.

Chuckling, Wells leaned up, putting enough space between them so she could accomplish the task of getting his pants down to his ankles, then returned his attention back to her chest. Satisfied, Brinley grasped him in her hands and began to pleasure him as he continued his assault on her senses.

After a few short minutes Wells released her. "Enough," he said hoarsely.

"What's wrong?" she asked innocently, pleased that she had him as on edge as much he had her.

"Tease," he grumbled as he stood up, scooping her body against his chest. Kicking the material of his jeans away from his ankles, Wells hurried to his bedroom, practically tossing Brinley on the bed when they entered. He finished undressing, then turned his attention to removing Brinley's clothes.

When he finally had her completely naked, he flipped her onto her stomach, kissing his way down her spine as she twisted in pleasure on the bed. Knowing they were both close to their release, he grabbed her hips and lifted until she was on her knees on the bed, her cheek resting on the blankets. Without hesitation, he climbed onto the bed, taking her from behind.

Brinley gave herself over to the pleasure Wells was creating between them. Explosive currents raced through her and her pulse quickened as together they reached the precipice before falling over in unison, their collective groans assuring her that she wasn't alone in her release. In fact, it wasn't until she felt his hands moving gently down her back that she realized she had completely zoned out in her euphoria.

Chapter Twelve

BRINLEY COVERED HER yawn as she looked out the truck window, watching the sun come up as they drove. It was comforting to be sitting next to this gorgeous man, her hand firmly tucked in his as the miles passed by.

Wells had been insatiable the night before. They'd barely gotten any sleep before his alarm went off at four-thirty and he forced her out of bed and into the shower. It was only the promise that he would stop for coffee at the first opportunity that had her moving more quickly to get in the truck.

True to his word, Wells stopped at the first exit that had a McDonald's and got them both a hot coffee and a couple of breakfast sandwiches. After eating they drove for several miles in companionable silence. Brinley was nearly asleep when Wells spoke.

"Are you going to be okay at the house?" he asked worriedly.

"Of course. Why?"

"You mentioned that you made arrangements to have the house repaired after the fire. Is it really, completely repaired? I hate to think of you going back to a burned structure."

"I haven't been back since they fixed it, but my insurance people assure me it was taken care of and the smoke damage addressed."

"So, it's been just sitting there? Unoccupied?"

"I pay someone to go in once a week to check on the inside, run the water and stuff. I also have a lawn company that goes over and mows and weeds once a week during the spring and summer. It's not been completely neglected," she said defensively.

Wells reached over the console and took her hand. "I wasn't judging you, Brin. I was just worried about leaving you if the house was a mess."

"Sorry. I'm feeling a little anxious about going back. I'll be fine in the house alone. I've been thinking of putting it on the market so I really need to see for myself what I'm dealing with before I can do that."

"You really want to sell it?" Wells asked.

"I do. Too many bad memories there. It's a beautiful house, though. Just not for me."

For the rest of the drive Wells left Brinley to her thoughts. She seemed to want to be left alone so he respected her silence. It wasn't until they got within the city limits that she spoke, and it was only to give him directions as they got closer to where she lived.

When he finally pulled into her driveway, they sat in silence staring at the house.

"You okay?" he eventually asked. "I'll go in with you," he said, reaching over for the door handle.

Brinley grasped his arm to stop him. "No. It's okay," she said weakly. "I need to do this on my own."

"You have your phone with you, right?" When she nodded yes, he reached over and touched her cheek to get her attention. "You need me, even if it's five minutes from now, you call me, okay? I'll come right back."

"I will. Thanks, Wells. I'm okay. Promise."

Leaning over he grasped her chin to turn her face toward his again. "I mean it, Brin. You need me, just call," he reiterated before placing a soft kiss on her lips. "You've got this."

"Right. I've got this," she smiled lamely, then reached for the door handle and got out of the truck. When she walked up the front steps, she turned to wave at Wells, then retrieved her keys from her purse and inserted it in the lock. Wells waved back, watching as she disappeared behind the door, worried about what nightmares she was about to face alone.

The first thing that Brinley noticed when she walked into the house was the smell of new carpeting. As hard as she tried, she couldn't detect one whiff of smoke, which surprised her. Whatever company the insurance people found had done a really good job.

Not sure where to look first, she moved to her right, avoiding looking at the steps leading to the second level, and walked into the living room where most of the fire damage had occurred. She stopped suddenly and looked at the space where she was told the fire had originated. And while the carpeting had been replaced and the walls rebuilt and freshly painted, she couldn't take her eyes off the spot where her husband had been found dead, his body burned beyond recognition. It was only by the wedding ring on his left hand and the hideous ring he always wore on his right hand that she knew the burned figure found in the living room was indeed her husband.

Shaking her head, she slowly walked from room to room on the first level. Everything was as it had been before the fire, only cleaned and polished. Fortunately, it was only the living room, hallway, and the stairs leading up to the bedrooms that had been severely damaged. It all looked like new, other than the fact that whatever furniture got burned had not been replaced.

Knowing there was no place else left to inspect, Brinley headed back to the living room and slowly walked up the steps. Timidly, she entered her daughter's bedroom and nearly collapsed as memories assailed her. Her crib was still intact but had been cleaned of soot by the cleaning crew as had the pictures on the walls and every surface of the room. The rocking chair where Brinley spent so much time snuggling and rocking Annie asleep was still there as well as all the little baby clothes and stuffed toys. Raggedly inhaling, Brinley dropped to her knees and sobbed uncontrollably.

Wells pulled into the parking lot of his condo and looked around. It all looked the same. The lawns were neatly cut, flowers lined the beds around the buildings, and fresh mulch gave off that earthy scent that he loved.

The first thing he did was head to the management office to pick up his mail. When he first moved in and they learned that he was military, the people who ran the property were kind enough to offer taking care of his mail. Knowing he would be deployed for long periods of time, it made sense to take them up on the offer. He chatted with the girl at the desk for a few minutes, thanked her for the mail, then headed to his place.

It seemed strange when he walked in. Everything had been neatly dusted and vacuumed—thanks to his mom who checked on his place regularly—but it didn't feel like home. He'd never experienced this feeling before, but for some reason this time was different. It was kind of sad to realize how sterile the place was. Other than a few pictures, there was nothing to signify his own likes or dislikes. It was bland, barren of any character. Not like Brinley's cabin, he thought smiling to himself. Even as a temporary place she'd made it her own, and probably hadn't even realized she had. With her girly magazines tossed around, her special teacup that he learned she'd brought with her—one of the few things she had left of her mother's—and an old blanket that had been hers as a little girl that was always on the back of her couch. That's what made a place special and something that wasn't reflected anywhere in his own condo.

Grabbing a bottle of water from his fridge, Wells sat on his couch and started going through the mail. Most of it was junk so it didn't take long to separate everything and toss what wasn't needed. Next, he checked his answering machine that was attached to his landline, grinning when he heard JP's voice practically yelling at him to call him back.

Jonah Perez, JP to those who were closest to him, was Wells's best friend. They'd met the day they were inducted together into the Navy. They had applied and were accepted to train as Navy Seals. And while Wells was close to all the brothers that were on his Seal team, JP was his ride or die. There was nothing JP wouldn't do for Wells and would, in fact, move heaven and earth to provide anything he needed. The same thing JP knew that Wells would do for him. Which made JP leaving a message on his home answering machine funny. JP knew his cell phone number and knew full well that that was the best way to reach him. But if by some odd chance he couldn't reach him, JP always made sure to leave a message on both phones. The man was quirky if nothing else.

Finishing the little chores he wanted to get done, Wells packed a few more clothes from his bedroom and headed back out to his truck. Within minutes he was pulling into the driveway of his mother's two-bedroom cottage.

Smiling, he took in the picture-perfect flowers and greenery enhancing the front. His mother's favorite thing to do was to putter in her yard when the weather permitted. It was the perfect little house, one level, and a second bedroom for when she insisted he stay with her. The grocery store was only a few minutes' drive in a little plaza that had anything she might need. Within walking distance were a little coffee shop and the public library that his mother visited often. Wells felt comfortable with his mother living here; it was the exact kind of place he would have chosen for her.

Knowing it was too nice a day for her to be inside, Wells headed around to the back and found his mother right where he knew she'd be—kneeling in her flower bed. Not wanting to startle her, he gently cleared his throat.

"You know I could hear your truck before you even pulled into the driveway," she said, pulling her gardening gloves off and looking up to smile at her son.

Wells walked over and reached out a hand to help his mother up. "So why didn't you come out to greet me," he teased.

"I knew you'd know where to look for me. Come here," she admonished, reaching her hands out to hug her son.

Ruby Kennedy was feisty woman who stood no taller than slightly over five feet high but could command a room full of people. Her hair was a soft pearl-gray and always perfectly coifed unless she was working in her garden. She was kindness personified but she did not suffer fools lightly. Her one weakness, which everybody knew, was her son. She made no bones about how dearly she loved him, but she also had no problem calling him out when she thought he was being, as she put it, an ass.

"How are you, sweetie?' she asked, pulling back so she could examine him closely.

"I'm good," he answered softly.

"No, you're not," she answered back. "Come on, let's go to the kitchen. I made chicken salad when you texted me last night that you were coming in. We'll have a nice lunch and you can tell me what's going on."

Wells followed his mom into the house and sat at the small kitchen table as she made their lunch. There was no way he was going to inform her that it wasn't even eleven o'clock in the morning yet. If his mom said they were going to eat, then they were going to eat. Besides, he was never stupid enough to turn down anything made by Ruby Kennedy.

"So, what's weighing on you?" she finally asked when they'd finished their sandwiches. The conversation while they ate was kept pretty light but evidently his mother was done with the pleasantries. "Are you finally ready to come back home? Maybe tell me what staying in that god-awful cabin in Green River is all about? I know leaving your team was hard on you but there's more to it than that."

"Mom, the time away has been good for me. But you're right, there's more to it, I just can't get into it right now. Please understand."

Ruby reached across the table and covered Wells's hand with her own. "It's okay, Wells. Tell me when you're ready. Are you at least safe?"

"I am absolutely safe, Mom. Except…there's this woman. She's staying in the cabin near mine."

"And you like her?" his mother asked hopefully. While she wasn't one to push, it was about time Wells gave her a grandchild to spoil.

"I do. Too much. I haven't exactly been completely honest with her and when she finds out—and she will—I'm afraid I'm going to lose her."

"It's not a true relationship unless you can be honest with her, Wells. Please, I'm begging you, before you get more involved you have to tell her the truth."

"I already figured that out, Mom. When I get back to Green River, I'm going to tell Brinley everything."

"I like the name," his mother smiled. "Is she why you left?"

"Yes. I thought she was involved with what I've been investigating but it turns out she wasn't. She's completely innocent in the whole thing and now I have to come clean because I really like her but I'm afraid she won't understand why I did it."

"You're being so cryptic, honey. Look, just be honest with her and if she feels anything for you, she'll understand. It may take a while, but you have to be patient. Just like I'm being patient with you and your non-answers. Since when did you become so obtuse?"

"Geez, Mom, cut me some slack, okay?"

"Of course, dear. I'm nothing if not understanding," she smirked.

"Come on, I'll help you clean up the kitchen, then you can lead me to those chores you wanted me to do for you."

Ruby patted her son's cheek and stood to help with the kitchen. When they were done, she handed him the list of things she needed help with and together they accomplished the tasks quickly. When he was sure that there was nothing else she needed done, Wells ran to the grocery store, picked up her items, and had them put away before she could shoo him from the kitchen. They shared a glass of iced tea before Wells looked at his watch and told her it was time for him to leave.

"Are you sure there's nothing else I can do while I'm here?" he asked for a third time.

"You've been awesome, honey. I'm all set. You go ahead and start the drive back. Just please, call me when you arrive safely at that cabin of yours."

"You know I will, Mom. I'll probably be back sometime next week but if you need me before, all you have to do is call. Okay?"

"Don't worry, I'm fine." Pushing the bag of leftover chicken salad into his hands, Ruby walked him to the door. "Thank you for taking care of all that stuff," she added. "You're such a good boy," she said kissing him on the cheek.

Wells hugged his mother, always feeling a little sad when he had to leave. "I'll call when I get back," he assured her. "Thanks for the leftovers," he added before kissing her one more time and heading to his truck. Taking his phone out, he texted Brinley that he was on his way back and pulled out of the driveway.

Traffic was light so it didn't take him long before he was back at Brinley's home. He slowly got out of the truck and approached her front door. He wasn't quite sure what he would find but when she opened the door, she was smiling at him.

"I just got your text. Come on in."

Wells followed her into the house, looking around as he went. Surprisingly, there was nothing to indicate that there had been a fire, much less that two humans had lost their lives in the house. The only things he was aware of were the scent of new carpeting and the echo of her empty living room.

"How are you?" he asked tentatively. "You look okay."

"I'm not sure what I'm feeling, to be honest with you. I was okay when I first walked in. The hard part was when I went upstairs to Annie's room. I literally had a meltdown. Took me a while to collect myself, it was just so difficult to be in there again. All of her things are still there. Her toys…her crib."

Seeing the tears in Brinley's eyes was his undoing. Wells quickly wrapped his arms around her and kissed the top of her head. "I can't imagine, honey. I'm so sorry."

Brinley absorbed the warmth of being in his arms for several seconds. Taking a deep breath, she pulled away and wiped at her eyes. "It's okay. I'm okay. Are you ready to head back?"

"Is there anything you want to take with you?"

"No," she said looking around. "My plan is to head back and spend some time thinking about what I want to do. There will be some things I want from Annie's room but until I figure out where I'll be, there's no point in taking anything with me."

Wells rubbed her back as they both quietly looked around, standing in the empty living room in silence.

"Hello, Brinley," a voice from behind them spoke.

The hairs on Brinley's neck instantly rose. She knew that voice. It was a voice from her past. It was the voice of a dead man.

Brinley jerked around and gasped in shock. There, as alive as anyone, stood her husband, Dean. A man she thought to be dead. A man whose ashes she had buried alongside their daughter's.

"How can this be?' she whispered, her knees nearly collapsing for the second time that day.

"I assure you it's me," he said acidly, watching as the man next to his wife put his arm around her in protection. "Hello, brother," he jeered.

Chapter Thirteen

Darkness started to descend as Brinley grappled with the words that she heard. Her husband was alive? Brother? Did she hear right that Wells was Dean's brother? Shaking her head to clear her brain, she stepped away from Wells, desperately needing space to try and figure things out.

"How can you be alive?" she asked Dean, addressing the foremost question in her head. "I buried you. I saw the rings on the charred body they carried out. They were yours. Where have you been these past two years? Why didn't you contact me? Why didn't you tell me you were alive? How could you let me grieve…think you were dead? How could you be so cruel?" she hissed.

Looking over to Wells, she laughed sharply. "And you. Was this some cosmic joke to you?"

"Brin, listen, please," Wells begged. "Dean isn't my biological brother. He was my stepbrother for about a minute back when I graduated from high school. We never even lived together…"

"I don't care," Brinley argued. "What's happening," she nearly sobbed as she clutched the sides of her head. "I can't believe what either of you have done."

"Brinley, please, I was going to tell you everything…"

"While this is all very charming," Dean said in a strained voice, "I really need to have a little chat with my wife. That is if you can stop trying to fondle her for two fucking minutes."

Wells lunged for Dean, grabbing him around the throat and knocking him down to the floor. Straddling his legs, he swung his right fist, connecting with Dean's nose. As the two men fought, Brinley grabbed her purse and ran out the door. When she reached the end of the walkway, she looked both ways, not sure which direction to go. The only thing she was certain of was the fact that she needed to get away. She'd been betrayed by both men and the last thing she wanted or needed was to hear any explanation from either of them.

The main highway leading out of town was toward her right, so she turned in that direction and started walking at a fast clip. She was almost to the end when she heard her name being called. Brinley turned and recognized a woman she had met when she and Dean first moved to the neighborhood. They hadn't been best friends, but Brinley had known her well enough that whenever she was out walking Annie in her stroller, she would stop and they would talk.

"Jennie?" she asked, the woman's name finally coming to her when she stopped in front of her.

"Yes, Jennie Markewitz. I haven't seen you in the neighborhood for so long, Brinley. Geez, there's been no activity at your house since the repairmen left, what two years ago? Except of course for the lawn people. Now today, all of a sudden, I see you and that guy. How are you?"

The woman must have taken her first real good look at Brinley's face because she reached out and touched her arm. "You don't look so good. What happened? Can I help you with anything?"

Jennie had always seemed like a busybody to Brinley but today, in this moment, she truly needed some help. "Actually, I could use your help. If you don't mind."

"Sure, honey. Come in the house," she offered, guiding Brinley to her front door.

Very quickly Jennie had Brinley seated at her dining room table with a glass of water in her hand. "Now what can I do? I'm sure it must have been hard to be back in the house where you lost your daughter and husband," Jennie speculated. "Is that what has you so upset?"

"Some of it," Brinley answered. "Jennie, it's very nice to see you again, but I was wondering if maybe you had a phone book I could borrow? I need to rent a car."

"Sure…sure, honey," the woman said, getting up from the table to fetch her phone book. Placing it in front of Brinley, she sat back down and pointed to the cell phone in her hand. "You could always google a rental company from your phone as well."

"Sorry, I was so upset that I didn't even think of it." Not wanting to explain that she really had thought of it but just wanted to get off the street in case either Dean or Wells stopped fighting long enough to come searching for her, she opened the book and searched for rental places. Finding one that was within a mile of her, she dialed the number and made the reservation.

"I can drive you over," Jennie offered when Brinley hung up. "I was on my way out to the grocery store when I saw you on the sidewalk."

"Are you sure it wouldn't be too much trouble?" Brinley asked. "I would really appreciate the ride if you have the time."

"You son of a bitch," Wells yelled down at the man on the floor, standing over him just waiting for him to try to get up again. He would love nothing more than to knock him back down. "Why did you do this to her?"

"It's not any of your goddamn business," Dean seethed.

Both men stared at each other, their chests heaving with the exertion of trying to pummel each other. The shock that Dean was alive was starting to wear off. Now Wells was getting angry thinking of the hoax the man played on Brinley. "You're a piece of shit," Wells barked, stepping away from Dean.

Slowly Dean rolled to his knees, taking several deep breaths before coming to his feet. Wiping at the blood rolling down his nose, he glared at Wells before looking around the room in search of Brinley. "Where is she?" he shouted.

"Jesus," Wells muttered, moving to the kitchen. Realizing she wasn't there, he raced back to the living room and up the steps, calling her name as he went. It quickly became clear to both men that she was nowhere to be found in the house. As Wells walked toward the front door, Dean grabbed his arm.

"You need to find her and bring her back. She and I need to talk."

"I'll find her all right, but I won't be bringing her back to you."

"Look, you moron, you better get her to talk to me. I can't go out there searching myself."

"And why is that?" Wells asked snidely.

"There are some very bad, angry men out there and if they realize that I'm still alive, they're going to come looking for me. Which means they'll come looking for her. She was safe as long as they thought I was dead but if word gets out to the contrary, we're both in danger."

Wells stared at him incredulously. "What have you done?"

Dean shoved a card at Wells's chest. "This is where I'm staying. Find her and have her meet me there in two days.

"I won't let you hurt her," Wells vowed.

"I only want the goddamn money," Dean yelled. "You can have her for all I care. But that money is mine."

"What money?"

"She'll know. She must have found it after the fire. I've searched everywhere and it's not where I left it. She's got it, I know it. Tell her to hand it over and I'll go peacefully. I need that money to disappear again. Two days, Wells. Get her to meet me or I'll hunt her down myself. And this time I won't fail," he threatened as he turned and walked to the back of the house and disappeared through the door.

The second the door closed, Wells ran out the front, desperately looking up and down the streets for any sign of Brinley. After making sure that she wasn't in his truck, he picked a direction and started walking along the sidewalk searching for her. He wasn't sure how long he walked before he switched directions and headed the opposite way. He'd just about given up when he passed by a house and a woman stepped from her front door and stopped him.

"You seem a little lost," she offered with a smile. "I've never seen you in the neighborhood. Can I help you with something?"

"Actually, I'm looking for a woman. She's about five feet four inches tall, brown hair, medium length, blue eyes, slight build."

"Goes by the name of Brinley?" the woman stated.

"Yes," Wells said excitedly. "You know her? Have you seen her around?"

"I met her when she moved into the neighborhood with her husband, Dean, several years ago. I just saw her today, in fact."

"Do you know where she went?"

"Not really, but I did drop her off at a car rental place a little less than an hour ago. She seemed really upset. I have no idea where she was heading once she got the car though. She never told me."

"Thank you," Wells said, shaking the woman's hand. "Thank you so much," he reiterated before racing back toward his truck. There was no doubt in his mind that she was heading back to her cabin in Green River. It was where she felt the safest.

The drive back, which normally would have taken a little under four hours, took Wells three hours and fifteen minutes. He'd broken so many speeding laws that he was surprised he hadn't gotten stopped. He could have done even better but he spent much of the drive back looking at the side of the road, worried she might have gotten in an accident. It was devastating enough to learn that a man you thought dead was alive but add on top of that the betrayal of another man you'd come to trust, and it didn't bode well for a clear frame of mind to navigate the long drive. It wasn't until he finally pulled into her driveway and saw the rental car sitting there that he was able to take a deep calming breath.

"Thank god," he whispered.

Chapter Fourteen

Wells jumped out of his truck and strode up to Brinley's cabin. Hesitating outside the front door, he could hear her sobs from where he stood. It nearly broke his heart. He knocked several times, but she obviously couldn't hear him. Trying the doorknob, he was surprised that it turned in his hand. He knew she wasn't happy with him and that he should probably give her space but there was no way he could walk away knowing that she was in such pain and that he had caused some of it. Taking a chance that she wouldn't kill him, he walked in.

It took him only a few seconds to find her in her small bedroom, lying on her bed, curled in a fetal position as she sobbed.

"Brin," he whispered.

Brinley jerked to a sitting position and gave him a hostile glare. "Get out," she screamed, throwing the words at him like stones.

"You have to listen to me, sweetie," he nearly begged.

"I don't have to do anything," she said, her lips thinned with anger.

"Please, Brinley. I think you could be in danger."

"The only danger I'm in is in possibly hurting you. I trusted you, Wells, and you betrayed me," her accusing voice stabbed in the air. "Get out!" The long deep look they exchanged infuriated her. He didn't deserve the time of day from her, much less an opportunity to explain. "Please, just get out."

Wells watched her face for any sign of forgiveness but found none. The only thing he could give her at this point was time. So, he did the only thing he could...he turned and walked away.

Brinley watched his shoulders sag as he left the room. Her breath burned in her throat as she held back the tears until he was gone. Hearing the door shut, she laid back down and let the sobs continue.

By the time she gained some control, it was dark outside. Food held no appeal, so she got out of bed long enough to grab a bottle of water. Shuffling into her bathroom, she took some extra-strength Tylenol from her cabinet and swallowed them. Changing into her nightgown, she crawled back into bed and stared at the ceiling, watching the shadows of the trees outside dance across the room as the moon came out.

Dean was alive. That was the most shocking revelation of the day. Aside from the obvious anger and betrayal that brought, so many questions popped in her head. Where had he been, why had he not told her, who was the man they found on the living room floor, and a host of others that just brought on more confusion. It was hard to fathom why her husband would perpetrate such a ruse? Did he not think of how that would impact her? And what of their daughter? Did he even grieve her loss? And most devastating of all…could he have saved her?

"Oh my god," Brinley whispered, covering her mouth in horror. If Dean was alive, then that meant he left their daughter to die. He hadn't even tried to save Annie. Much less his own wife!

Shocked at realizing what his actions disclosed, Brinley curled onto her side. How could he? She thought he was a good man. Maybe distracted and perhaps a little thoughtless but this? It was almost too much to believe. This was criminal!

The fact that Wells would never abandon them flitted through her mind. But it was true. In looking at the two men she knew deep down in her soul that Wells would never betray his family like Dean had. For all intents and purposes, that's exactly what her husband had done. But she knew without question that that wasn't the type of man Wells was. She hated that he had misled her but there had to have been some underlying reason why he had.

Brinley's eyes gradually started to close around two in the morning. Her head ached vilely from all the tears she'd wept and the ugly truths she'd come to realize about her marriage. The one thing she had concluded, though, was that she needed answers. From both men.

The sun had just started to rise when Brinley woke up. Her eyes felt grainy from lack of sleep. The few hours she'd managed were restless and plagued by horrible dreams. Tossing the covers aside, she got out of bed, grabbed her robe and went to her bathroom in search of more Tylenol.

She put water on the stove to make a cup of tea and wondered over to look out her front window while she waited for it to boil. Gasping in surprise, she saw Wells sleeping awkwardly in a chair, a tarp pulled around his shoulders to ward off the cold. He'd scooted the chair closer to her door in an obvious attempt to bar anyone else from possibly getting to her. He'd been trying to protect her!

"Oh, Wells," she mumbled, moving to her front door and opening it quietly.

He must have heard her because he jumped from his seat and was wildly looking around for an intruder. "It's just me," Brinley said softly.

Wells rubbed at his eyes and let the tarp drop from his shoulders. "Sorry, I'll head back to my place. It's light now," he said by way of explanation.

"No," she said stopping him. "Come in, Wells. We need to talk." Stepping back inside, she waited by the door until she was sure he had followed her. "Would you like some tea? I'm making a cup for myself."

Wells really would have preferred some strong coffee but at this point anything with caffeine would help. The chair he sat in guarding her cabin was more uncomfortable than any foxhole he'd slept in when he was a Seal. It was a brutal night, but he would have done anything to make sure she was safe. He really didn't believe that Dean knew where she had been living the past two years, or he would have certainly made an appearance before now, but there was no way he was going to take a chance. "That would be great. Thank you," he added.

Brinley made quick work of making the tea, then sat at the table across from Wells. After taking a few sips she looked directly at him. "You said I was in danger last night and I have some questions on that, but first I want to talk about us. Why did you do it, Wells? Why lie to me? I'm guessing that our crossing paths wasn't an accident."

"It wasn't, although finding you on the trail, hurt, was not the way it was supposed to play out. I'd intended on us casually meeting, but finding you like that threw me for a loop. Now that I think back on it, I'm glad that it did."

"Explain."

"You were vulnerable. I got to see the real you. The prickly, standoffish, genuine you."

"Gee, thanks," she said sarcastically.

"Not what I mean," Wells corrected. "There was no pretense with you. Because you were vulnerable, I saw the real you. Being able to take care of you, get close to you, I watched the walls start to come down and when I got to know you, I knew there was no way you were involved."

"Did you know that Dean was alive?"

"God, no! That came as a shock to me as well."

"Involved with what then?" Brinley asked.

"I'll start from the beginning. When my dad passed away, when I was in high school, Mom was pretty lonely. I was about to go away to the Navy, and I think she was struggling. My dad worked for McGill & Son Construction—before you worked there—and he and my mom were friendly with James, Dean's father. I don't remember Dad saying very much but I know there were things bothering him at work. Then he died, suspiciously, and Mom was alone. Before I know it, I get this call from my mom saying that she and James McGill were seeing each other. I knew that toward the end my dad didn't like the guy so knowing that Mom was going out with him pissed me off. I came home on leave and tried to talk to her about it, but she basically told me to mind my own business. Politely, of course. So, I did. She seemed happy so who was I to tell her what she could do? Next thing I know she married the guy, making Dean and me stepbrothers. We never lived together as brothers and I only saw him a few times, but I disliked him on sight.

"What happened? When I started working at the construction company, your mother was nowhere around. I hadn't even heard of her. James was single," Brinley added.

"I don't really know. A little over a year went by and Mom called and told me she had left James. When I asked why, she wouldn't say anything. Told me it was over, and she didn't want to talk about it. She changed, though, just in the short time they were together. She was withdrawn when we spoke on the phone, didn't seem very happy. I flew home on emergency leave to help her find a place to live and even face-to-face she wouldn't say anything. She got agitated when I pushed it. I asked if he hurt her and she said no but that was all I could get out of her, so I dropped it."

"Okay, I get the connection between you now. But that doesn't explain what it is you thought I was involved with. What exactly did you suspect me of doing?"

Wells suddenly felt ridiculous for the suspicions he'd placed on Brinley before he knew her. How do you explain to someone you cared about that you thought horrible things of them? Especially without proof of those accusations?

Brinley crossed her arms over her chest and stared at him. "Well?" she asked impatiently.

"I think James, and now Dean since he took over after his father's death, were involved with taking kickbacks and bribes from some unsavory people. I think their construction company is a front for some very bad characters and I think my father found about it and was killed before he could go to the police."

"Oh my God," Brinley gasped, covering her hand over her mouth. "Are you serious?"

If Wells had any doubt in the recesses of his mind of Brinley's innocence—which he didn't—her reaction would have quelled it then and there. "Dead serious," he answered.

"How do you know? What proof have you found? Have you spoken to the police?" she asked, firing questions at him as fast as they came to her.

"First, I don't have any proof. Yet. I remember my dad, before he died, sitting in his office at home looking over some papers and he seemed really upset. If you remember I told you how we were going through a bad patch and weren't really speaking. I didn't question it at the time but when I think back on it, how upset he was, it had to have been about work."

"Have you asked your mom?"

"I tried but she shuts me down."

"What about the police?"

"I went to them when I was on leave once and raised questions about my dad's death, but they couldn't help me. His death certificate said it was a heart attack and there was no reason to suspect otherwise."

"So, you need more proof and that's where I came in. Because I worked for McGill & Son Construction and was married to Dean, you assumed that I was part of whatever dirty dealings that were going on."

"I was wrong," Wells emphatically stated.

"Obviously. I was personnel, Wells. I never handled payroll or any billing to know what was going on. Basically, my responsibility was dealing with employees. Their health insurance, 401K plan, making sure we were OSHA-compliant, and the myriad of grievances against the supervisors. I wasn't in a position to see much of anything else. I stayed in my lane and did my job. When I was eight months pregnant with Annie, I quit working. Come to think of it, Dean was insistent that I stop working all together. I had planned to go back but he never wanted me to. Now I'm wondering why," she said, her voice drifting off in thought.

"You believe me," Wells said in wonder.

Brinley glanced over at Wells and saw the look of surprise on his face. "Of course I believe you. I'm really pissed at you for suspecting me of some pretty horrible things and not being honest with me from the beginning, but I know you to be an honest man. You've had to rely on your instinct as a Navy Seal, Wells. I trust that. If you think your father's death was suspicious, then we need to find the evidence you need. Especially given the fact that Dean has just proven himself to be an avid liar. Which brings me to the next question. What happened between you two? What did he say and why am I in danger?"

"He wants me to bring you to him. He says you have his money, and he wants it back. Did you ever find any in the house?"

"Oh my God!"

"You know about the money?"

"No," she said distractedly.

"Then what?"

"The insurance company paid out on his policy. The life insurance money wasn't much, around eighty thousand, but I used it for the cremation and burial for both him and Annie. There's some left but they're going to want the money back. It's fraud," she panicked. "I helped him perpetrate a fraud."

Wells got up from his seat at the table and knelt at Brinley's feet. "It's going to be all right, Brin. You had no idea he wasn't dead. That's on him and they'll know it."

"So what money is he talking about?" Brin asked, confused. "There was no other money. The homeowner's policy paid for the repairs to the house but that went directly to the contractors. There was no other settlement. There is no other money."

"We need to go to the police, Brin. Tell them everything. Tell them what happened, and that Dean isn't dead."

"I need to talk to Dean first," Brinley said, getting up from the table to pace. "I want some answers. I need to know what I'm dealing with. The police will think I'm just being hysterical. I'm going to meet with Dean, then I'll take everything I learn to the police and let them take it from there."

"I don't think that's wise," Wells advised. "He's desperate, Brin. From what he told me there are men who would love to know he's alive so they can get whatever money he's talking about from him. Sounds like he stole from them and they're not happy about it. Dean's scared and scared men do stupid, dangerous things. I don't want you involved with any of it."

"It may be the only way we can get any evidence of what really happened to your father," Brinley said, hoping to coerce Wells to her way of thinking.

"I don't care about that anymore. I can't change that Dad's gone but I can sure as hell make sure you stay alive," he said vehemently.

"I want to meet with him, Wells. I have to…don't you see? I need answers that only he can provide. I promise, after that I'll go directly to the cops and tell them everything."

Wells completely understood why Brinley needed to meet with Dean, but he didn't like the danger it placed her in. His instinct was to stash her someplace safe, somewhere he knew she couldn't be found, and let the authorities handle things. But he also knew that there was no way she would be able to handle the resurrection of her husband unless she had her answers. Besides, looking at the pleading look in her eyes—begging for his understanding—there was no way he could deny her. Maybe there was a way that he could let her meet with Dean and still find a way to keep her safe.

"Fine," he capitulated. "We'll meet him, but I need your promise that we'll do it my way. No questions asked," he admonished. "And before you get all pleased with yourself for getting your way," he added, seeing the look in her eye, "there's one other thing you have to agree with."

"And what exactly is that?" she asked crossly.

"You stay with me until then."

"Because you're worried I'm not safe."

"Because I love you…and you're not safe," he admitted.

Brinley sighed and walked into Wells's arms. "Oh Wells, what are we going to do? I'm still married and there's so much unknown right now."

"You're only married on paper," he groused. "As for the rest, we'll figure it out together."

Unsettled by the thought, he held on tightly, praying that extricating her from her louse of a husband and working their way through this mess would not prove difficult. It would have been so much better if the man had stayed dead!

Chapter Fifteen

BRINLEY SNUGGLED AGAINST Wells' s chest trying not to wake him. The nightmare that startled her from her sleep was so graphic that the taste of fear lingered with her. No matter how many times she tried to shake the terror from her mind, it wouldn't go away. Not only was Dean still alive, he definitely wasn't the man she thought she had married and to her disgust, probably never had been.

He was alive! It was still so unfathomable to her that the man she thought was dead was actually still alive. But why? So many questions came to her that she knew sleep was going to be impossible. Not wanting to wake Wells, she slowly moved away from the warmth of his body and slipped from beneath the covers. Grabbing the shirt he'd taken off a few hours before, she pushed her arms through the holes and walked into the living room as she buttoned it.

How had her life become such a mess? She'd grieved when she thought Dean had died. She felt the loss as surely as she felt the loss of her parents. But now that he was back—alive—the thought of seeing him again sent shivers up her spine. There was no happiness that her husband had survived, no euphoria that the man she married was still her husband. Just a profound sense of fear and anger. And so many questions it made her head spin.

Confused, she wandered restlessly around the room. The more she thought about her circumstance, the more she felt the screams of frustration at the back of her throat. The gamut of perplexing emotions ran riot as she paced, her feet not even registering the cold smoothness of the hardwood flooring.

Disappointment seeped through her as she thought back to how she had settled so easily for a man who had obviously cared nothing for her. How could she have been so wrong about Dean—even marry the man—and yet be so sure of Wells and the type of person he was? Being with Wells, making love with him, thrilled her in a way that it never had with her husband. Why couldn't she have seen that before she married him? Was she so desperate not to be alone that she ignored all the signs? Obviously, but why him? Of all people.

And now there was Wells to consider. He didn't deserve to be put through any of this. Who knew how dangerous and ugly things were about to get and the thought of placing him in that kind of danger terrified her. She felt a momentary panic as her mind jumped to the very real possibility that he could get hurt. He was still recovering from his injuries and should probably be resting, not traipsing around the state putting himself in danger. With a pang, she realized she was going to have to let him go. It wasn't safe for him to be near her. She would never be able to live with herself if something happened to him because of her mess. She couldn't let that happen so the only solution was to leave now while he was still asleep. She knew if he were aware of her decision, he would fight for her to stay.

Deciding on her course of action, Brinley began searching for the piece of paper that Dean had given Wells with the information of where they were supposed to meet. Once she found that, she would sneak out, walk back to her cabin to get the rental car, and start the drive back to Casper. The sooner she disentangled herself from Dean the better off everyone would be. All she needed to do was to explain to Dean that there was no money and that would be the end of it. Then she would report him to the police, call the insurance company and explain that her husband wasn't dead, and then just deal with whatever consequences there were. They would understand it wasn't her doing, right?

Brinley quietly searched the living room for the paper Wells had had in his hand earlier. She couldn't remember exactly where he had put it but surely it had to be close.

After a thorough search of the living room and having no success in locating it, she made her way into the kitchen. Maybe on the dining room table, she thought as she picked up the placemats, shaking them in the hopes that it might fall out. Moving to the counter, she opened the drawer where she had seen him put his keys and had just lifted them out when she heard Wells ask quietly, "What are you looking for?"

Jumping at the sound of his voice, she dropped his keys back in the drawer and looked over to where he was lounging expectantly against the doorway.

"Jesus," she whispered, placing her hand against her chest. "You scared me."

"I woke up and you were gone. What's going on, Brin?"

Deciding that the best way with him was straightforward, she looked him directly in the eye. No subterfuge, no lying, just simple honesty. "I'm leaving. I need that address where I'm supposed to meet Dean. Where is it?"

"We're leaving in the morning," Wells answered cautiously, coming to the quick conclusion that something was up.

"No. I'm leaving now and you're staying here. I need to handle this on my own. It's the best way. You'll just make him mad and right now I need him calm. I need answers and it will be easier if I do it without you. Where is it?" she asked again.

There was no way Wells could miss the fear that was clearly in her eyes. This wasn't about her worry at pissing Dean off because he was there. It was something else entirely…something he needed to get to the bottom of. There was no way he would ever let her go alone to meet her psychotic soon-to-be ex-husband. There was something else driving her panic.

Calmly, Wells walked to where Brinley was standing. He reached out and touched her cheek. "What's going on?" he asked softly.

"I told you," she answered defensively.

"Talk to me," he encouraged gently. The tears that swam in her eyes were nearly his undoing. "Please."

Wells watched as a battle took place within Brinley. He watched as her shoulders finally dropped, defeat weighing on her. "I can't let you get hurt," she whispered brokenly, the tears she tried to hold back rolling down her cheeks.

He should have known that she was more concerned for him than she was for herself. Touched at her concern, Wells kissed her forehead, then led her over the kitchen island and onto the barstool. "I'll make you some tea."

Busying himself with the task, Wells thought of what to say to Brinley to reassure her. He didn't want to divulge his entire plan until he was sure of it working out, but he needed to come up with something to get her off the idea of handling things on her own.

When the water came to a boil, he filled her cup and went to sit beside her. As she took her first sip, he gently rubbed her back. "Do you think I can handle myself?" he asked quietly.

Brinley looked over to him in surprise. "Of course, I do."

"And you know that I've spent the greater part of my life handling dangerous situations. Dealing with terrorists, putting the bad guys away, generally being a badass Navy Seal, right?"

Brinley couldn't stop the smile that came to her lips. "So you've told me," she mused.

"So, what makes you think I can't handle that whiny ass Dean?"

"It's not that," Brinley said, turning in her seat to face Wells. "He's scared, angry, unpredictable. If you got hurt because of my situation, I wouldn't be able to live with myself. I love you, Wells, and I couldn't handle losing you because of something that was my responsibility to deal with. This is my mess."

Wells smiled. Finally, the words he'd wanted to hear! Leaning in, he kissed her gently on the lips. Pulling back, he took a strand of hair and tucked it behind her ear. "First off you didn't create this situation; your lying bastard of a husband did. What he's done is not your responsibility to shoulder. It's on him, Brin, not you. Besides, if you will remember, I have a stake in this too. I need answers about my father's death and I'm quite certain Dean knows something. Tomorrow we'll head back to Casper and figure out how to proceed. For now, let's head to bed and get some rest. It's going to be a long day tomorrow."

Brinley sipped the last of her tea and set the mug down. "Fine," she said, allowing Wells to help her from the stool, her moment of insanity dissipating under the calmness that he exuded. He had that special way of making a person feel that things were going to be okay as long as he was around. Maybe it wasn't smart to succumb to his belief that things would work out, but she couldn't help but want to believe him.

Wells climbed into bed and immediately reached out for Brinley, pulling her body close to his. Hearing her finally say the words that he wanted to hear had done something to him. He'd never felt this way with any other woman and knowing she loved him made him more determined to keep her safe and to find a way through their situation. After years of wondering if he would ever find his person—the one he wanted to build a life with—to lose her would be untenable.

Lost in his thoughts, Wells felt Brinley move against him and glanced down at her, only to see a grin on her face. "I can't sleep," she murmured, running her hand over his chest.

As seductions went it wasn't much of one, but he wanted her so badly that desire quickly flared in his eyes. Reaching up he grasped her hand in his. "And just what is it that you expect me to do about it?" Wells grinned back.

Deciding not to play coy, Brinley leaned up, swung her leg over his hip and perched herself on his muscular thighs. Reaching up she slowly unbuttoned the shirt she'd put on earlier. Pushing it off her shoulders, she let it drop behind her, then leaned down so that her breasts were brushing against his chest. "We could chat for a while," she said, staring into his sapphire-blue eyes, "or we could…," she whispered leaving her sentence unfinished as she kissed him, lingering, savoring the moment.

Feeling his hands run up her back, Brinley shivered, loving the feel of his touch. Pressing closer, she deepened the kiss, losing herself in his embrace.

"Jesus," Wells uttered, feeling Brinley's hand grasp his penis and guide him to her entrance as she raised herself up. This woman was going to be the death of him.

He watched her face as she slowly lowered herself onto him, reveling in the sheer joy it reflected. Not able to help himself, he arched up and took one of her nipples into his mouth, gratified at the moan of pleasure escaping her lips. She was such a responsive woman, it made being with her all the more exciting. Her responses when he touched her overwhelmed and delighted him.

His tongue caressed her sensitive swollen nipples as Brinley held his head against her. His hands were seeking, gliding over her body, his ardor surprisingly, touchingly, restrained.

Her tormented groan was a heady invitation as Wells's impatience finally gave way. Flipping her onto her back, his body drove her into the mattress as he settled firmly inside of her. "Wells," she sighed as he took her lips in a ravenous kiss.

Her body squirmed beneath him as she tried to get him to move. An electric shock scorched through her body as he acquiesced to her demands and started a punishing rhythm. She was fully aware of the hardness of his thighs brushing against hers with each thrust. Involuntary tremors of arousal began, making her soar higher until the peak of delight was reached. Shouting out her release, Brinley was gratified when Wells quickly followed her.

After several minutes, he raised his head and gazed deeply into Brinley's eyes. Contentment and peace flowed between them. "I love you," he vowed, brushing a strand of hair from her cheek.

"I love you," she echoed sincerely.

Chapter Sixteen

As before, Wells and Brinley were up early the next morning making the drive to Casper. They drove in silence, only speaking or commenting on the hour, the weather, or something they had just passed. For her part, Brinley was just trying to keep her feelings under control. The thought of encountering Dean, much less speaking to him, brought a myriad of emotions to the surface. As much as she wanted to have a calm conversation with him, at least enough to have her questions answered, the urge to throttle him was tantamount to taking her next breath. That was something she would have to control. She'd never been the type of person to get into a physical confrontation, but he was sorely testing her resolve.

For Wells's part, he was busy planning how to go about the upcoming confrontation and running through every possible scenario in his head. As a Navy Seal, he was trained to anticipate every angle and to have a contingency plan in place. Ensuring Brinley's safety made the preparation even more imperative.

Before entering Casper, Wells stopped at a gas station. As he stood by the pump waiting for the tank to be filled, Brinley glanced over to see him tapping on the screen of his phone. She waited patiently until he finished paying for the gas, then quizzed him when he was back in the truck.

"Were you trying to reach out to Dean?" she asked.

"No. There's another stop we need to make," he answered as he pulled back on to the road.

"Is there a time we have to be there?"

"Do you trust me, Brin?"

"Of course, I do. I wouldn't be sitting in your truck if I didn't, and you know it."

"Then be patient," he advised.

"You've not been very forthcoming with the plan and I…wait," she said as he pulled into a driveway. Looking at the little cottage, she turned sharply to gaze at him. "Where are we? Whose place is this?"

"My mom's," he answered succinctly.

"Your mom's? Now is not the time for a visit, Wells. We need to meet Dean. I don't want to be late," she stressed.

Wells turned and took a hold of Brinley's hand. "We're going to meet with Dean tomorrow."

"But he specifically said today," she reiterated, quickly becoming agitated. "He was clear with you, Wells. We have to go today. You're just going to make him angry and then I won't ever get my answers."

"Listen to me, Brin. I'm not about to go into a situation I'm not in control of. Especially with you. Quite frankly Dean needs this more than we do. You're right…he's desperate so he'll wait. At least until tomorrow. There are a few things I need to have in place before we meet with him. Trust me, he'll be there."

Releasing her hands, Wells got out of the truck and walked over to open her door. When she hesitated, he reached out, his palm up. "Please."

Knowing there would be no arguing with the man, she sighed heavily and grasped his hand.

"Good girl," he said as he kissed her temple when she came to stand beside him.

Brinley didn't have time to get nervous about meeting Wells's mother. Before she knew it, they were up the walkway and entering the quaint cottage through the front door. She watched as a slight woman with gray hair came from a back room and enveloped Wells in her arms. She was fascinated watching the interaction between mother and son. It was terribly sweet watching Wells stoop lower so his mother could put her arms around his neck and sweeter still when the woman kissed him on the cheek, patting his chest as she stepped back.

"Well, who do we have here," his mother asked when she caught sight of Brinley hovering by the front door. "Come in, dear," she invited.

"Mom, I'd like you to meet Brinley Crew," Wells introduced, waving Brinley forward. "Brin, this is my mom, Ruby Kennedy."

"It's nice to meet you, Mrs. Kennedy," Brinley responded, respectfully holding out her hand.

Ruby Kennedy took the offered hand, shaking it briefly before enveloping Brinley in a hug. "It's so nice to meet you, dear. Wells, why didn't you tell me you were bringing a friend. I would have dressed a little better," she laughed, patting her hair into place. "What can I get you two to drink?"

"I'll grab us all something, Mom. Why don't you take Brinley out to the back patio?"

"Of course," she said, glancing curiously at her son. "Grab us some of those cookies in the snack drawer while you're at it. Come along, Brinley."

Not really given a choice, Brinley followed Ruby out to the backyard.

The view was stunning. There wasn't much space to the yard, but the landscape was beautifully designed. The small amount of grass she had was lush and green and would require little time to mow. Flower beds sloped around the house and boasted bursts of color from the flowers planted in the beds. Further out toward the back of the yard were birdhouses and feeders strategically placed so that anyone on the deck could watch the tiny creatures from the patio table or the lounge chairs placed on the bricked area.

"This is so lovely," Brinley complimented as she settled on her chair.

"Thanks, honey. I love it back here. When I'm not working on my flowers, I'm sitting here reading or working on my puzzles. It's kind of my own oasis back here. Wells helps me when he can. I love all the flowers but keeping the weeds out can be a bear. So, tell me, how do you know my son?"

The twinkle in the older woman's eye told Brinley that she knew more than she was letting on. How much she knew, though, was the mystery. It would have been nice if Wells had forewarned her of the visit and prepared her by letting her know exactly how much his mother did or didn't know.

"Actually, he saved me," she answered, deciding that honesty was always the best way to go. Besides, if she and Wells had any sort of future once this mess was cleared up, this woman would be a big part of it. For that very reason, she deserved the truth.

"Oh, do tell," Ruby encouraged.

"I'm renting a cabin near his in Green River. I was out hiking, totally unprepared for basically anything, when I fell and hurt myself. Wells found me on the trail and carried me back to my place. He took care of me until I was back on my feet. That's how we met."

"Such a nice boy," Ruby grinned as Wells cleared his throat to get their attention.

"Someone care to open the door for me?" he asked.

Brinley quickly stood up and opened the door, holding it as Wells carried a tray out and put it on the table. After placing a glass of fresh lemonade in front of each of them, he sat down next to Brinley and grabbed a handful of the cookies he'd put on the plate.

"Nutter Butter?" Brinley laughed.

"They're his favorites," Ruby offered, grabbing one for herself. "Have been since he was a little boy. I always keep them on hand."

"Spoiled," Brinley admonished as she popped one in her mouth.

"So, want to tell me what's going on?" Ruby asked after a few minutes of companionable silence. "You were just here, Wells. And while you know I love your company, I can tell by both your faces that's something's going on. How can I help?"

"You just get right to it, don't you, Mom," Wells hedged.

"I find it's always best," she replied.

"I want to ask you about James McGill."

Seeing how Ruby tensed up made Brinley cringe. She hadn't expected that Wells would bring that up with his mother, especially with her—practically a stranger—sitting right next to her. She knew he had questions but wasn't exactly sure what Dean's father may or may not have to do with her current circumstance. Besides, she really liked

Ruby Kennedy and discussing something that could hurt the woman didn't sit well with her.

"Why do you ask?" Ruby asked cautiously. "I thought we already discussed this years ago, Wells."

"You didn't really discuss anything with me, Mom. I've let it go but I think it's time you told me everything."

"Why now?" she asked, a shadow of annoyance crossing her face.

Wells hated pushing his mother on this but if there was anything she could tell him that would give any insight into Dean's or James's actions over the past five to ten years, it might help Brinley. He needed to go into the meeting with Dean armed with as much information as he could get. "What happened, Mom?"

"Mrs. Kennedy," Brinley interjected softly. "I used to work for McGill and Son Construction a while back. It was after you had already divorced James McGill, so we never met. But it would be helpful if you knew anything that he or his son were involved with that you could tell us about."

"But why now?' Ruby implored Wells. "They're both dead. Let it alone."

"Mom, Dean is still alive."

"No…" she exclaimed. "How do you know that? I heard he died in a fire."

"I was married to Dean," Brinley explained. "I, too, thought he died in that fire, Mrs. Kennedy. But he didn't. He's back and he wants something from me, something I don't have."

"Oh, you poor dear," Ruby said, grasping Brinley's hands. "I heard a little girl died that night. She was your daughter?"

"She was. Her name was Annie."

"Mom," Wells chimed in. "Is there anything you can tell us about either James or Dean?"

"Oh, honey. I don't really know anything. James was a horrid man. Sure, he was all nice when he started courting me but once we got married, he changed. He was a hard man, Wells. I have a lot of suspicions, things I heard, but nothing I could prove. I thought he and your father were friends but after I married him it became clear that he couldn't stand my late husband. He started saying awful things about him. I started thinking that maybe Jeremy had had something on James and that he only married me to find out what I knew...to see if Jeremy had ever said anything to me. I never said anything to you, Wells, because I only have my suspicions. Nothing to back it up. But once I figured out he married me for reasons other than love or affection, I left him. Your father was the love of my life and there was no way I was going to spend another second listening to James disparage his memory. That's when I packed up and left and filed for divorce. Besides, I'd already come to realize that I only married him out of loneliness. That's not a good reason to be with anybody," she said sadly.

Wells grasped his mother's hand in sympathy. It saddened him that she had felt she needed to take that step. Maybe if he hadn't joined the service, she wouldn't have felt the need to marry the awful man. "Did you ever look through any of Dad's things, Mom? Afterwards to see if he left behind anything incriminating against the McGills?" Wells asked.

"I did but there was nothing that I could find. To be honest with you, though, I didn't look all that hard. I didn't really want to rehash what turned out to be the worst decision I ever made. I'm really sorry for your loss, though," Ruby said turning to Brinley. "I can't imagine losing a child."

"Thank you," Brinley responded quietly.

"Mom, would it be possible for me look through some of Dad's old boxes? Maybe I'll find something that might help."

"Help with what?"

"We're meeting with Dean tomorrow..."

"That's dangerous," Ruby interrupted. "You need to head to the police and tell them that Dean's alive. Let them deal with everything."

"That's the plan, Mom, but first Brinley wants to meet with Dean to find out why he disappeared like that. We still have no idea who that man was who actually died in Brinley's home. She has a lot of questions and quite frankly, I agree with her that if we turn him in, he may clam up and she'll never get her answers. The plan is to get what information we can tomorrow, then head straight to the police. I'm hoping that if I can find something in Dad's things, when we go to the cops, there will be even more evidence to put Dean away other than faking his own death."

"Oh honey, I don't like this. Not one bit."

"We'll be careful," Wells assured his mom.

"There're two boxes in the garage, top shelf. It's everything of your dad's that I haven't gotten rid of. You're welcome to go through them."

"Thanks, Mom. I promise I'll bring them back."

"Why don't you stay with me tonight? You can go through the boxes and Brinley and I can get to know each other. I'll fix us a nice dinner."

"I appreciate the offer, but I think it's safer if we stay at a hotel. I don't want to take any chances of bringing Dean to your door or, quite frankly, my condo. I have a room booked already. I promise, though, that as soon as we get things taken care of, both Brinley and I will come back and stay longer."

It was obvious that Wells's mom was not happy with the arrangements, but she graciously acquiesced. They stayed for a while longer before Wells went to the garage to get the boxes and placed them in the back seat of his truck. The hug that Ruby gave Wells when they were ready to leave was extra tight, her concern for what they were facing the next day foremost in her mind. It almost made Brinley cry over the fact that Wells could be in danger because of her. The guilt she started to feel, however, dissipated when Ruby held on to her even longer.

"You stay strong and let Wells take care of you. He's good at what he does," she whispered in Brinley's ear.

Pulling out of the driveway left Brinley feeling sad. What little time she had with Wells's mom had meant so much. The woman was exactly what she had imagined the person who raised Wells would be like. It would have been so much nicer to have met her under better circumstances. What must she think of Brinley getting her son involved in this mess after everything he had already gone through?

Wells reached over and took Brinley's hand. "It's going to be okay," he assured her.

Brinley merely smiled at him, hoping against hope that he was right.

They arrived at the hotel in less than ten minutes, parking in the back corner of the lot, and made their way to the front desk. As Wells checked them in, Brinley looked around the lobby. It wasn't exactly the Ritz-Carlton, but the main floor looked clean and well kept. Lost to her own thoughts, Brinley jumped when a hand touched her shoulder.

"All set," he informed her before turning to walk a short distance down the hall. She followed him to the elevator, standing silently as they rode to the top floor.

When he unlocked the door, she walked in and sat on the bed. Wells carried what little luggage they had and placed it on the credenza. Brinley watched as he took out his phone and sent a quick text. Not really caring about the communication, she stood up and wandered around the room. Pushing the curtain aside, she looked out the window, watching as dusk began to settle.

"You're being very quiet," Wells said, coming to stand behind her.

It was hard to explain to him exactly what she was feeling when she herself couldn't quite figure it out. On one hand she was grateful that Wells was with her, helping her to deal with her resurrected husband. On the other hand, she was beginning to feel as if her life was out of her own control. There was Dean, who lied and betrayed her in the worst possible way, and Wells, who took control and made plans to deal with the situation without even consulting her. It was her life and yet she was being impacted by others and their decisions and actions. After standing on her own two feet for so long now, she was finding she much preferred her independence. She'd handed everything over to Dean when they met and married all those years ago, something she'd vowed never to do again.

"Brin..." Wells started before a knock at the door stopped him. "Hang on."

After checking the peephole in the door, Wells opened it and ushered a man inside. Brinley watched as they hugged tightly, slapping each other on the back as they pulled away.

"How the hell are you, man?" the blond Adonis asked as he carefully looked Wells up and down.

"Stop mothering me, I'm fine. JP, I'd like you to meet Brinley Crew. Brinley, this is my best friend and former Seal teammate Jonah Perez.

"It's nice to meet you," Brinley said, shaking the man's hand. Lord, but he was tall. Tall and extremely good-looking. From his almost white-gold hair to his sharp blue eyes and muscular build, it was obvious this was not a man you would want to mess with. And she had thought Wells was tall—this man stood at least two inches above him. But it was the twinkle in his eye when he had hugged Wells that said so much more to her about the man. He was Wells's best friend and in just that one look it was obvious the tight bond they shared. The type of friend she'd never had.

"I brought food," he said, pointing to the bags he'd placed on the credenza when he and Wells hugged.

"Awesome," Wells said, grabbing the bags and carrying them to the small round table near the window. "Let's eat then we can talk about tomorrow."

"What about tomorrow?' Brinley asked, her voice brittle at the thought of this stranger knowing her business. It was embarrassing enough to have her life fully displayed for Wells to see but to have this man as witness was almost too much.

"You didn't tell her I was coming?" JP admonished Wells. "Seriously, dude?" he said in disgust. Turning to Brinley he gently shook his head. "I'm really sorry," he said. "You'll have to forgive Wells. Sometimes he just doesn't think. Why don't I leave you two to hash this out and you can let me know later what you need me to do tomorrow."

"You're not going anywhere," Wells informed him, tossing a wrapped burger in his direction. "Sit, let's eat." Turning to Brinley he took her hand and forced her to sit next to him on the bed facing the small table. "I absolutely refuse to take you into a situation that I don't have some control over," he explained. "I trust JP with my life, and now yours. We need to have a second set of eyes and ears when we meet with Dean tomorrow. That's why I delayed the meeting. I needed this extra day to get more prepared. What did you see?" he asked turning to face JP.

When JP started talking it became clear that he'd spent several hours surveilling Dean. He described the rundown, abandoned house they would be going to the next day, areas to steer clear of, and Dean's extreme agitation as he nervously moved around the house and property checking for intruders.

"You'll have to tread carefully," JP continued. "It's obvious that the man is unstable. He's nervous as hell and quite jumpy. I didn't see him carrying a firearm, but it doesn't mean he doesn't have one."

"I'll have mine," Wells stated firmly. "How close could you get?"

"The man's an idiot. Sorry," JP said, glancing over to Brinley. After all, technically it was still her husband he'd just insulted. "I was ten feet from the house, and he had no idea I was even there. He's scared and he's careless. Whoever he's hiding from will have an easy time getting to him if they learn he's alive. I still think you should just go to the police. Why take a chance meeting with him?"

"Brinley and I need some answers and I agree with her that the second he's in police custody he'll go silent. I'm hoping that we can get information from him by using the money as a bargaining chip. Money he thinks Brin has."

The two men continued to discuss the plans for the next day while she sat quietly, absently chewing on the fries Wells handed her. It really was quite distressing to think of what her life had become.

As she sat listening to them it became clear that both men had thought of every possible scenario and prepared as much as possible to mitigate any danger. No wonder Wells wanted the extra day! The poor man was trying to get her the answers she needed and do it in the safest way possible.

"I think that does it," Wells said, bringing Brinley back from her thoughts. "You good?" he asked her.

"I am," she said glancing to JP, hoping neither man saw that she had been distracted. "Thank you so much for helping us," she said sincerely.

"I'm happy to help," JP answered. "You won't see me tomorrow, but I'll see you," he grinned before slapping Wells on the back. "Get some rest," he advised, then saluted as he walked out the door.

"You really think Dean is that far gone?" she asked when the door shut.

"I don't presume to know anything about that man," Wells said irritably. "But I won't take any chances."

"Then why go to your mom's? Why take the chance that he might follow us there? You could have gotten those boxes after our meeting with Dean."

"First, as I told Mom, I want to see if there's anything in those boxes that might give us a heads-up on what Dean or his father was involved with. Secondly, you two are the most important people in my life and I wanted you to meet. Besides, JP was watching us the entire time."

Brinley inhaled sharply, surprised that she hadn't even realized that they were being watched.

"What? You think I would honestly take a chance with either you or my mother?" he smirked.

Chapter Seventeen

STRANDS OF LIGHT peeking through the hotel curtains allowed Brinley to quietly search for her clothes. She didn't want to wake Wells because she knew he would stop her from leaving. She just wanted an hour at the most to do what she needed. Hopefully, she would be back before he even realized she was gone.

Grabbing his keys from the dresser, she quietly unlocked the door, glancing back to make sure he hadn't moved. When she was certain he was still asleep, Brinley slipped through the opening, being careful not to slam the door as she left. She quickly made her way down to the lobby, out the front entrance to Wells's truck.

The drive took less than fifteen minutes. By the time she arrived the skies were just beginning to lighten. Slowly she made her way through the gravestones until she found the one she was looking for. Dropping to her knees, Brinley let the tears flow as she lovingly cleaned around the granite marker.

The shrill sound of his cell phone ringing brought Wells out of a deep sleep. When his hand finally came into contact with the cold plastic, he hit the connect button and lifted it to his ear. "What?" he grumpily whispered in an effort not to wake Brinley.

"Where's your girlfriend?" an amused voice asked.

"What? Who is this?" he asked, confused.

"Where's your girlfriend?" he asked again.

"JP? What the hell are you talking about? She's right he…." Wells stopped when he looked over and realized that the other side of the bed was empty. "Brinley," he shouted, hoping that she was just in the bathroom.

"Stop yelling, she's not there," JP informed him.

"Then where is she and how the hell do you know?" Glancing at the clock on the bedside table, he saw that it was not quite five in the morning. "Aren't you heading out to set up a perimeter around the house to watch Dean?"

"I was heading out when Stevens called and said your girl was slipping out of the hotel. I'm in the parking lot. Get dressed and get your ass down here. I'll drop you off to your girlfriend on my way out of town."

"Stevens? But…"

"Get dressed. I'll explain on the way," JP barked before hanging up.

Jumping out of bed, Wells hurriedly dressed, brushed his teeth and grabbed his wallet. As he waited for the elevator, he silently cursed Brinley for going off on her own. Was she in danger? And knowing that Dean was out there, why would she do something so asinine as sneaking out?

The elevator seemed to take its sweet time getting him to the bottom floor. When the doors finally opened, he rushed out through the exit and searched for JP's car. Hearing the light tap of a horn, he turned to his left and rushed toward it. When he got in, JP handed him a to-go cup of coffee from the local gas station.

"Thanks," Wells murmured taking a sip. "Where is she?"

"Don't get mad at her, Wells. She's safe. Stevens is with her. He followed her to the cemetery and has been standing outside making sure no one is around. Hell, Brinley doesn't even know he's there watching over her."

"The cemetery? Christ! And just how did Stevens come to know to follow her? Mind explaining?"

Conrad Stevens was another one of his Seal team members and a man that he counted as a close friend. They didn't stay as close in contact as he and JP, but Wells knew if he ever needed someone, Conrad would be there. Case in point…the disappearing Brinley.

"I wanted to make sure you guys were safe so as a precaution I had Stevens outside watching the entrance door to the hotel. He's pissed, by the way, that *you* didn't ask him to help. Anyway, he watched as Brinley left, called to give me a heads-up, and followed her to make sure she was all right. Look, man, I can tell you're upset but go easy on her when you see her. Her whole life has been turned upside-down. She's confused, angry, and worried about what's going to happen. Being back here where it all took place is bringing back a lot of feelings for her. Losing her daughter is at the top of the list. According to Stevens, she's been crying over her daughter's grave so I'm telling you…go easy."

"Why didn't she just ask me to bring her here if it meant that much to her? I would have brought her, and she should have known that!"

"And exactly how much have you consulted her about this whole plan with her husband? Have you one time inquired what she thought or wanted?" When Wells opened his mouth to argue, JP shut him down. "You're a fixer, man. That's what we're trained to do. But she's not in the military. She's a civilian and this is her life. For some reason she needed to visit her daughter, so she did what she needed to. This has nothing to do with you so don't take it as a personal slight."

Wells silently sipped at the hot coffee, mulling over what JP had said. When they pulled into the cemetery, JP parked next to a vehicle Wells recognized as belonging to Conrad Stevens. He got out of the car and went over to his friend. "Thanks, man," he grunted as they fist-bumped.

"No worries," Conrad answered back. "Now I'm going with JP to help cover the back side of the abandoned house. Got a problem with that?" he asked, raising his eyebrows in question.

"Nope," Wells assured him. "No problem at all. I appreciate your help."

"You're an ass," he grimaced. "And go easy on that woman," Conrad lectured as he got back in his car and followed JP out of the parking lot.

When the taillights of both vehicles vanished in the distance, Wells turned and walked toward the front of his truck and leaned against it.

He could see Brinley in the distance kneeling at the gravesite of her daughter. From that far away it was difficult to see but he thought he could make out her lips moving in conversation.

Respecting her need to be with Annie, he stood vigilant ensuring she remained undisturbed. When another ten minutes came and went, he slowly made his way to where she was kneeling. Not wanting to scare her, he cleared his throat and gently called her name.

"You're not going to yell at me, are you?" she asked, not turning to look at him.

"No, but you could have told me what you needed. I would have brought you here myself."

"I needed to be alone."

"You weren't alone."

"Who was he? JP must have brought you since I took your truck. So, who was the guy who watched over me?" she asked curiously.

"Jesus Christ," Wells nearly exploded. "You knew you were followed and yet you still came?"

"I didn't know I was followed," she corrected. "I didn't realize anyone else was here until right before you and JP pulled up. I realized a man was staring at me from the parking lot. I was beginning to feel scared until you showed up and I saw you speaking to him. Who was he?"

"Conrad Stevens, one of my former teammates and a very good friend. JP had him watching the hotel during the night. He saw you leave and followed to make sure you were safe."

When Brinley didn't say anything else, Wells stepped closer and held his hand out to help her stand. She hesitated for a few seconds before placing her hand in his. When she was at her full height, he merely wrapped his arms around her and held on tightly. She stood stiffly for several moments before giving in and settling into his warmth.

"I'm sorry," she whispered into his chest.

"Did it help? Coming here?" he asked.

"I haven't been here since the funeral. I thought it would help me to face today but when I got here and saw Dean's name on the marker next to hers, I just got so angry. There's a stranger buried next to my daughter's ashes, Wells. It makes me sick."

"We'll make it right," he promised. "Let's just get through today and then we'll work on making sure Annie is taken care of. Okay?"

Grateful that he understood, Brinley nodded and kept her arm around his waist as they headed to where she had parked his truck. When they arrived back at the hotel, Wells ordered room service, then took a quick shower. By the time he got out, breakfast had been delivered. They sat in silence and picked at the food. Neither of them seemed very hungry but it was important they had some sustenance to get them through the next few hours.

When Brinley had had her fill, she took her turn in the shower, standing under the hot water, trying to calm her mind. She had to get her anger under control before meeting with Dean. In hindsight, going to the cemetery and seeing Dean's name just infuriated her further. Although being able to speak to Annie, to tell her how much she was missed and that her mommy always kept her in her heart did help to a certain degree. Now her main priorities were meeting Dean, going to the police, and making arrangements to either have Annie or the stranger moved. Only then would she rest easy.

Exiting the bathroom, she cautiously glanced in Wells's direction. While he seemed sympathetic to the reason she felt she needed to visit the cemetery, she knew there was some frustration and anger at the risk she took. Not to mention the fact that she stole his shiny big truck without his permission. He didn't seem like the type of man to be all possessive with things but—he was, after all—a guy, and it was his truck.

"I'm not mad," he sighed heavily. "So stop looking at me like I'm going to explode. We do need to talk about our communication skills, though."

"I'm sor…"

"Me, not you," he interrupted. When she looked confused, he walked over and took her hand, then led them to the bed and encouraged her to sit beside him. "I know I've kind of taken over and made plans on how to deal with this without consulting you and I'm sorry. It's the military in me. I see something that needs to be handled and I handle it. It's what I do. But I should have taken your thoughts and feelings into consideration. I just feel this need to protect you. Not knowing Dean and what he's capable of scares me. Making sure you're safe took over and I didn't stop to consider the very person I was protecting."

Brinley stared at Wells's handsome face, amazed at what an incredible man he was. He had no reason to apologize to her when all he'd been doing for the past several days was to look out for her. And yet, here he was, trying to understand her side of things.

"Wells," she whispered. "You've done nothing wrong."

"I didn't ask what you felt, Brin, but I'm asking now. Is there any part of today that you're uncomfortable with? It's not too late to make changes."

"There's nothing to change. I'm the one insisting that we meet with Dean before going to the police. Your plans just ensure that we do it in the safest way possible. How can I find fault in that? Going to the cemetery this morning was just something I needed to do. It had nothing to do with you or any plans you made."

"You're sure?"

"Absolutely," she smiled at him.

After giving her a lingering kiss, he stood and held out his hand. "Then it's time to go."

When they were less than a mile out, JP called to inform Wells that both he and Conrad were in place. It came as no surprise when he told them that Dean seemed highly agitated as they watched him pace around the dilapidated house.

"He's definitely alone, Wells, but be careful," JP said. "He seems unstable even from this vantage point. We've got your six but watch out for any quick moves, traps like loose boards in the house, or objects that could become weapons. I don't trust him. I still don't see a gun, but you never know."

"Got it. Thanks, JP," he said before hanging up.

When they arrived near the location, Wells parked nearly a quarter mile away. Reaching to open the glove box, Brinley was shocked as Wells pulled a gun out and placed it in a holster under his jacket.

"Wells," she sputtered. "Is that really necessary?"

"Yes," he answered tersely as he put a small device in his ear and looped the wire around. "Can you hear me, JP? Stevens?" he asked. Brinley assumed they confirmed because she heard no responses herself. "Good," he responded, then got out of the car and proceeded to open her door.

Without speaking they began the short walk to where they were meeting Dean. As they got closer and the house came into view, Brinley couldn't help the shivers that raced down her spine. Anxiety spurted through her with each step that took her closer to seeing Dean. She breathed in shallow, quick gasps, her chest feeling as if it would burst at any moment.

Wells, feeling her tremble, grasped her hand and held on to it for encouragement. They had gotten nearly fifteen feet from the front porch when Dean, with bloodshot eyes and wrinkled clothes, stepped out onto the worn, pitted wood.

"You were supposed to be here yesterday," he growled angrily.

"And you were supposed to be dead." Wells's entire demeanor changed with those few short words. His voice was absolutely emotionless and it chilled Brinley to her core. This was the warrior…the Navy Seal that she knew he had been. Seeing the change in his face, his stance, and his overall tone comforted her more than she cared to admit.

It was obvious that Dean had no liking for the comment. He came to his full height, took a step forward, and placed his hand near the pocket of his trousers. In that moment the tension between them escalated with frightening intensity.

"Go ahead," Wells dared.

Brinley's pulse began to beat erratically at the threat in his deep voice. She silently prayed that Dean grasped the danger he was in. Both men continued to stare at each other, anger and hatred radiating off their bodies. Her breath seemed to have solidified in her throat as she waited to see what would come next.

To her utter relief, Dean let out a deep breath and took a step back. "Inside," he said gruffly.

Wells placed Brinley behind him as they made their way through the door. Looking around, they could see cans of soup that had been opened and eaten from and tossed carelessly to the side. Wrappers from sandwiches bought at a gas station were strewn around as well as containers and bottles of various drinks.

"Love what you've done to the place," Wells said snidely.

"Cut the shit," Dean threatened. "Where's my money?" he demanded, staring at Brinley.

Brinley swallowed with difficulty, then found her voice. "I want answers first."

"I'm not playing games."

"Neither am I," she answered sternly.

The two stared at each for a few moments before Dean acquiesced. "What do you want to know?"

"Who was the man who died in our house and is now buried next to Annie? What happened that night?"

Dean seemed to hesitate briefly before he began. "I was in trouble at work. When Dad was alive and running the company, he started doing some underhanded deals with some pretty shady characters. Buying low-grade materials but charging the customer the higher price. The kickbacks were good but then one of the councilmen who was working on the new courthouse construction job got wind of what was happening. I have no idea how, but he demanded a sizable payment, otherwise he was going to report us. And that started the downward spiral. We were awarded more and more jobs because of the councilman's endorsement and the demands for higher kickbacks got worse. When Dad died it all became my responsibility. The company, the overbidding for higher kickbacks, and the demands for more payouts. McGill & Son Construction was drowning in debt with no way to recover. I started refusing to pay the councilman, which didn't go over well. So, I did the only thing I could. I cooked the books, didn't report all of the income, and started stashing money away knowing I was going to have to disappear and soon."

"So, you were just going to take the money and run? Leave Annie and me alone?"

"Come on, Brinley, we didn't have a marriage and you know it. I hated coming home to the little domestic scene you had going but Dad insisted I get married. Then when you had the kid, that pissed me off. I never wanted a child. I didn't want that pressure in my life. I had enough to deal with."

"Oh my God," Brinley gasped in horror.

"I had just about enough money put aside but I got wind that the councilman found out what I was doing. No idea how that happened, but that night I came home to get the money and run. What I hadn't planned on was the council guy sending someone after me that very night. You were sick upstairs, and the kid was in her crib. I was in the living room with my bag ready to walk out the door when this guy grabs me around the throat from behind. We struggled for a bit, traded punches back and forth. I thought I was done for, but you had left a candle burning on the end table, which got knocked over when we were fighting. The guy saw the flames and got distracted long enough for me to grab the marble statue on the coffee table and crush his skull with it. I knew the only way I was going to survive was if everyone thought I was dead. So, I quickly removed the rings from my fingers and put them on the dead guy. When I went to retrieve the money, the flames had taken over almost the entire living room. I decided to get out when I saw that the man's clothes were starting to burn. My plan was to go back for the money later, but by the time things cooled down enough for me to slip back in, the money was gone, and so were you. So, I'll ask you again, where's my money? It was hidden in the floorboards near the kitchen, but when I looked it was gone. What did you do with it?"

"You just left Annie and me there to die?" Brinley croaked. "You didn't for one second think to save us? Our daughter is dead, and you could have done something to save her," she nearly screamed.

"That was unfortunate. I may not have wanted a kid, but I certainly didn't mean for her die."

"Unfortunate!" Brinley whispered as tears slid down her cheeks. How could this man…this father…be so callous and unfeeling?

Snapping his fingers, Dean glowered at Brinley. "Pay attention. The money…I want my money."

Wells put his arm around Brinley to give her support. To hear how this man spoke about his wife and daughter, how uncaring and cold-hearted he was, made Wells want to hurl him off the closest bridge. What could make a man become so heartless to the very people who had loved him?

"There's no money, you bastard. There never was," Brinley revealed.

Dean took a step back like he'd been slapped. "What do you mean?"

"I never found any money. There's nothing. Whatever you left behind was either burned in the fire or someone else got to it. There is no money!"

When Dean took a step toward Brinley, Wells stepped in front of her to block him. "Don't even think about it."

"God damn it, I need that money. I'm a dead man without it. You better come up with something because if those guys find out I'm alive, they're going to come after you for the money I took. Hell, I couldn't find you, although God knows I tried. You come back to Casper to stay and they'll be on you like nothing you've seen before. They'll assume you have their money. The only reason you're probably still alive is because you pulled that little disappearing act."

"So, here's the thing," Wells volunteered. "There really is no money. I imagine it's been long gone since the fire. Who knows, maybe the repairmen hired to fix the house after the fire found it. I don't know, nor do I care. The only thing she has is the insurance money that was paid out for you when you were presumed dead. Give us a few days and we can come back with it."

"That was only worth about two hundred thousand. I can't live on that," he screeched.

"It's all there is. Take it or leave it," Wells replied calmly.

"I had almost half a million stashed away," Dean whined.

"What's your plan? Take what she can give you and disappear or walk away with nothing? It's your call," Wells pushed.

Dean paced the small confines of the old house. To give up didn't really sit well with him, but then again, the two hundred thousand was better than nothing. For that much he could find a way out of the country and start a new life. It was something at least. Besides, he had this awful feeling that he was being watched, and the need to get away from Casper, Wyoming, was becoming paramount. The possible chance of being seen was uppermost in his mind.

"Fine," he agreed grudgingly. "I'll take it. Meet me back here tomorrow morning."

"We need time to get the money out of the bank," Wells insisted.

"Fine, tomorrow late afternoon. Don't keep me waiting or I swear to God I'll make sure the councilman knows where to find you both," he threatened.

"Which councilman?" Brinley asked.

"Like I'd give that up to you. Besides, you're so smart, you figure it out. You have nine to choose from," he said snidely.

When Brinley started to reply, Wells took her elbow and led her to the door. "Let's go."

When they got several yards from the house, Brinley glanced sideways to Wells. "I never received the two hundred thousand. The policy was only for eighty thousand and a large portion of that went for the funeral, cremation, and burials."

"It doesn't matter, honey. He's not going to see a dime. The only way he was going to let us leave safely was if he thought we were going to get him some money."

Sadly, Brinley knew the truth of his statement. It was obvious that the man she married had just proven how selfish and callous he really was. A true monster with no regard for others and an overwhelming need to satisfy his own needs.

Chapter Eighteen

When they got back in the car, Wells quickly said into the device to "meet back at his place in an hour" and removed it from his ear. Putting the earbud and his gun back in the glove box, he started the engine and slowly pulled out on to the dirt road. Reaching over, he took Brinley's trembling hand, bringing it to his lips for a soft kiss. They looked at each other briefly before he turned back to watch the road.

They drove in silence until Wells pulled into a small complex of about twelve condominiums. The grounds were neatly kept, with fresh flowers and earthy-smelling mulch in beds around each condo. To the left she saw a building with a sign indicating it was the complex office, as well as a gym and a laundromat for any of the tenants. Behind the office, Brinley could see a tennis court and a pool with several people lounging in chairs enjoying the sun.

"Nice," she murmured as Wells drove to furthest building to the right and parked in front of the last condo.

Getting out of the truck, she followed him to the front door and stood patiently by as he unlocked it, then motioned for her to proceed him.

The first thing that caught her eye was how neat everything was, just as it had been at the cabin. Knowing it was the military in him, she moved to the kitchen and took in the clean, uncluttered counters. The colors were in muted tones of beige and brown throughout his place, with accents of color in the artwork on his walls and the furniture he'd chosen.

Heading back into the living room, she walked over to a desk he had in the corner. Running her fingers over the wood, she imagined him sitting there paying his bills or working on his laptop. "This is beautiful," she said quietly.

Wells, who had been watching as she examined his home, came to stand next to her. "Thanks, my dad made it," he said proudly.

"It's amazing. You're lucky to have such a beautiful piece."

Walking over to his couch, she sat down and clasped her hands nervously. "So why didn't we go straight to the police?"

"Because I wanted to talk to JP and Conrad first. I want to hear their impressions of Dean, learn anything they might have found out while they were watching him. I also want to know if anyone else was watching him. There are some awful people out there who would love to get hold of him. Which makes them a danger to us. I'm not so certain that they don't already realize he's alive."

"I hadn't thought of that," Brinley mused.

Sitting next to her on the couch, Wells put his arms around her. She seemed completely out of sorts, and he had no clue how to help her. There was no easy way around this mess except to deal with things head on. He couldn't begin to imagine all the thoughts that were going through her head so the only thing he could think of was hold her and love her.

When she settled against his chest, he kissed the top of her head. "It's going to be okay, Brin, I promise."

"You can't promise me that, Wells," she mumbled into his shirt. "But it helps that you're here."

They sat quietly like that for a short while. When Brinley eventually pulled away to use the restroom, Wells went into the kitchen to get them something to drink. By the time she made her way back into the living room, there was a knock at his door.

After checking to make sure who it was, Wells opened the door and stood back as JP and Conrad entered. After the guys exchanged their manly one-armed embrace and backslaps, JP walked over to Brinley without hesitation and gave her a hug. When he stepped back, Conrad took his place in front of her.

"We haven't officially met, but I'm Conrad Stevens."

"My guardian angel who watched over me at the cemetery. It's nice to meet you, Conrad."

"It's nice to meet you, Brinley Crew," he answered back before giving her a hug. "Don't sneak out like that again, okay?" he said in her ear before pulling back.

"I won't," she promised, winking at him.

"She's trouble," Conrad said turning to Wells. "I like that in a woman."

"So did you learn anything about Dean?" Wells asked, frowning at his friend. He was standing entirely too close to Brinley, and while he knew Conrad would never cross a line, he didn't like the fact that his friend seemed taken with her.

JP grabbed a bottle of water from the fridge and, after asking if anyone else wanted one, stood next to Wells and twisted the cap off. Taking a long drink from the bottle, he finally lowered it and took in the group at large. "Someone else knows he's alive."

"What?" Brinley exclaimed.

"Explain," Wells said simply.

"There were other sets of footprints about a hundred feet from the place. We watched Dean and never at any point did he venture that far from the house. I didn't see anyone, but the tracks looked to be recent. It could be just some kids or hikers in the area, but I don't think you should take the chance. I'd head to the police now. As much of a sneaky bastard as that man is, he's completely unaware of his surroundings. Anyone could sneak up on him and he'd never know it."

"I agree," Wells added. "Anything else we need to know?"

"That's about it," Conrad informed him.

"Then we need to head to the police now."

"Want us to come with you?" JP asked.

"No, we got it from here. But thanks for everything you guys have done. Brinley and I both appreciate it."

"No worries, man. You know where to find us if you need anything else. JP and I won't be deployed for at least another week or two. Call if you need us," Conrad said as he winked at Brinley, fist-bumped Wells, and walked out the door.

"What he said," JP said as he followed his friend's lead and hugged Brinley, fist-bumped Wells, and exited the condo.

When the room was quiet again, Wells looked over to Binley. "Are you hungry? I can fix you something to eat before we head over to the police station."

"I can't eat," she said quietly. "My stomach is in knots. I'd rather get this over with."

"Then let's go," he said, brusquely ushering Brinley out the door.

When they arrived at the police station, Wells explained to the sergeant at the front desk that he needed to speak with the chief of police. He mentioned that he had evidence of fraud being perpetrated and would only speak to the man in charge about it. The sergeant pointed to the waiting area and told them to have a seat.

When fifteen minutes had gone by, Wells stood up and approached the desk again. He was just about to tell the man that they were leaving when a tall, nearly bald, heavy-set man approached the desk. He looked at Wells and Brinley, obviously taking their measure, before holding out his hand.

"I'm Chief Dubois."

After some hesitation, Wells shook his hand. "I'm Wells Kennedy and this is Brinley Crew."

"I remember the name," the chief said curiously. "You came here about your father's death a while back."

"I did," Wells confirmed.

"Humph," he responded. "So, you have some information for me about some fraud that's taking place?"

"It's a rather sensitive issue. Is it possible to speak in private?" Wells asked.

"Come with me," Chief Dubois commanded.

They followed the chief down a small hallway and into the room marked *Chief of Police.* When Wells and Brinley were seated in front of the massive desk, the chief simply stared at them and waited for them to speak. So much for small talk. It was obvious he was a man of few words. Or was he a nonbeliever as he had been before when Wells spoke to him about his father.

With Wells holding her hand, Brinley began. "My husband died a while back in a fire at our house. I filed for the insurance money, which they paid, and had the house repaired with the money from our homeowners policy. A few days ago, I found out that my husband didn't really die in that fire, the body that burned was someone else's, and now he's coming after me to give him money because he's running from some bad people who tried to kill him for siphoning off money that he illegally obtained that they think belongs to them."

Other than the sound of breathing, the room remained in silence as Chief Dubois mulled over what Brinley had just revealed. After several moments, he looked at her with suspicion in his eyes. "How do I know that you weren't in on this scheme from the beginning and are now coming forward because it went sideways, and you want some payback."

Brinley inhaled so swiftly at the insult that she nearly choked herself. "How dare you," she seethed as Wells grabbed her hand and tried to get her to calm down. It was an obvious question, and one he had expected to be asked.

Shrugging out of his grasp, Brinley stood and leaned over the older man's desk. "First off, I would never do something like that. You don't know me, Chief Dubois, but that is as far from my character as you can get. Secondly, my daughter died in that fire. She was my life, and I would never, EVER do anything that could possibly hurt her. To suggest that I would is just…well…it's unconscionable!"

"Please, Ms. Crew, have a seat. I didn't mean to offend you, but I had to ask the question."

Brinley stared at him for a few seconds before relenting. When she sat back down, he looked at her kindly. "I truly am sorry, but you should know how these things work. We have to look at everything from every angle. And I'm sorry for your loss, by the way. I can't imagine what it would be like to lose a child."

"There's something important you should know before we go any further," Wells interrupted.

"What might that be?" the chief asked.

"One of Casper's city councilmen is involved. We don't know who it is or how deep it goes but there's some corruption going on."

"And yet you still came to see me. How do you know I'm not involved as well? You just took a pretty big chance, Mr. Kennedy."

"I had you investigated. There's nothing in your background or lifestyle to indicate you are. You lead a quiet, unassuming life, no large debt and no sudden deposits in the past five years. No offshore accounts that I could find and the car you and your wife own is a 2015 Camry, bought used a few years back. Your two children, a son and daughter, worked their way through college and are now paying back their student loans. You should be very proud. Since they took over the payments, neither of them has been late one time," he finished smugly.

"Well, aren't you a wealth of knowledge," the chief scoffed. "Who are you, exactly?"

"I told you: Wells Kennedy."

"I knew that," he said hotly. "What do you do for a living, Wells Kennedy?"

"Former Navy Seal. Retired early due to an injury on the job."

"That explains it," Chief Dubois chuckled, relaxing in his chair. "Thank you for your service, young man."

Wells acknowledged the comment with a nod of his head as the chief stood up. "If you don't mind, I'd like to invite Detective Bob Morris to join us. I think he'll be very interested to hear what all you have to say."

After the detective joined them, Brinley once again explained everything that had transpired, from Dean's supposed death to everything he told her when they met at the ramshackle old house earlier. She left nothing out, from the beginning of their relationship to seeing Dean again at the house alive and well. When she'd explained every minute detail, she fell silent as Wells picked up the story.

"He's a loose cannon," he advised. "Dean's desperate for money and I'm worried he's going to come after Brinley for coming here today. He's dangerous."

"If you're correct that someone else knows he's alive, he's very dangerous," Detective Morris agreed. "He say where he's been hiding all this time?"

"Not a word and to be honest, we didn't ask."

"I'm going to pull a team together, get SWAT involved. We'll go in and take him into custody tomorrow morning. If we're lucky, he'll give us the name of which councilman is involved if it will help to save his own ass," the chief theorized.

"So you know," the detective added. "We've had McGill and Son Construction under investigation for some time. We knew there were shady deals going on, money passed for payoffs and bribes. We were holding off on arresting McGill and some of his employees, hoping to get a lead on who on the city council was involved. Then he died in the fire and our case literally went up in smoke. It was only a matter of time before we arrested him if he'd survived."

"What do I do about the insurance money I received? I had no idea he was alive, or I wouldn't have taken it. He made me a part of the fraud charges, right?" Brinley asked.

Chief Dubois handed Brinley a card with his and Detective Morris's name and contact information. "When you go home, call your insurance company and ask to speak with a supervisor. Explain what happened, tell them an investigation is ongoing, and McGill's arrest is imminent. Give them our contact information and they'll take it from there."

"What will happen?"

"Anything from your homeowners policy related to the house repairs will be okay since it really was damaged in the fire. For the life insurance policy, they'll take back the death benefit, usually plus interest," the detective answered. "It will be referred to the fraud department and they'll go after Dean for it. There's what they call soft fraud and hard fraud. The amount the policy paid out makes it a felony. He'll have to pay restitution to the company as well as jail time that will be added to whatever he gets for the other charges."

"Do you have someplace safe to stay until we arrest your husband?" Chief Dubois asked.

"She'll be staying with me," Wells answered, bristling at the reference that Dean was her husband. "I gave you my contact information. Will you let us know when Dean's in custody?"

"Of course," he replied. "You'll be my first call."

By the time Wells and Brinley left the police station, dusk was settling over Casper.

"I'm scared," Brinley whispered when they started the drive back to his condo.

"It's going to be all right," he assured her as he took her hand, hoping like hell that he hadn't just lied.

Chapter Nineteen

Wells pulled Brinley closer to his body, smoothing strands of her glossy hair away from his face where it tickled his nose. It was two o'clock in the morning and so far sleep was eluding him. He was worried. Not just a passing concern but deep-in-his-gut worried. He knew going to the police was the right thing to do but now Brinley was exposed. It was difficult enough worrying about Dean, but his associates caused another whole level of concern.

When they'd gotten home, Brinley did as the chief suggested and reached out to the insurance company to explain the situation. The original tone was a little threatening until she gave them the phone numbers of the chief and the detective involved. It took everything he had not to grab the phone and deal with them himself, but he knew this was something she needed to handle on her own. She was so stressed that the dinner he made for them went nearly untouched. Brinley merely pushed it around her plate until finally she gave up and put her fork down.

Not wanting to crowd her, Wells cleaned the kitchen, giving her time to wrap her head around the day. When he walked in the living room, she was standing by the window looking lost. He called her name and that seemed to be all that was needed for her to give in to the tension that had been building all day. She finally broke down and he did the only thing he knew to do and that was to hold her as tears streamed down her face. She grasped his shirt as wracking sobs tore from her throat, giving vent to the fear and uncertainty that plagued her. He'd never felt so helpless!

When she had eventually calmed, he gave her an over-the-counter sleeping pill and tucked her into his bed. Not able to sleep himself, he wandered back to the living room to call his mom and check on her. He didn't think that Dean would do anything stupid like go after her, but he needed to make sure she was okay. To his great relief, JP and Conrad had dropped by for a visit and stayed for dinner and watched a movie with her. They chatted for a while and by the time he hung up he felt much better. Not only was his mom okay but he had the best group of friends a man could ask for. He hadn't even had to ask them to watch out for his mom…they simply stepped up to the plate and did it, for which he was extremely grateful.

With nothing else to do, Wells brushed his teeth and crawled into bed, pleased when Brinley gravitated to him in her sleep. For now, he could hold her in his arms and keep her safe. Unfortunately, thinking of what the next day would bring kept him awake until just before the sun began to rise.

Brinley woke up with Wells wrapped around her, his soft snores blowing the hair near her ear. Looking at the clock she realized that it was not quite six in the morning. Not wanting to disturb him, she crawled out from under the covers and padded out to the living room.

Today was the day. Very soon Dean would be arrested and then maybe…just maybe she could move on with her life. Her first priority was to file for divorce from her wretched husband; her second priority was to have her daughter moved to a new resting place so that she wasn't buried next to a stranger. And then? Who knew? The thought of possibly having a future with Wells excited her but would he want a future with her? It seemed she came with more baggage than most women. There was the divorce she was going to have to obtain, probably court hearings, and her name was going to be spread all over the news. Who would possibly want to sign up for that?

She must have paced and pondered her future for an hour before she felt warm arms wrap around her waist. Wells nuzzled her neck, then turned to plant a kiss on her lips.

"How long have you been up?"

"Maybe an hour or two?" she answered.

"I'm going to make some coffee. Can I make you a cup of tea?"

Nodding her head, Brinley followed him to the kitchen and watched as he put water into a kettle and put it on the stove. As he moved about the kitchen getting his coffee ready, his motions were fluid and graceful. Brinley could have watched him for hours, enjoying the distraction.

"Eggs for breakfast?" Wells asked, turning around to catch her watching him. Amused, he leaned in for another kiss. "Were you ogling my ass?"

"I don't ogle," she said grumpily.

"I ogle you every chance I get," he joked.

"That's because you're a very sick man. And no eggs, thank you anyway."

"You need to eat something. I have cereal, some instant oats."

"My stomach's not feeling so well this morning. I think I'll just stick to the tea if you don't mind."

Wells frowned at her. "You didn't eat dinner last night either. It's not good to go without food. Especially with the stress you've been under," he lectured.

"I'll eat once we hear from Chief Dubois and I know that Dean is in custody. This uncertainty is getting to me."

Not wanting to push her, Wells had a bowl of cereal and finished his coffee. They took turns showering then sat around watching random sitcoms on television. When that began to bore them, Brinley picked up an old magazine to leaf through while Wells went through his mail and paid some bills online. Together they did a couple loads of laundry and sat back on the couch waiting for one of their cell phones to ring.

When the quiet became too much, Brinley went into the kitchen and made a light lunch of ham sandwiches and grabbed a bag of potato chips to add to it. She watched as Wells ate his, then tossed hers onto his plate when she couldn't get past the second bite. When lunch was done and the kitchen tidied again, Brinley looked over to Wells.

"Should we call? We should have heard from him by now. Maybe he forgot."

Knowing there would be no peace until they heard something, Wells pulled out his cell phone and called the Casper police station. When the officer at the desk answered, Wells explained who he was and asked to speak to Chief Dubois.

"The chief hasn't been in all day," the man answered. "We haven't heard from him but if you like, you can leave a message and I'll have him call you back."

Wells left his name and number and hung up, turning to see that Brinley was looking at him with concern and disappointment in her eyes. "Don't go reading anything into that," he started. "I'm sure the chief is very busy with interviews and paperwork. He'll get back to us as soon as he can," Wells assured her.

Not wanting to dispute his claim, Brinley shrugged and went in search of a book to read to occupy her mind. She lasted almost an hour before she tossed it aside and searched for his remote to turn the television on. "Maybe there's something on the news about an arrest," she defended when Wells raised his eyebrow at her.

For the next hour she skipped from channel to channel in search of news reports. When nothing came up, she began all over again, starting back at the lower channels. Wells was about to snatch the device from her hand when there was a knock at his door.

"Thank God," he muttered as he got up and went to the door, peeking through the hole to see who it was. "It's Chief Dubois," he answered as Brinley came to stand behind him.

When he opened the door, he knew immediately it wasn't good news. Chief Dubois looked tired and haggard as he stood looking at them both. There was dirt on his shirt and pants and his badge hung precariously off his belt.

"Please, come in," Wells offered and stood back to allow him room. "Can I get you something to drink?"

"I'd love some water if you don't mind," the chief answered.

Brinley hurried off to the kitchen to get the water while Wells ushered the chief into the living room. When he was settled in a chair, Brinley handed him the drink and watched as he took a long draw from the bottle, sighing in relief.

"Thanks," he said, tipping the bottle in their direction. "I've needed that for hours now."

"What happened?" Brinley asked urgently.

"When we got there this morning, McGill was gone," the chief stated bluntly.

"Gone?" Brinley practically yelled. How could that be?

"There was sign of a struggle when we got there. There was fresh blood on the floor and it was obvious, despite the disrepair of the house, that something had happened. SWAT and my guys combed the woods for most of the day looking for evidence and/or a body. We found blood but no sign of McGill. There were tracks all around the house of varying sizes so we know that whoever was after him showed up in force. We've got samples at the lab already hoping to find out whose blood it was."

"Oh my God," Brinley whispered.

"It may be good news that we didn't find a body," he assured Brinley. "McGill could still be alive."

"Or somebody has him," Wells filled in.

"To what end?" the chief asked. "If what you say is true and McGill has no money, whoever was after him will find that out pretty quickly and simply kill him."

"Or Dean will mention that Brinley has money and they'll come after her," Wells fired back. "I'm sure it's not just about the money," he continued. "They'll want to know what Dean knows like names of the city council member involved or others and if he shared any of that information with, say, his wife?"

"There is that," Chief Dubois agreed. "Which is why I'm putting a detail out front to watch your condo. I suggest you lay low for a few days, let us do our thing. Stay close to home and I'll be in touch as things progress."

"Just stay here and do nothing?" she asked incredulously.

"That's exactly what I'm telling you," he said, getting up from the chair. "And I mean it," he warned. "Let us handle this. I'll stay in touch," he said brusquely as he walked out the door.

Wells engaged the locks and turned to face Brinley. He watched her for a few minutes, waiting to see her reaction to what the chief shared with them. When she said nothing, he took her hand.

"Are you okay?"

"Not really. I don't know what this means. Is he still alive? Is he on the run? Does someone have him? I have no idea. And what does that mean for me? Am I in danger like the chief thinks? Is Dean going to lead them to my door by lying and saying that I know something I don't? Or that I have money that I don't? I didn't do anything wrong and yet my life is in limbo."

"I'm right here with you, Brin. You're not alone."

"But I should be," she answered quickly. "It's insane for you to be anywhere near me. Not after today. Not now," she swallowed hard, lifted her chin, and boldly met his gaze. "I have to leave. I can't put you or, God forbid, your mother in danger." Turning, she rushed into his bedroom.

Wells followed her and leaned against the doorway watching as she rushed around grabbing her things. "We've had this conversation before, Brin. You're not going anywhere without me."

"I love you, you idiot, and I will not stand by and watch you get hurt because of this."

"And I feel the same way about you so you can just stop what you're doing. For now, we do what the chief says and lay low. Together. You know damn well I wouldn't walk away from you so what makes you think I'll let you walk away from me?"

Brinley paused for a second, then plopped on his bed, dropping the clothes in her hand. "I know. I panicked," she admitted.

Wells smiled as he sat next to her and took her hand in his. "I know. It's a lot to take in but I'm glad you heard me. We'll handle it together. Although," he added, "if you want, we could go back to Green River and ride it out there. I'm sure the chief would agree to that."

"No," Brinley said, squeezing his hand. "But thanks. I need to stay here. It's time I stuck around. I need to see this through. No matter how it ends," she said determinedly.

Chapter Twenty

Two weeks, Brinley huffed. Two weeks of sitting around, lying low and waiting. It was starting to drive her slightly insane. Chief Dubois was good about keeping in touch with them about what was going on, but the problem was…nothing was happening. It was as if Dean had disappeared off the face of the earth. No contact, no body, nothing. The cooler temperatures of mid-September only brought relief from the heat, not the stress of waiting and worrying.

The only time Brinley felt any type of peace was in Wells's arms. He was exceedingly good with her, understanding when she needed to be left alone and when she needed him nearby. They made love just about every night, the exertion helping to calm both their frayed nerves. She'd never felt so close to another human being. The nights she spent with his arms around her were some of her best moments, even though concerns of the future were never far behind.

They fell into a good routine. They woke up together, ate breakfast together, then split up to read, work on the computer, or do what little housework there was. Every third or fourth day they would go over to visit Ruby Kennedy. Wells would do chores around his mom's house that needed to be done while Brinley spent the afternoon sitting on the back deck with the older woman, chatting and getting to know her while they watched Wells work. Those were special times for Brinley. She hadn't realized how much she missed having a mother and Ruby was nothing if not motherly toward her. She easily accepted that Brinley was a part of her son's life and welcomed her without reservation. They formed a tight bond, so much so that Brinley felt comfortable talking about her previous life, what it was like to lose her parents at the age of fifteen and having to live with a family friend when what she really needed was a mother. There was no topic off limits between them and the more time they had together, the closer they became.

Which made today frustrating because as much as she wanted to spend time with Ruby, she wasn't feeling all that great, so Wells went to his mom's by himself. He was willing to postpone the visit but Ruby needed something fixed on her car, so Brinley insisted he go over to help. It wasn't right to leave the woman without a running vehicle so Brinley pushed him into going. It was only after she promised to stay put and just relax that Wells relented and headed over to his mom's. He stood outside the door listening to make sure she engaged the lock before he felt okay about leaving her.

Two hours later he called to let Brinley know that it was going to be a while longer. He needed to go to Auto Zone to pick up a part and it would take another thirty minutes or so. Assuring him she was fine, Brinley hung up and paced the condo. Glancing out the window, the cool air and sunshine called out to her. Staying inside was rather boring so she grabbed her book and her cell phone and a towel. It wouldn't hurt to sit by the pool and read in the sun for a while, would it? The complex was usually busy with men working on the grounds and there were constantly tenants coming and going. It wasn't like she was going to be alone, she justified as she opened the door and stepped out.

Halfway through the parking lot, she caught herself glancing uneasily over her shoulder. Disgusted that she was allowing her imagination to get away from her, she flipped the towel over her shoulder and continued toward the pool. A warning voice whispered in her head just before a voice called out her name.

"Brinley…is that you?"

Turning, Brinley looked at the woman whose face looked familiar. It took her a few minutes before it dawned on her who it was. Relief surged through her. "Jennie Markewitz?" Brinley puzzled, looking at her former neighbor. "What are you doing here?"

"I have a friend who lives in this complex and stopped by to visit. What about you? Are you living here now? I thought when I saw you a while ago that you would be moving back to the old neighborhood."

"Well, I..."

A noise sounded behind her. Before Brinley could turn around to see what it was, she felt a sharp pain at the back of her head and then blackness consumed her as she crumpled to the pavement.

Coming into consciousness, Brinley felt sharp pain radiating from the back of her head and nausea that made her want to retch. The room she was being held in was completely dark.

Feeling around, she realized that she was on a mattress that had been thrown on the floor. The room was cold and had a damp, musty smell to it. Rolling to her knees, Brinley took a few deep breaths to get the nausea under control, then slowly came to a standing position. Holding her arms out, she walked around the room, feeling for any objects and to learn the size of the space she was being held in. By the time she made her way around the entire circumference, she knew two things. One...there was nothing in the room except for the mattress and two, the walls were wet with condensation so she must be in some sort of basement or cellar. Which was terrifying given the fact that she had no idea where she was, how long she'd been out, or who was keeping her hostage. If this place was below ground, how on earth was she going to get help and, more importantly, where was Jennie and did she get away in time to notify the authorities?

Just as panic started to set in, she heard the faint sound of a key being inserted into a lock. She backed against the wall as the door finally swung open and light flooded the room, causing her to blink from the brightness. It took several seconds before her eyes adjusted and she was able to see the man standing in the doorway. Dean!

Brinley noticed that her usually neatly groomed husband looked nothing like himself. He had awful bruises on his face and his left eye was swollen nearly shut. His lip was split, and his right arm was wrapped in white gauze that had stains of red from where he had been bleeding. It was his eyes, though, that made her blood run cold. He was furious… and it was all directed at her.

As Dean stepped toward her, Brinley stepped sideways to get away from him until her shoulder hit the other wall. When she had nowhere else to go, Dean closed the distance until he was directly in her face. He stared at her for a few seconds before raising his hand and slapping her hard across her left cheek.

Brinley hadn't seen it coming and had no opportunity to protect her face. She cried out in pain as her head bounced off the wall, injuring the same spot from before. If Dean hadn't grabbed her arm she would have collapsed at his feet. Instead, he dragged her like a rag doll across the cement floor and out into another room. Pushing her onto a sturdy metal chair, he quickly tied first her hands behind her back, then secured her feet to each leg of the chair. To make sure the bonds were tight, Dean wiggled them back and forth, then stepped back to admire his work. When he felt she was secure, he gave her another good slap across the face, this time on her right cheek, and stepped back.

"You betrayed me," he snarled. "You went to the cops, you stupid bitch!"

Brinley swallowed the despair in her throat and stared at the man who had once been her husband. It was so hard to fathom what he once was compared to what he had become. If she weren't so terrified it would have been almost funny to see the dichotomy between the past and present.

"Did you honestly think I would help you after everything you've done?" she proclaimed. "Especially where Annie was concerned?"

Dean bolted toward her and placed his hands around her neck and started to squeeze. A sensation of intense sickness and desolation swept over her as the lights in the dank basement began to dim around her eyes. In that instant she knew she was going to die. There would be no saving her this time. She'd angered him beyond reason and Wells was nowhere near to help her. Her mind quickly went to Annie. Knowing that she would finally be able to see her again gave her the calmness she needed before taking her last breath.

Only it turned out not to be her last breath. Something came over Dean that caused him to release her throat. When she realized he stepped back, she took in a gulp of air, clearing her vision and causing her to cough repeatedly. When she was finally able to take more breaths, she looked to Dean and saw the crazed look in his eye, the anger on his face, and watched as he wiped his shaking hands down the front of his shirt. He started ranting at her at that point, pacing back and forth as he called her names and blamed her for his current situation. He spoke vilely about her as a wife and mother and a human being. He blamed her for everything that had gone wrong in his life and lamented the day he met her. He spoke so viciously that she wondered how she could have ever thought him kind.

When his tirade finally ended, Brinley heard a door from upstairs open and watched as a set of women's heels appeared at the top step. Shock registered when the woman came to stand at the bottom step and sent a smug look in Brinley's direction. "Jennie?" she croaked.

"Hello, sister," Dean greeted.

Sister? Brinley couldn't grasp what Dean meant by calling her sister. Jennie was their neighbor, not a relative…wasn't she?

"I prefer stepsister but to be honest," she beamed, "lover is a truer description."

As Jennie walked over to Dean and rubbed against him, Brinley tried to shake the cobwebs from her brain. "I…I don't understand," she whispered.

"You always were a bit too slow and trusting, now weren't you, Brinley," Jennie purred. "Not much to understand actually. My mama married James McGill a while ago and that made Dean here and me related. The marriage lasted just a short time, but I found I rather liked having my stepbrother in my bed."

Brinley knew James McGill had been a womanizer, but it was becoming clearer and a little shocking at the number of stepchildren he'd accumulated over the years. How many more were there?

"Were you sleeping together when we lived in the same neighborhood?" Brinley stuttered as she began to put the pieces together.

Jennie glanced at Dean. "She sure is slow, isn't she?" Dean merely shrugged as Jennie continued. "He bought the house for me, darlin'. Liked to keep me real close so when you were busy with the brat or too tired to pay attention to him, I was always close at hand. I befriended you so you would never suspect what was going on. Good thing you were so naïve. You came by one day and there Dean and I were, in the middle of the day in my living room naked as can be. You never suspected a thing…told you I was under the weather and off you went, back home to make me some chicken soup. What a joke!"

Brinley couldn't believe what she was hearing. It seemed like nothing from her life before was what she thought it was. Not her marriage with Dean and not the friendship she thought she had with Jennie. How could she have been so stupid?

"But then Dean died," Jennie continued. "Or at least I thought he died. My life went to hell. I almost lost the house because he wasn't there to pay for it. I had to get a job…learn how to live on next to nothing. I was thrilled when you left town. I knew Dean here was hiding money so at night when the workers left I'd sneak over and search for it."

"You took the money?" Brinley exclaimed.

"I never found any money, so I assume you have it?" she said menacingly.

"I told Dean I never found any cash and I'm telling you the same. There was no money!" Brinley insisted.

Both Dean and Jennie studied Brinley, looking for any signs of deception. Finally, after a few minutes, Dean shrugged. "I believe her, unfortunately."

"Damnit!" Jennie burst out. "What do we do now? Those men who attacked you are not going to give up. They know you're alive now, Dean. They want their money."

Dean turned and stared at Brinley. "She's going to get some for us. I can't replace what I took from them but I sure as hell can get enough to disappear."

"For *us* to disappear," Jennie corrected.

"Yeah, sure, us," Dean muttered.

"I don't have that kind of money," Brinley stressed.

"Maybe not but your boyfriend does," Dean sneered. "I bet he would give just about anything to get you back in one piece."

"We're not that close," Brinley lied. "I'm not worth anything to him. Especially when it comes to giving away the only money he has. He's been released from the military. He has no job and no money."

"You better hope that's not true or you're a dead woman," Dean seethed before taking a knife out and cutting the rope from around her ankles that anchored her to the chair. With her hands still tied behind her back, he roughly yanked her from the chair and marched her back into the tiny room. Pushing her onto the mattress, he quickly left the room and slammed the door shut, the clank of a lock echoing off the walls.

A flash of wild grief ripped through her as a high-pitched laugh reached her ears. *Please, Wells, please be careful,* she whispered softly, curling into herself on the torn mattress. Because one thing she knew for certain…Wells would not take her abduction lightly.

Chapter Twenty-One

Wells left his mom's house satisfied that he was able to get her car up and running. He felt bad leaving Brinley to fend for herself for most of the day but knew that she understood that he needed to take care of his mom. She was good like that and it gave him a great deal of pleasure to see them together and how well they got along.

By the time he walked through the front door, he was anxious to see Brinley. After years of living alone and not really being attached to anyone, it was a good feeling to be so happy to see someone. He liked her being in his space and knowing that she was there waiting for him.

"Brinley," he called, tossing his keys on the table by the door. When she didn't say anything, he walked back to the bedroom expecting to find her napping on the bed or soaking in the bathtub. It wasn't until he realized that both the bed and the bathtub were empty that he started to get worried. His condo wasn't all that big and if she was there, he would have found her by now.

Rushing to the front door, he paused long enough to grab his keys. Locking the door, he pulled his phone out, found her number in his contact list and hit the call button. He stood anxiously on his front step praying that she would answer her phone. When it went to voicemail, he started walking to the parking lot, unsure where to start his search. He was just about to get in his truck when he glanced over to his left and saw something on the pavement. Shutting the driver's door, he went over and knelt down. A chilling, black silence surrounded him as he lifted the book and read the title, *The Catcher in the Rye* by J. D. Salinger. The book Brinley had been reading when he left this morning.

With a sense of dread, Wells scanned the parking lot, finding a beach towel that he knew came from his own closet and several feet further away a broken cell phone. Lifting it, he realized it was in fact Brinley's, causing fear to snake up his back.

Holding the items close to his chest, he searched frantically for her, hoping he would find her somewhere nearby with a completely logical explanation as to why her things were scattered in the parking lot. He spoke to several of the groundskeepers who were working around the area, but they had no recollection of seeing her. He spotted a woman who was just leaving the pool area with two kids in tow. He approached her to see if she had seen anything.

"Well now, I did see a woman who fits your description. She was over there near the red car, talking to a woman. I got distracted with these two," she said, nodding to her children, "so I didn't see where she went after that. Sorry I can't be of any help. Come on, kids, dinner won't make itself. Sorry," she apologized before corralling her children and heading them toward her condo.

The red car was exactly where he had found Brinley's book. But it didn't make sense to him. Surely, it would have been Dean who would want to get to Brinley, not a woman.

Confused by the new information, Wells continued to search for another twenty minutes. When he had covered the entire complex and spoken to everyone who was around, he gave up and hurried back to his own place. He did one more search around the condo, hoping that she might have returned while he was out looking for her and when he came up empty, he reached out to Chief Dubois.

Within ten minutes the chief arrived at his condo with two officers in tow, directing them to scout the complex and start knocking on doors to speak with the tenants. He joined Wells inside and sat on the couch asking him questions. He grilled Wells for a while before he glanced over apologetically. "Could she have simply run away? Maybe she needed some time apart from you," he suggested.

"Don't be ridiculous," Wells huffed. "Brinley is a strong, independent woman. If she wanted time apart, she would have just said that. She doesn't play games and speaks her mind. I know her, Chief. Something's happened to her. She wouldn't make me worry like this. Besides, she wasn't feeling well this morning, which is why she didn't come with me in the first place. She wouldn't just go off like this."

Just then the two officers who had been out canvassing the complex returned to inform the chief that there was no new information. Brinley was nowhere to be found and no one they had spoken to saw anything that might be of help.

"I'm sure she'll be in touch with you soon," Chief Dubois advised. "Could be she went out shopping and lost track of time."

"You're ignoring the broken cell phone and the book and towel," Wells argued. "She wouldn't just leave those things on the pavement." Hearing his phone ding with an incoming text, he got up and went to retrieve it from the table. "Besides, Brinley wouldn't make me worry like this. Something has got…son-of-a-bitch," he exclaimed, reading his screen.

"What is it?" the chief asked as he came to stand beside Wells.

"Still think she went shopping?" Wells asked tersely, turning the phone toward Dubois revealing a picture of Brinley's bruised and bloodied face with a demand for five hundred thousand dollars.

Two days and still no word. No information on where to drop the money—in fact, no communication whatsoever—and no signs that the police had come up with to try and locate her. The waiting was agonizing. Not knowing if she was still alive, how bad her injuries were, or if she was still being beaten annihilated him the most. His nights were spent pacing the confines of his condo and staring out his windows. Sleep eluded him so after a while he simply stopped trying. The days he spent going out and searching for her, visiting the police station to check for updates, and trying to convince his mother to stop delivering food that he knew he wasn't going to eat. Nothing would be right again until he had Brinley back safely in his arms.

They still had no idea who exactly had Brinley. Was it Dean? Was the woman, whoever she was, involved or just a passerby? The text came from an untraceable phone and the chief suspected it was probably one of the men Dean had stolen from. But they still had no clue which scenario it was, which made looking even more difficult. Even Detective Morris was running out of ideas of where to go next.

It was out of sheer frustration that Wells finally decided to reach out to JP to see if maybe he could help. Being military, the guys had access to certain intelligence and elite technology that just might be more helpful. His call went immediately to voicemail. Assuming that JP was still out on a mission, Wells hung up without leaving a message. Within an hour, his phone rang, and the screen indicated it was an incoming call from JP. He'd no more than said hello before his friend interrupted.

"What's wrong? You always leave me a message when you call."

Hearing the sound of rotor blades in the background, Wells sighed. "It's fine, I can hear that you're out on a mission. Stay safe and give me a call when you get stateside."

"Cut the shit, Kennedy. We're on our way back home now. Just waiting for the transport to be cleared for takeoff. So, what's going on? You sound weird."

"I am weird," Wells joked lamely, not wanting to cause concern when the guys were coming off an op that was probably more stressful and chaotic than someone missing. He knew firsthand the toll it took when the team was out on a mission and how important downtime was to their peace of mind. There was no way he would infringe on them, knowing how bad it could get out there.

"Wells…"

"Everything is fine here. I'll give you a call next week and we can meet up for a beer or two, okay? Be safe flying back and tell the guys I said hey," Wells added before disconnecting the call.

He knew he'd done the right thing but the feeling of helplessness that overcame him when he'd hung up was absolute. If there was ever a time he needed his brothers, now was it.

Wells paced until it was well past dark. Finally, out of sheer exhaustion he fell asleep in a chair, his neck contorted at an odd angle. The sun was just starting to peek above the horizon when a loud banging on his front door brought him awake. Grabbing his neck in pain, Wells dashed to the door and swung it open, hoping that by some miracle Brinley had escaped on her own and found her way back home.

"Nothing wrong my ass," JP grumbled, taking in the dark circles under his friend's eyes, his wrinkled clothes and disheveled appearance. "What the hell happened?"

"You should be home resting," Wells admonished.

"Obviously we need to be here," Conrad countered as he brushed by JP and walked into the condo.

"Stevens, what the hell are you doing here? I've got this. Both of you, go home and rest," Wells insisted.

It shouldn't have surprised Wells that when JP moved to the side, there were four other members of his former Seal team standing near his front door. Robert "Papa Bear" (because he was a large man and looked out for everyone) Anderson, Jack "Romeo" (because he loved the ladies) Burns, Ben Welsh (because he was stern and refused a nickname) and Henry "Yoda" (because he was the go-to guy for information) Johnson. All there, willing to help out, even after what he was sure had been a long and arduous deployment. It humbled him.

"Going to invite us in?" JP suggested.

Wells hesitated a few seconds before he motioned them in, emotion clogging his throat. "I know you guys are exhausted but I'm beyond grateful for the help. Brinley's missing," he said as he closed the door.

"What happened?" Conrad asked as they all settled in the living room.

Wells gave them all the information he had, which unfortunately wasn't all that much. He told them what he and the local police had done, where they looked and about the untraceable cell phone number. When he shared the picture of Brinley's beaten face, he saw them cringe at her injuries, then become angry that she had suffered such abuse.

"So, what's the plan?" JP asked. "How can we help?"

"Chief Dubois is good, but his department only has so many resources. Is there any way that we can do a deeper dive on the number of the burner cell that was used to contact me? I know the Navy was working on some technology that might help with that. Maybe we can recanvass the complex again as well. I can't believe that no one saw anything that might help. The camera in the parking lot was broken but certainly we can use cameras from other locations, maybe across the street."

When Wells finished speaking, JP took out his phone to make a call. The rest of the guys stood and exited the condo to speak to the neighbors again while Conrad left to see about any working cameras that might give them some information on Brinley's disappearance.

Within two hours they had gathered more intel than the police had in two days. The first bit of help came from one of the neighbors who remembered the red car in the parking lot. She knew it wasn't owned by anyone in the complex since she had never seen it before. Conrad took that information, then used the camera from across the street at the gas station and began tracing it back, camera to camera. From one angle they were able to get a license plate number, which they gave to the military police who agreed to run it through their system. When it came back belonging to a Jennie Markewitz, it didn't register with Wells until he recognized the address on her driver's license.

"That's Brinley's street," Wells exclaimed. "Wait, I met that woman. Why would her car be here? What's the connection?"

"Were they friends?" JP asked.

"More like acquaintances according to Brinley. They talked whenever she was out walking Annie, but I didn't get the impression they were all that close."

"Someone should have a talk with the woman," Conrad interjected. "The question is, should one of us go or do we hand it over to the local cops?"

"I'll talk to Chief Dubois, see if one of his guys can handle it. I think a uniformed officer as opposed to one of us would get a little further," Wells answered. Hearing his phone ring, he pulled it out of his pocket to look at the screen. "Shhhh…" he said to the guys in the room. "It's them. Thank God, finally. Hello," he answered hoarsely.

It didn't really come as a surprise when a female voice began to speak but the connection was still a mystery. "Drop the cash off tomorrow at Rotary Park. Be at Garden Creek Falls by 6:30 p.m. Hike up the Bridle Trail until you reach Split Rock. Leave the bag on the last overlook platform you come to. Not on the platform but a foot before you step onto it. Don't try anything stupid or Brinley gets dumped off the side of the mountain. Leave the money. When we're sure you're gone, she'll be released at the base by the falls. She'll have a phone to call you once we leave."

Hearing the click, Wells shook his head. "Is she kidding?" he asked to the room at large. "The hours for Rotary Park are from sunup to sundown. This time of the year it gets dark at seven o'clock. That's cutting things close."

"Did you pick up that she used the plural *we're*? It's obvious now that there's someone else involved," JP added.

"I'm calling Dubois and Morris. Between all of us, maybe we can sit down and come up with a good plan to get Brinley back safely," Wells said urgently.

"Sounds like a solid idea, especially with all of us working together," JP agreed.

Please God don't let me lose her, Wells whispered as he dialed the chief's number.

Chapter Twenty-Two

BRINLEY COULD BARELY take in a breath. Her ribs were killing her from the last time Dean and Jennie took her out of her holding room. It seemed for Jennie's part she merely liked the idea of inflicting pain. In fact, the last time she was taken back to her mattress, Jennie delivered a swift kick to her ribs that she was sure cracked at least one of them. The pain was excruciating but Brinley refused to give in to it, not wanting either of the two to get any satisfaction out of seeing her hurt. Although after her last encounter, Brinley glanced toward Dean as she was being led back to her room and swore she saw guilt lingering in his eyes.

Taking a shallow breath, Brinley sat up and cautiously rolled to her knees. It took several seconds before she could come to a stand, feeling her way to the damp wall, then shifting left toward the corner.

She knew her way now, even in the darkened room. She knew the old mattress was on the floor in the middle of the room. She knew that once she stood it would take five steps to hit the far wall and that if she sidestepped another six steps there would the bucket in the corner for her to relieve herself. She was given a bottle of water once a day and food twice a day, but the meals consisted of a piece of bread with either peanut butter or mustard smeared on it. That was it. No other sustenance allowed, just enough to barely keep her going.

The worst part of her incarceration was the waiting. The silence seemed deafening. Then she would hear the sound of footsteps coming down the stairs and she would tense up. She never knew who it would be, but she was certain that pain was soon to follow. Both Dean and

Jennie knew there was no money, no information she could provide to lead them to it, so the abuse was done merely because they enjoyed inflicting pain, a payback for something she had nothing to do with.

After making use of the bucket, Brinley slowly made her way back to the mattress and was about to lie back down when she heard footsteps thundering across the hallway upstairs. She heard the rattle of a lock being disengaged as voices were raised in anger. Cringing at what was to come, she backed against the furthest wall and waited. Within a minute she heard the key inserted into the lock on her door. When it swung open, she raised her hand to shelter her eyes from the bright light.

It didn't surprise her when Dean and Jennie walked into the room, grabbed her arms, tied her hands at her back, and began dragging her out. She had learned quickly that fighting them was useless. She'd already tried to once and paid a very high price for her insubordination.

Expecting to be pushed into the heavy metal chair, she shuffled that way only to be redirected toward the steps. Shocked at this new development, she mounted the steps one at a time with the aid of Dean at her side and Jennie behind holding her by the rope around her hands. When they reached the landing, they continued toward the front door where Dean opened it and ushered her outside. Looking around furtively, Brinley realized that they were at Dean's father's old home. The place had been abandoned since his death. It was as if evil lived here. She felt its very presence. She knew that Dean had tried to sell it a while ago but no one was interested in it. He left it alone, completely abandoned. Neither time nor elements had been kind, according to what she could see.

Opening the trunk of the red car, Dean motioned Brinley to get in. She raised her chin with a cold stare in his direction. "I'm not getting in there," she vowed.

Dean shot her a twisted smile. "Wanna bet?"

He'd no more than finished his response before Brinley was pushed in the back by Jennie and awkwardly fell into the trunk. Hissing at the pain the shove caused, she held the tears back as the cruel woman angled her legs in, forcing her to roll to her side before the trunk was slammed shut.

As the engine turned on, she could just make out voices from the front seat. The car jerked into motion as their voices got louder and carried to where she lay in the trunk. Brinley could make out some of the words, knowing by the tone that they were having a fight. Jennie seemed angry that she had to retrieve the ransom while Dean waited in the car with Brinley. Evidently, she was worried because she was taking the chance of getting caught and felt she deserved more of the cash. By the tone she could tell that both Jennie and Dean were starting to lose their grip. Which made her situation even more dangerous.

It was obvious that someone—most likely Wells—was paying to get her back. Which warmed her heart that he would do so, but terrified her at the chance he was taking.

By four-thirty everyone was in place. Wells was waiting a mile from the entrance to the park, ready to move in and hike to Split Rock. JP and four officers were stationed where the money was to be picked up, while Conrad, the chief, and two other men waited at the bottom of the falls. With all their bases covered, they settled in to wait for the arranged time.

At exactly six-thirty, Wells entered the park, left his car near the falls and started the hike up. Fortunately, Chief Dubois spoke to the people who were in charge of the park and gained their permission—not that they really needed it—to be in the area well after closing.

Even given the physical limitations that kept Wells from remaining active duty, he was still in great shape. The hike, which would typically take forty-five minutes for a normal person, took less than twenty-five minutes for him. All those hikes at Green River had paid off.

The quietness of the wooded area struck Wells as incongruent with how fast and loud his heart seemed to be beating. With effort, he brought his breathing under control and looked around the area. He had reservations about just leaving the bag of money near the steps of the observation deck, but he knew that there were men watching everything from a short distance away. He desperately wanted to be there when the money was retrieved but the directions were clear, and it was more important that he was at the bottom of the waterfall to get Brinley. There was no telling what shape she would be in, and he needed to be there for her.

Hiking back down the trail, Wells listened intently as JP relayed what was happening.

"There's a slight figure to the left of the steps that watched as you put the money down. Must be the woman who gave us the directions. Good thing we came in quiet. Clearly she arrived early as well."

"Probably Jennie Markewitz," Wells breathed into the mic as he continued down the path.

"We don't know that for sure," JP answered as he watched the woman slip from her hiding spot.

"Hell of a coincidence if she isn't," Wells countered. "What's happening now?"

"She's approaching the bag. Are you close to the falls yet?"

"Just about," Wells answered. "Take her when you can. Don't wait for me. If she's working with someone, and they are the ones who have Brinley, we can't let her warn them. They can't know that we have her. I need to have Brinley with me before they realize what's happened."

"Just stay hidden," JP warned. "If they see you they'll never release Brinley."

For the next fifteen minutes Wells stood by the waterfall, hidden behind a large bush, listening as JP and the officers took the woman into custody. She put up a fight and nearly managed to drop the bag of money over the side of the mountain in her struggle to break free. After what seemed an eternity JP finally spoke into the mic.

"It's Jennie Markewitz. She's denying it right now but based on the picture we have, it's her. Any sign of Brinley?"

"No. They must have had a signal worked out if and when it was safe to leave her at the falls. Can you get Jennie to tell you what it was?"

Wells listened as JP questioned the woman. She staunchly refused to cooperate and after ten minutes it was clear that she wasn't going help them. She tried to tell them that she was an innocent bystander and had merely walked to the abandoned bag, curious to see what it was. It was utter nonsense, and Wells knew it for the lie it was.

In agreement, JP and the officers kept Jennie at the top of the trail, hoping that by not bringing her down, whoever she was working with would give up and show themselves. Ideally, they would simply let Brinley go. At the very least they were hoping he or she would make a move to depart and they would be able to follow them back to wherever they'd been hiding.

Unfortunately, nearly an hour came and went and there was no sign of any other activity. It was obvious nothing was going to happen at that point. The best thing they decided was to get Jennie back to the station so they could interrogate her properly.

Wells felt angry and frustrated that he was no closer to Brinley than he had been two days ago. It was agony not knowing where she was or if she was okay. All their careful planning and organizing did nothing to get him answers.

By the time JP and the officers appeared at the base of the falls with Jennie in tow, it took everything he had not to throttle the woman. JP had to literally pull him away from her before he did something stupid. Wells was always respectful to the opposite sex, but this woman had the answers he needed and her keeping silent only served to antagonize him further.

"Cool it, man," JP repeated for a second time as he stood between Wells and Jennie, his hand on his chest pushing back. "This isn't going to help."

Dean watched from his hidden alcove as Jennie was brought down to the base of the falls, handcuffed and struggling between two officers. He knew things hadn't felt right but she wouldn't listen to him. She had to get her greedy hands on that money so badly that she wouldn't listen to reason. He tried to tell her to be patient. To wait until they could come up with a better plan, but the crazy bitch wouldn't listen to him. Now the money was gone, and he had no idea where to go from here.

His one advantage was that he still had Brinley as a hostage. If Wells was willing to pay to get her back, there was still a chance he could get his hands on that cash and be able to disappear.

Taking a deep breath, he watched as Wells lunged toward Jennie. It amused him to a certain degree to see the big guy so incensed over a mere woman. Hell, he'd been married to Brinley and never felt that much emotion toward her. It was interesting to see and made him wonder if there was something in his wife that he had missed. Not that it mattered now. His feelings had long since been dead and now she was merely a means to an end. His father had taught him how useless women were. It was something he now lived by.

Popping a Tylenol in his mouth, Dean took a swig from the bottle of bourbon he brought with him and leaned against the headrest of the driver's seat. It was a good thing Jennie had insisted they arrive so early to the dropoff site. Otherwise, he might have been caught as well. The fact that neither of them had seen Wells and the officers arrive unnerved him. How they got to the falls or the dropoff point at the top without them being aware of it was a mystery to him. As it was, he was stuck sitting in the overheated car, unable to turn it on to get relief from the air conditioner because it would alert the men to his presence. While the two large boulders provided the perfect spot to pull the car between, it left no way to get a breeze through the windows. Even the branches he used to cover the entrance from view blocked any hope of circulation. It was a great hiding place for a vehicle…not so comfortable for humans.

Grinning to himself, Dean shifted in the seat to get comfortable. It was a good thing that as a kid he'd spent so much time roaming this park. What at one time had been a refuge to avoid his father's abusive, angry rants was now saving him from getting arrested. Strange that his life had become this. He was once the guy in charge, controlling things around him, making deals, bending people to his will. Now he'd just be grateful to get out of this alive.

As the sun slipped beneath the horizon, Dean watched and waited for Wells and the officers to leave. He knew they lingered to watch the area in case he or Brinley were near, ready to flee at the first opportunity.

Well, the joke was on them. He could wait until morning if he needed to. He had water, crackers, all he needed to wait them out. His only concern now was Brinley. She was no good to him as a bargaining chip if she were dead. And he hadn't heard a peep from her in hours.

Chapter Twenty-Three

WELLS PACED OUTSIDE the interrogation room, impatiently waiting for Chief Dubois to finish with Jennie. He'd been denied access to the observation room and as time slowly ticked by, he was getting more irritated. It had been hours since they had entered that room and yet still no information on Brinley's whereabouts.

JP and the rest of his former team members were lounging on the hard chairs in the waiting area of the police station. He'd long since given up trying to get them to go home since they'd all adamantly refused. As brothers they always had each other's back. It gratified Wells that even though technically he was no longer a part of this team, they still included him in that pact.

His mother continued to do an hourly check, both on the progress on finding Brinley and to see how her son was doing. At one point—a few hours into the interrogation—she appeared at the station with coffee and sandwiches for everyone. It was only when Wells insisted she go back home that she left, admonishing him to call her with any news.

Wells whirled around at the sound of the door opening and carefully watched Chief Dubois's face. By the lines and the turn of his lips, Wells knew he hadn't had any luck in getting Jennie to talk.

"What happened?" he asked.

"She's not talking. I want to make a quick call to the DA. Maybe if we can offer a deal of some sort she'll be a little more cooperative. Give me a few minutes," he said, walking away.

"What's going on?" JP asked, coming to stand next to Wells. "She say anything?"

"Not a thing. Dubois is going to talk to the DA to see if he can make her a deal of some sort. Maybe then she'll give us what we need," Wells grunted.

"Hang in there," JP encouraged, patting his back in support before returning to his seat.

It took nearly twenty minutes before the chief came back from his office. Seeing Wells anxiously waiting he raised his hand. "They're willing to offer her a deal. The DA is on her way here now. Just sit tight for a little longer." When Wells started to argue, Chief Dubois placed his hand on his shoulder. "Head into the observation room next door. You can watch from there but I'm warning you, stay quiet and let things play out. I know you want to help but right now you need to let us do our jobs."

Grateful that he was allowed that much, Wells nodded and headed into the small room. When he entered, he was surprised to see Detective Bob Morris already there. "You've been here the whole time?"

"I have," the detective responded. "She's a tough one," he added.

Wells turned to look through the large window. Jennie sat, handcuffed to the table, looking like she didn't have a care on the world. It was obvious she was nervous, but her spine was ramrod straight and she was glaring at him through the window as if she sensed he was there watching.

"Don't worry, she can't see us," Bob reminded him.

Wells simply stared at her, wondering what had made her turn into the person she'd become. What type of person would hurt another human being just for money? He'd seen some pretty horrible things in the military, but this was America, for God's sake. She lived in a beautiful house, wore nice clothes. It didn't make any sense to him.

Deep in his own thoughts, it surprised Wells when the door to the interrogation room finally opened and the chief walked in alongside a stern-looking woman dressed in a plain gray suit and black high heels and a briefcase in her hand. After a brief introduction, the woman got down to business addressing Jennie with a coolness that had Wells silently applauding her. Suddenly, Jennie wasn't looking so confident.

As the DA listed the charges she was facing, Jennie became more agitated. Besides the federal criminal offense of kidnapping, which could bring a sentence of at least twenty years in prison, she was being charged with extortion and physical assault, proven by the picture Wells had been texted.

Obvious panic started to set in as the words sunk into her head. Jennie pulled on the chains that had her cuffed to the desk and looked wildly around the room. "You have no proof," she sputtered. "I was just in the area and saw that bag sitting on the ground. I was curious what was inside, that's all."

"Your red car was in the parking lot where Brinley Crew was abducted. You were seen on video footage, Ms. Markewitz."

"I…I…"

"You're going down on these charges, but I can help if you cooperate with Chief Dubois."

"Help how?" Jennie asked.

"Tell us where Ms. Crew is being held and give us the name of the person who's working with you. Do that and I can reduce the charges. You'll still have to do time, but you'll be much younger when you get out. You have two minutes before I walk out that door and the deal is off the table."

Wells held his breath as Jennie considered her options. It didn't take long before she caved in under the pressure.

"He's not working *with* me. Everything was his plan, not mine. He asked for my help, and I gave it to him for a cut of whatever he got."

"He who?" the DA insisted.

"Dean McGill. It was all his idea."

Wells inhaled sharply at hearing Dean's name. He had suspicions all along that Dean had something to do with Brinley's disappearance. He also knew in his heart that what Jennie had said was true. Dean was the mastermind of everything that had happened. He had the wherewithal to disappear for a few years; he certainly had enough intelligence to plot a kidnapping.

"What's your relationship to Dean McGill?" Chief Dubois asked.

The expression on Jennie's face at the question was one of discomfort. She hesitated for nearly a minute before she finally answered. "He was my stepbrother for a short time. Then we became lovers."

"Were you lovers while he was married to Brinley? Did you know that he hadn't really died in that fire?" the DA probed.

She hesitated again before letting out a huff and rolling her eyes. "Yes…we were lovers while he was married. But I really thought he was dead until six months ago. I came home one night after work and he was asleep on my back porch. He asked for my help, offered me a cut of what he got and that was it. I needed the money, so I said yes."

"According to our sources, Dean had money hidden in his house when the fire started. Did you take that money?" the chief asked.

"I knew about his stash. He bragged about it all the time before the fire incident. After the fire, when Brinley left town, I would go over to the house at night after the construction crew left to look for it. Honestly, I never found any money. Someone else took it."

"Where's he been staying? And does he keep Brinley with him or at a separate location?" Jennie shook her head as if to refuse to answer the question. "As I said before we started, give us what we need and I can help with the charges. If you don't tell us, the deal's off and you're on your own."

When the lady stood up and grabbed the handle of her briefcase Jennie nearly growled. "Fine, he's been staying at his father's old house. Brinley is being kept in the basement in a small room. At least he was. I'm sure he saw you all at Garden Creek Falls. He was parked between two boulders with branches covering the spot. If he saw that you arrested me, I'm sure he'll go somewhere else. That's all I know," she said, leaning back in her seat and letting out a breath.

"Do you think Dean trusts that you wouldn't betray him?" the chief asked. If Dean felt Jennie wouldn't rat him out, they just might have a chance of finding them still there.

"Dean's scared and knows people are out to kill him. But he came to me and asked for my help. So yeah, he trusts me. Which makes him the dumbest man on earth," she sneered.

"Why's that?"

"He betrayed me first when he married Brinley instead of me," she said angrily.

Sweat was running down Brinley's back and arms. The sweltering heat inside the trunk was making her nauseous. She'd found some reprieve when she fell asleep from the pain and exhaustion, but when the car engine started again, she awoke with the urge to vomit.

As the car rocked her back and forth in movement, she knew that whatever had happened wasn't good. Dean was driving erratically, taking turns sharply causing her to slide from side to side. It felt like she'd been in the trunk for hours and when she had drifted off to sleep, she just knew that her next vision would be of Wells lifting her from the car. Which to her utter dismay was now clear that that wouldn't be the case.

After what seemed like hours, the vehicle slowed to take a right turn. She listened as gravel crunched under the tires, signaling that they were no longer on the highway. When the car came to a full stop, Brinley heard a door slam and the latch being released on the trunk. Grateful for the fresh air that filtered in, she took a deep, cleansing breath.

"She lives," Dean said snidely. "I was beginning to wonder."

Too weak to respond, Brinley simply looked up at the stars praying for strength. The pain was becoming unbearable, and she could tell that her body was protesting from lack of food and water.

"Get out," Dean insisted.

"I can't," she whispered. "Not on my own."

"Jesus," Dean groused as he reached in and grabbed her shoulders. Not caring for her injuries, he dragged her out of the trunk, hitting her head on the lid and her ribs on the latch. By the time she was standing next to the car her body was swaying in agony. It took everything she had not to drop to the ground.

As Dean pushed her to the house, she finally glanced around and realized that they were back at his father's house. Back where they had started just hours before.

Surprisingly, when they entered the house, he guided her to a wooden chair in the kitchen instead of dragging her down to the basement. He deftly tied her to it, then stood back, leaning against the counter. Brinley got her first good look at his face and what she saw terrified her. He was coming unglued. His clothes were stained with sweat and his breath reeked of alcohol. But it was the look in his eyes that worried her the most.

"Wh..what happened?" she fretted.

"Your fucking boyfriend screwed me, that's what happened," he jeered.

"Where's Jennie?" she quavered.

"In jail as we speak. I watched them drag her out in handcuffs."

"What now?"

"Now? I have no idea. I should just kill you and get it over with. You're like this albatross hanging around my neck that I can't get rid of. Not quite sure if you're worth keeping around just to get the money. You're bad luck."

"Are we leaving?" Brinley queried.

"Naw…we have time. Jennie's been in love with me for a while. She'd never betray me. I always could get her to do whatever I wanted. So easy! No," he laughed. "I think we'll hang here tonight until I get a plan together. I'll figure someplace else we can go. Once we're settled, I'll reach out to Kennedy again and set something up. By then he'll be so desperate to get you back he'll do exactly as I say. I'll get that damn money and disappear just like I wanted. Only now I won't have to worry about splitting it with anyone."

It was on the tip of her tongue to question him about leaving Jennie behind, the one person who was willing to help him, but Brinley already knew the answer to that one. If he could betray his own wife and child, he was capable of betraying anyone!

"Can I have a drink of water," she nearly pleaded. "Please."

It was clear that Dean thought to refuse her but eventually after looking her over he acquiesced. Taking a glass from the cupboard, he filled it with tap water and moved to hold the rim to her lips. Brinley drank thirstily, grateful for the cool liquid sliding down her throat. Before she had her fill, Dean pulled the glass away and placed it on the counter. Frowning at her briefly, he exited the room, leaving her strapped to the chair. It was dark outside, and the air was chilly. The chair was hard and uncomfortable, but Brinley was relieved that at least for this night, there would be no more physical pain inflicted.

The sun was just starting to rise as both cruisers and unmarked cars pulled into the driveway of James McGill's old house. Seeing Jennie Markewitz's red car sitting on the gravel gave Wells hope that he hadn't felt in hours. Brinley was here!

In a matter of minutes the house was completely surrounded, making any escape impossible. When the signal was given that everyone was in place, the negotiator brought to the scene took out his bullhorn and called out Dean's name.

At first there was no sign of movement, then a curtain in one of the second-floor rooms fluttered slightly.

"He's in there," a voice called out.

Inside the house Dean quickly stepped back from the window. "Shit…shit…shit," he ranted. Careful not to pass in front of a window, he rushed downstairs and into the kitchen. He breathed a quick sigh of relief that Brinley was still in her spot, tied to the chair. He couldn't afford to lose his ace in the hole. Maybe he could still get out of this intact, as long as he had her to bargain with.

Quickly pulling the curtains together to block their view, Dean paced around the small kitchen, his anger building with each step. "This is your fault," he seethed at Brinley. "Why couldn't you just get me the money when I asked for it. You caused this by going to the police. If you had just cooperated it wouldn't have gone this far. I should kill you now."

Wisely, Brinley kept her mouth shut but watched in fear as Dean removed a knife from the butcher block. He continued pacing, the weapon against his leg.

"And that Jennie. She betrayed me too. She must have told the cops everything. Stupid bitch…I shouldn't have trusted her."

"Mr. McGill," a loud voice penetrated the kitchen. "We know you're in there. The house is surrounded with snipers in every area. Please, come out now so we can end this peacefully. No one needs to get hurt today."

"Great negotiating skills," Dean sneered. When Brinley shifted in her seat, he turned toward her and raised the knife. "If I'm going down today then so are you. We're both as good as dead. You know that right?"

As the man behind the bullhorn tried to coax Dean to give up, time came and went. Dean was refusing to listen to anything they said or offered, and only responded by informing them that if anyone tried to come into the house, he would kill Brinley.

Wells spent much of his time listening to the negotiator and fearing for Brinley's safety. He tried several times to get them to let him try to talk Dean out, but the chief refused, going so far as to threaten to have him removed from the scene if he didn't step back. Wells's frustration mounted as the day wore on with no results.

As the sun began to set, the futility of his position began to hit Dean. There was no way out of this. There was no way he would survive in prison. The council member he'd stolen from had friends in very dark places and his reach extended well beyond the state of Wyoming. He'd been stupid to even think he could get away with taking that money. Who knew the guy had someone close to McGill Construction watching him so closely and reporting back to him? You couldn't trust anyone these days. At this point, death would be preferable to enduring whatever pain was ahead of him. He was quite certain that even jail couldn't protect him from the man.

Having made his decision, Dean grabbed the meat mallet from a kitchen drawer and went over to the gas stove. After making sure the gas was on, he pulled the stove out from the wall and swung a few times at the valve that connected the gas line to the appliance. Hearing a hissing sound, he stepped back with an evil grin on his face. Taking a candle from a drawer, he snickered as he lit it.

"Shouldn't be long now," he surmised.

Brinley tried to jerk free from her restraints. "What are you doing?" she yelled, terrified. "You're insane."

"Careful dear *wife*," he snarled. "You don't want to cause any spark that might make us go boom before I'm ready."

"Please," she begged.

Losing patience, Wells slipped away from Chief Dubois while he was talking to the negotiator. Something in him told him that one way or other, things were going to end soon. His first and only priority was to get to Brinley before something horrible happened. If they weren't willing to make a move, he would.

"Where are you going?" JP asked before he made it to the side of the house. "You know there are snipers watching every movement around the house."

"Just heading over to the living room window on the side of the house. I want to take a quick look to see if I can see anything."

"The curtain isn't pulled there. Give me a minute and I'll distract the sniper watching that particular window so you can get closer," JP advised.

"Thanks, man."

Wells gave JP a minute and a half before he made his move. When he got to the window, he saw Brinley in the kitchen. He could tell by the angle of her arms that she was tied to a chair and her face looked bruised and swollen. Rage enveloped him when he saw her condition. Taking a deep breath to calm himself, he checked to see if he could see Dean. When he was sure the coast was clear, he carefully removed the screen with his pocketknife and tossed it aside. Testing the window, Wells was relieved when the frame gave way and he was able to slowly lift the glass.

Brinley was starting to feel the effects of the gas as it began to fill the kitchen. Her head was beginning to feel swimmy, and her stomach was starting to roll. She heard a sound from the living room and glanced up in time to see Wells crawl in from an open window. Concern set in because there was no way to warn him of the gas without alerting Dean that he was in the house.

Once he was safely in the living room, Wells got a good whiff of the air and immediately knew that gas was filling the house. There wasn't much time to get Brinley out, so he carefully approached the kitchen, listening for any sound to indicate where Dean was. Knowing what Wells was listening for, she nodded her head to the left, where Dean was standing muttering to himself.

Looking around, Wells saw a small statue on an end table. Picking it up, he checked his surroundings to judge how close Brinley's chair was to the kitchen door leading outside. If he timed it right, he could have them both outside safely before Dean realized what was happening. He was fairly certain that by now JP had warned the snipers that he was inside. Bursting through the door to a spray of gunfire wasn't exactly a safe plan. At this point, though, he could only count on his friend to do what he himself would have done. And trust.

Saying a silent prayer, he lifted his arm and tossed the statue down the hallway. As he'd hoped, Dean ran toward the hall to check out the noise, allowing Wells to run into the kitchen undetected. Grabbing Brinley, chair and all, he moved to the opening and kicked his foot out, splintering the wood of the door. As he took his first step outside, Wells could hear Dean's footsteps running toward them, swearing as he approached. They had gotten no more than ten feet from the house before a loud explosion boomed and hot flames rushed toward them. The heat on Wells's back stung as he fell to the ground, covering Brinley with as much of his body as he could while debris rained down around them.

Chapter Twenty-Four

Wells groaned as hands tried to lift him from Brinley's body. He knew he needed to get his weight off her but the hands pulling at him irritated the burned skin.

"I got it," he groaned, grateful when the hands on his back disappeared. Placing his arms on either side of her, he carefully lifted his body up and moved to her side. She was lying at an odd angle, pieces of the chair she'd been tied to scattered about her. The chair had broken apart on impact, leaving only the back still attached to her with her hands still tied. Wells worked at the ropes to release her hands, swearing at the tight knots. From somewhere behind him a knife appeared so he grabbed it and cut her loose. Rolling her gently onto her back, he brushed aside the hair covering her face and gently called her name. "Brinley," he urged. "Baby, wake up for me. I need to see those beautiful blue eyes of yours."

As he tried to coax her back to consciousness, sirens blared in the background. Before he knew it, Wells was being forced away from Brinley as paramedics surrounded her. When he fought to get next to her, JP took his arm and pulled him back.

"Let them do their job, man. She needs to be taken care of. I know you were a medic but they know what they're doing and they have the equipment."

As much as Wells knew his friend was right, it was hard to relinquish her into their care. He wanted to be the one to take care of her, to make sure that she was all right. Stepping aside just made him feel helpless.

"What the hell were you thinking?" a loud voice boomed behind him. As Wells turned, Chief Dubois approached him with a scowl on his face. "You could have gotten everyone here killed. I told you to stand down god-damnit!"

"I couldn..."

"You're lucky that your friend here warned us you were in the house. Do you realize you came within seconds of having your ass shot?"

"But I..."

"Seconds I'm telling you. Don't they teach you military guys how to follow orders? Is that how you responded to orders when you served? You think just because you were a Seal that you didn't have to listen to me?"

"No, sir. I..."

"What in the Sam Hill do you think I would have done if you had gotten yourself killed because of your harebrained interference? How would I have explained your death to your mother?"

"My mother, sir?"

"Just look at this mess," he roared.

Wells turned back to the house. There was hardly anything left to it. The second floor had completely pancaked onto the first level. Where once there had been walls, now there were jagged pieces of wood protruding from the floor. Burnt parts of the kitchen appliances could be seen as well as water spraying from disconnected hoses. Littered all around were chunks of debris still in flames. The fire department was working valiantly to get it all under control.

"Get that back looked at," the chief grumbled. "They're loading your girl in the ambulance now. Ride in with them and get checked out."

"Dean?" Wells questioned.

"Dead," the chief said brusquely. "Found his body near the door. Burned to a crisp. The blast was so intense he never had a chance."

Wells hesitated a second before looking at the chief. "You're going to check DNA, though, right?"

"He does have a history of not really being dead, doesn't he? I'll have the coroner run it just to be certain. Go," Chief Dubois said, motioning his head toward the flashing lights.

Wells raced toward the ambulance and jumped into the back, settling where the paramedic indicated. Before taking off they checked his back, then decided that he was good enough that he could wait for treatment until they got to the hospital.

The ride seemed to take forever. Wells silently sat by, watching as they worked on Brinley, checking her vitals and starting IV fluids. He spoke to her softly, hoping she would wake up if she heard his voice. Unfortunately, when they pulled up to the ambulance bay at the emergency room, she still hadn't regained consciousness.

Before he could protest, Brinley was whisked away to be treated in one direction and he was ushered in another. He endured gentle poking and prodding as they checked him over to be sure there were no injuries other than the mild burns on his back. They found some cuts and bruises, which they treated. Then they ordered an echocardiogram when they read his history and knew that he had suffered a pericardial effusion a while back. He fought the order at first, only wanting to get back to be with Brinley, but when two cardiologists appeared at his bedside expressing their concerns and facts on what could happen if his heart were injured in any way—death being one of them—he agreed and let them do their thing.

An hour later he was pronounced perfectly fit and allowed to return to the emergency room where he found JP, Conrad, and his mother waiting.

"Oh Wells," Ruby exclaimed, rushing over to give her son a hug. Remembering the burns JP told her about, she stopped short, looking him over for other obvious injuries.

"It's okay, Mom. I'll hug you," he said wrapping his arms around her. "I'm fine," he assured her.

Looking over the top of his mother's head he glanced at JP. "Any word?" he asked.

"Not yet. I checked with a nurse about ten minutes ago. They were taking Brinley for x-rays. She was still unconscious. The doctor will be out to talk to you as soon as he knows more. They know to talk to you about her condition. I told them you were engaged to be married. If I hadn't they would never have let you be her point of contact."

"Thanks, man. I appreciate it."

"Conrad picked me up and drove me here," Ruby informed Wells, as she stepped out of his arms. "Such a good boy," she smiled, reaching up to pat Conrad on the cheek. "Are you okay, Wells? What did the doctor say?"

"I'm fine, Mom. A few cuts and bruises and that's it. My back got the worst of it. The burn was minimal and should be fine in a few days."

"I guess for now we just wait. How about I go down to the cafeteria and find us some coffee." Ruby offered. "I know I could use it."

"I can go grab it," Conrad offered respectfully.

"You're sweet, but I need to keep these old bones moving," she laughed as she got up and exited the waiting room.

Brinley wasn't sure what woke her: the constant beeping or the voices coming from somewhere near her. The one thing she was sure of was that she was no longer tied to a chair. In fact, she was horizontal and in a soft, clean bed.

Opening her eyes, she quickly realized that she was in a hospital and that the beeping was coming from a machine that was attached to her. The voices were coming from a man in a white coat and a woman in a nurse's uniform. She tried to speak but nothing seemed to come out. Clearing her throat, she started again but stopped when the doctor turned to her.

"You're awake finally," he said coming to her side.

The nurse he had been speaking to went to her other side, producing a cup with water. After a long draw on the straw, Brinley put her head back. "That tasted good," she said gratefully.

"What do you last remember?" the doctor asked.

"Well…I'm not sure. My head feels kind of fuzzy."

"You have a concussion, Ms. Crew. That's to be expected," he said kindly.

"Wait a minute," Brinley began. "I remember I was being held in a small room. That's right, I've been tied to a chair, beaten. He stuffed me into the trunk of a car. Wait a minute, I was at a house. There was gas filling the kitchen…I remember Wells trying to get in to help me. Oh, God, there was an explosion. Oh, God, what happened to Wells? Is he okay? He tried to save me," she said panicked.

"Mr. Kennedy is just fine," the doctor assured her. "He was burned but he's being taken care of. Nothing serious. You can see him as soon as we finish taking care of you."

"What's wrong with me?" Brinley asked quietly.

"With a lot of rest, you're going to be fine. You have the obvious bruising, cuts, and scrapes that look worse than they actually are. The most serious of your injuries are the three broken ribs and the concussion. The ribs will take longer to heal. You were severely dehydrated when you got here so we're pumping fluids into you as fast as we can. From the looks of your skin, something tells me food wasn't part of your captivity."

"Just bread with mustard or peanut butter on it."

"Not exactly a healthy diet but something that can be improved on quickly. With your condition, it's imperative that you get into a solid routine of eating healthy now that you're free."

"My condition?" Brinley questioned.

The doctor observed Brinley for several seconds before glancing at the nurse still in the room. It was obvious that there was something he needed to tell her, and the hesitation was starting to scare her.

"Ms. Crew. One of the tests came back that you're pregnant. Did you not know before this?" he asked gently.

"Pregnant?" Brinley stammered. "I had no clue. I mean, before all this happened, I was feeling a little sick, but I chalked it up to…oh God…this can't be happening."

"We ran the test twice to be sure. You are most definitely pregnant. I would suggest that you don't make any decision right now about anything. Obviously, you're in shock at the news. Let things stand for a bit. You've been severely traumatized and should get back on your feet before making any decisions about your future," he suggested.

"Please, don't tell anyone about this," she pleaded.

"Your condition is your business, Ms. Crew. Neither I nor any staff member here at the hospital will give out any information on you. It's your news to share. Now, there's a young man out there who's been driving the nurses crazy trying to get in to see you. Is it okay to let him come back? It will be another hour or so before we can get you settled in a room upstairs. I want to admit you at least for tonight. If everything goes as I expect it to, you can go home tomorrow."

Brinley nodded absently as both the doctor and nurse left her alone. Pregnant! How on earth could she have allowed that to happen? She'd been very careful each time she and Wells made love. She wasn't ready to be a mother again. No one could replace Annie…she wasn't ready for another baby! Was she?

Hearing a noise around the curtain, she glanced up in time to see Wells rush toward her. His hair was askew, remnants of ash were still smeared on his neck and cheek, and there was a look of despair on his face. When he reached her side, he leaned down and pushed hair from her forehead to place a gentle kiss there.

Seeing him so upset tore at her heart. It looked as if he endured as much hell from the horrific experience as she had. "I'm okay," she whispered as he examined her closely. "Wells," she said gently, grabbing his hands. "I'm okay, really."

Grabbing a chair from the corner, Wells pulled it next to the bed as close as he could get and leaned over, holding one of her hands and using his other to smooth the hair from her face. "I was so scared," he admitted. "What did the doctor say?"

Brinley told him everything the doctor said to her—except of course about the pregnancy—and assured him that she was going to be fine with a little rest. When she asked about Dean, he hesitated before explaining that he was dead. Not that Wells thought she'd be devastated by the news, but the man was, in fact, her husband and someone that she had once loved.

Brinley was silent for a short bit after hearing that Dean had died. Finally, she looked up at Wells. "Doesn't it seem a little eerie that he died by fire? The exact way he once faked his death?"

More like karma, Wells thought to himself. The man was a piece-of-shit husband, a worse father, a liar and a thief. He possessed no redeeming qualities, but Wells wasn't going to say that out loud. It didn't seem prudent to speak ill of the dead. "Very strange," he murmured instead.

"I'm sorry I went outside," Brinley whispered. "You told me not to but I didn't listen. What happened is all my fault."

"It's no one's fault, sweetheart, certainly not yours. The blame lies directly on Dean's and Jennie's shoulders. They did this. Not you."

"What happened to Jennie? Dean went on a rant about how she betrayed him."

"She was arrested when she tried to take the money. At first she refused to give up any details about Dean or where you were being held. When the DA showed up and clearly explained the charges against her and that she could make it easier on herself if she helped us, she sang like the proverbial canary. That's how we found you."

"How are you?" she asked, stifling a yawn. "The doctor said you were being treated for burns. Should you be sitting here?"

"Minor," Wells informed her, brushing her concern aside. "The house exploded just as we got a few yards away. The heat was pretty intense, caused first-degree burns on a few places on my back."

"Oh Wells, I'm so sorry."

"Stop, this wasn't your doing. A little ibuprofen and cool showers and I'll be fine in a few days," he reckoned.

"Knock…knock," a voice called before the curtain shielding her cubicle was pushed aside. "They said it was okay to come in and say hi," JP said as he and Conrad walked in. "You look a little better," he said before leaning down to kiss Brinley's cheek. "How are you feeling?"

After Conrad kissed her other cheek, she smiled up at them both. "I'm better now. Thank you so much for stopping in to check on me."

"They didn't exactly stop in," Wells countered. "When you were taken, I called them for help. The guys were on their way back from a deployment and came as quickly as they could. We worked with the police to get you back. They discovered the information that led us to Jennie. I couldn't have gone through this without them."

"I can't believe you did that," Brinley uttered. "Thank you…"

"Don't thank us," Conrad mumbled. "Someday we're going to need Wells's help, and he'll be there for us just like we were for him."

It was obvious that neither man was comfortable with any expression of gratitude, so she left it at that.

Once again, the curtain was pushed aside and Ruby Kennedy rushed in, making a beeline for the side of Brinley's bed. Kissing her cheek, the elderly woman fussed over Brinley, fixing her pillows, pulling her blankets up and patting her hand. "You poor baby. I was so worried about you. How are you? Are you okay? What can I do for you?"

Brinley absorbed Ruby's loving gestures, so happy to have another female in the room. And while it made her miss her own mom, she was beyond grateful that this kind woman truly seemed to care about her. Tears filled her eyes as Ruby continued to fuss.

Wells noticed the look on Brinley's face and knew she was becoming overwhelmed by all the attention. Stepping in, he urged both JP and Conrad to head home for some much-needed rest. After they departed, he gave his mom a few more minutes before he mentioned that she also should go home so Brinley could get her rest. Another ten minutes and a tearful goodbye and they were finally alone.

"You should go home and rest too," Brinley encouraged him. As much as she wanted to be close to him, she needed some space to think about her life. So much had happened that she was struggling to get a handle on things. First Dean and Annie's death, Dean coming back to life, finding out he wasn't who she thought he was, falling in love with Wells and now…now she was pregnant.

"I thought I'd stay with you tonight."

It took some convincing on her part but once they had her settled in a room on the sixth floor, he finally gave in to her wishes. Kissing her softly on the lips, he exited her room, not leaving the hospital grounds until he was assured that the staff had his telephone numbers in case anything came up during the night.

Brinley fell asleep for a short time, but it really was difficult to rest with so much activity going on at all hours. A plan had formed in her head before she fell asleep, and she needed to be up early to put it in to place.

When six o'clock finally rolled around, Brinley pressed the button to call a nurse. When she arrived a few short seconds later, it took everything Brinley had to convince the woman of her seriousness. She was leaving the hospital with or without their permission. Finally, the doctor on call was brought in and tried to convince Brinley that she should stay at least until later that morning. Demanding her release, Brinley got out of bed and took the IV needle from her arm. When they realized that she was not going to back down, paperwork suddenly appeared releasing the hospital from any possible future lawsuits if anything happened to her. Once she accepted full responsibility for herself, a pair of scrubs was delivered to her room and a cab arrived out front to take her wherever she wanted to go. Handing a piece of paper to the nurse and asking her to see that Wells received it, she walked out just as the sun was starting to rise.

Chapter Twenty-Five

Wells spent most of the night tossing and turning in his bed. The burns irritated him when he flipped onto his back, and whenever he reached out and realized that Brinley wasn't with him, he became irritated once again. He should have stayed with her. He'd felt it in his bones when he left the hospital, but Brinley was so insistent that he leave that he gave in, hoping she would rest better not worrying about him.

There was something in her demeanor that didn't sit well with him, though. He couldn't put his finger on it, but she had seemed distracted and sad. Granted she'd been through an awful lot, with Dean coming back and then kidnapping her, but it was more. More than just the ordeal she'd been through.

Giving up on sleep, Wells got out of bed and took a long, tepid shower to cool off his back. When he was dressed in jeans and a loose, soft blue T-shirt, he went to the kitchen and made himself some coffee. He sat staring out his front window, sipping the hot liquid as the sun started to come up. When he'd waited as long as he could, he grabbed his keys and headed out to his truck. Visiting hours weren't even close to starting but he didn't give a damn. He needed to be with Brinley so he could assure himself that she was okay. He dared anyone to stop him from going in!

Being so early he found a parking spot close to the front entrance of the hospital and walked in. No one stopped him as he entered the elevator, nor when he arrived on the sixth floor and headed to her room. With anticipation, he walked through the doorway and stopped short when he saw that the bed was empty. Figuring she was out getting some sort of test done, he went to the nurses' station to inquire. It wasn't until the nurse on duty glanced up and saw who he was that he began to get nervous. The look on her face was one of resignation.

"I'm here to see…"

"Good morning, Mr. Kennedy. I remember you from yesterday. You're here to see Brinley Crew."

"I am, but she wasn't in her room."

"She left," the nurse informed him.

"Left?" Wells asked, confused.

"She checked herself out of the hospital this morning, almost two hours ago. Against doctors' wishes I might add. I have no idea where she went. Just that she was insistent on leaving."

Wells stared stupefied at the nurse, trying to understand what was going on. How could she just leave like that and not tell anyone? Tell him!

"I don't understand," he stated.

Taking out a sheet of paper, she put it on the counter. "She left this for you. Maybe it will explain things. I'm really sorry, Mr. Kennedy."

"Thanks," Wells responded, taking the paper and heading to the elevator. Sitting on the bench next to the doors, he opened it up to see Brinley's handwriting.

> *Wells,*
>
> *I'm so sorry to leave you like this, but I need some time to get my thoughts together. Things have been so messed up since we met. I'm struggling to process everything right now. Please understand, I need to be alone for a while.*
>
> *Brinley*

Wells inhaled sharply at the shortness of her words. It was as if the relationship they had built meant nothing to her.

Balling the letter up in his fist, he punched the elevator button and waited for the doors to open. When it took longer than he wanted, Wells searched for the stairwell, slammed the door open, and pounded down the steps until he reached the first floor. Exiting the hospital, he stalked to his truck, slamming the door shut once he was in. Revving the engine, he tore out of the parking lot, tires squealing as he rounded the corner and made his way back home.

By the time he entered his front door, his anger hadn't dissipated. He prowled around the condo, taking deep breaths to try to calm down. He knew that anger never solved anything, but he was reeling from the abrupt dismissal of Brinley's letter. Needed to be alone? For what? What was she thinking? Was she suddenly afraid that he would become like her now-dead husband? He'd not given her a single reason to think that he would. In fact, he'd been nothing but kind, supportive, and understanding. Other than their meeting under less than desirable circumstances—one he had plotted for his own benefit—things had been great between them.

Okay, maybe their original meeting was a little underhanded, but he'd explained all that to her. And he thought she understood why he felt he had to handle it that way. She knew him. Better than anybody. So what was she questioning now?

Eyeing a bottle of Henry McKenna Single Barrel Bourbon he'd left on his kitchen counter, he made his way over to it. It had been a birthday gift from one of the guys on the team and to this day hadn't been opened.

"Good enough reason now," Wells grumbled as he opened the bottle, grabbed a glass and headed over to the couch.

The first taste made him cough and his throat burn. Alcohol wasn't something he typically imbibed on, so it was a little abrasive at first. By the third tumbler the smooth liquid was beginning to go down a little easier. Everything else ceased to exist. Not the quietness of the silent condo, the loneliness of the living room, or the sting of rejection from Brinley's letter. The more he drank, the less he hurt. Which was fine with him. He didn't need anybody.

As the sun began to set, Wells finished the bottle and tossed it aside. His phone was ringing from somewhere in the house, but he let it go to voicemail. He didn't want to explain or justify his actions to anyone. He needed to wallow for a while, then he'd get his act together.

Standing up from the couch, he swayed a little, and when he was sure he wouldn't fall over, he stumbled back to the bedroom. When his knees hit the mattress, he fell face first onto the pillowy softness and promptly began to snore.

A loud horn blaring woke Wells the next morning. Groaning, he rolled over and realized that he was still fully clothed, shoes and all, lying on top of his comforter. How the hell did he get here?

It took several seconds before the events of the day before came back to him. Tossing his arm over his eyes to block the sun, Wells inhaled slowly attempting to settle his stomach.

"Shit," he hissed as he jumped up and raced to the bathroom, making it just in time to lose the entire contents of his stomach. Somewhere in the distance his phone started to ring but he was too busy to pay any attention to it.

"So stupid," he grumbled, sitting on the floor next to the toilet, waiting to see if there was anything else in his stomach that wanted out. This was why he didn't drink. The day after was hell on his head and body.

Wells gave his stomach a few minutes to settle before he forced his body into the shower. He felt slightly better with clean teeth and clothes, but his head ached violently, which was no less than he deserved. Once in the kitchen he looked for something that might help his stomach. After deciding that at that moment, anything he tried to eat or drink would just come back up, he grabbed his phone to check messages.

There were a few from JP and Conrad wanting to know where he was and if he was all right. One was from Chief Dubois asking him to return his call and no less than four distraught messages from his mother.

It was stupid to have used alcohol to ease his pain. It was worse that he caused his mother so much worry. Deciding it would be best to go over so she could see that he was fine, he grabbed his keys and headed to his truck. On the way, he returned the chief's call and was told that the DNA came back and it was absolutely confirmed that the body was in fact Dean McGill's. He spoke briefly to JP and Conrad, assuring them that he was fine, that Brinley was okay but needed time to think. He brushed it off as if they had decided together to be apart for a bit so his friends wouldn't worry. When he saw them in person, he would explain what happened. That is, if he ever got to understand it himself.

Pulling into his mother's driveway, Wells shut the truck off and sat for a few minutes. With his head clearing up a bit from the alcohol, he was starting to feel that he was missing something. Brinley's note hurt but he was beginning to think there was something more to it. She wasn't the type of person to flake out on him. Sure, she tried to protect him in her own way, but she was always honest with him.

Wells found Ruby in her backyard, tending her flowers. When she looked up and saw him standing there, she got up and walked over to him, a frown marring her face. "You've had me worried," she accused. "I went to the hospital to see Brinley and they told me she checked herself out. I tried calling you because I was worried and suddenly, I couldn't get you on the phone. What happened?"

"It's a long story, Mom. Why don't we sit on the deck and I'll tell you?"

"Oh, honey, you don't look good," Ruby said as she put her arms around her son. She hugged him briefly before pulling back. "Good Lord, you smell like a brewery."

"Sorry about that. I was upset and decided to bury myself in a bottle of bourbon," Wells answered sheepishly.

When they sat down he explained to his mother everything that happened. He showed her the wrinkled note, told her about his reaction to it and how just now he was beginning to think it wasn't him that had Brinley upset, but something more.

"Don't you think you should go find her? Nothing will get resolved unless you two talk about it."

"I was just coming to that conclusion," Wells agreed.

"Do you know where she is?" Ruby asked.

"Not really but I have a few places to check. I tried her cell but there's no answer."

"Then go, honey. Go find her."

Wells got up and went to hug his mom. "I'm going. I just wanted to make sure that you knew I was all right."

"You won't be all right until you two talk, so go. And honey, you might want to get some lifesavers before you find her," she wisely advised.

Wells grinned at his mother, gave her another hug, and raced out to his truck.

His first stop was at the house Brinley had shared with her husband. He didn't really think she would be there but needed to make sure before he went to the next possibility. When he confirmed that the house was empty, he went back to his condo and quickly packed a few things. There was only one place left that Brinley had felt safe, and he knew that was most likely where she had gone.

Back to Green River…back to the cabin where she had healed herself…and where they met.

Chapter Twenty-Six

When Brinley woke up the next morning, she knew she'd made a mistake. She should have stayed instead of running out on Wells. It was the shock of being pregnant that hit her more than anything else she'd gone through. For some unknown reason, her first reaction was guilt because there was suddenly this new baby while Annie, her firstborn, wasn't alive anymore.

No doubt after everything Dean had said and done, her trust was shaken in the male species. That had played a small part in her bolting, but after the first hour on the road the day before, common sense invaded her thoughts. Wells was nothing like Dean. The kidnapping, the injuries inflicted on her, and the look in Dean's eye as he disconnected the gas line, knowing they were going to die, she had every right to be frightened. Certainly, she couldn't be blamed for having a knee-jerk reaction to all that had happened.

But it was the thought of Wells's face that had her going into the small bedroom and packing what little she'd brought. She needed to get back to him. To make him understand why she ran out on him and to beg if necessary for him to try to understand. It would have made her life so much easier if she'd thought about taking her cell phone with her. It was stupid to make the long drive back to Green River without a way to communicate with anybody. Especially given her condition. It was the height of stupidity and one she sorely regretted now.

When her bag was packed, Brinley took one last look around and headed to the front door. Locking it behind her, she made her way to the rental car, then turned when she heard another vehicle approaching. Holding her bag in her hand, she was shocked as Wells's truck came into view.

Brinley stared as he came to a stop and slowly got out of the truck. Unsure of his feelings, she watched and waited to see what he would say or do.

Wells was relieved to see that Brinley was in one piece. He'd worried about her the entire drive to Green River. She had been in no shape to drive and looking at her now, seeing the bruises on her body and the pain in her eyes, was nearly his undoing. Taking a few more steps, he came to stand just a few feet from her, but not touching her.

"Why did you run?" he asked quietly.

"I panicked. But I was coming back," she answered, raising her overnight bag for him to see.

"You didn't bring your cell phone. I was worried when I couldn't reach you."

"I'm sorry."

"Your note wasn't very helpful," he continued.

"I know," she said, hanging her head down. Thinking of the note and the phrasing of it as she drove up here, she came to realize it was a shitty thing to do, especially to the one man who had been nothing but kind and loving toward her.

"Please don't make me chase you again. Talk to me, Brin," he insisted.

Dropping her bag on the ground, Brinley walked to Wells, wrapped her arms around his waist, and laid her head on his chest. When his arms encircled her, she sighed in relief. This was where she belonged. This was home. For her and their baby.

Wells held on to Brinley, holding her close as he kissed the top of her head. He'd never been so grateful to have a woman in his arms. She hadn't rejected him. Which led him to believe—once again—that whatever had been bothering her, it wasn't him.

After several minutes Brinley released him and stepped back. "We need to talk."

Wells merely nodded as she led him into the small cabin. When he stepped inside, so many memories assailed him. Most importantly was the night they made love for the first time. That was a moment he would never forget.

"Do you want anything to drink?" she asked as they passed the kitchen.

"No thanks," he said as he led her to the couch and sat down, keeping her hand in his. "Talk to me. Why did you panic?"

Collecting her thoughts, Brinley sighed heavily. While she didn't think Wells was the type of man to run out on a pregnant woman, she also knew that he would be shocked when he found out. "First, I was so wrong on how I handled everything and I'm truly sorry for that stupid note. You didn't deserve that and I wish I could take it back. I was upset with everything that happened."

"Understandable."

"I know you're not Dean—not even close to it—but seeing how he was at the end, it scared me. If you could have seen his eyes, Wells. They were blank, like he was dead inside. He was content to kill himself and reveled in the idea that he was going to take me with him. It was awful."

"What did he do to you while he held you?" he asked, concerned.

"It was always physical, not sexual," she inserted, wanting Wells to know she hadn't suffered in that way. "Dean was pretty rough at first but after that first day it was Jennie who did most of the abuse. She hated me and I still don't understand why."

"She was in love with Dean and thought he was going to marry her. When he asked you instead, she became angry," Wells informed her.

"They were sleeping together the whole time we were married. She loved telling me that," Brinley acknowledged. "Anyhow, that freaked me out a little. His willingness to die, her anger at me when I did nothing wrong. Being taken…I was overwhelmed by everything."

"I'm so sorry," Wells apologized.

"But I could have handled all that. I knew you would be beside me and that things were going to be okay because I had you," she confessed.

"Then why?"

"Guilt," she answered simply.

"I don't understand."

"Guilt because Annie is dead. And this baby," she stated, taking his hand and placing it over her abdomen, "will be taking her place."

Wells looked at her, confusion worrying his brow. "Brinley, what are you saying?"

"Wells…I'm pregnant," she informed him. "The doctor told me at the hospital. They found out when they were running some tests on me. I had no idea until then."

"You weren't feeling well that day I went to help Mom," he surmised, starting to put everything together.

"You have to know, Wells. That was a momentary reaction. I was surprised to find out. We were so careful to prevent this, so it was a shock. Now that I've had a little time to digest it, I don't feel guilty anymore. It kills me that Annie isn't with me any longer, but this baby means everything to me. It's a new beginning, Wells," she said hopefully. A wonderful new beginning but only if he wanted it too.

"Oh my God," Wells whispered. "A baby."

At first Brinley couldn't decipher his reaction. She stared wordlessly at him, her heart pounding until a smile spread across his face.

"A baby!" he exclaimed with intense pleasure. He felt an indefinable feeling of rightness surround his heart. She was carrying their baby!

Reaching over Wells grabbed Brinley and pulled her onto his lap. Wrapping her in his embrace, he breathed her in, too emotional for any words. It was enough to feel her heartbeat against his chest and to know that she was his. This amazing woman who had endured so much was his…and she was pregnant with his child. He wasn't sure if life could get any better.

"So, you're not upset?" Brinley smiled as he placed soft kisses on her neck and cheeks.

Wells took Brinley's face between his hands to make sure she could see into his eyes. "I've never been happier about anything in my life. *You* make me happy," he asserted.

"I'm glad."

"But…you went through so much. What did the doctor say about the baby? Is everything okay?" he asked worriedly.

"From what he could tell yes but I need to schedule an appointment with an OBGYN. My doctor retired so he gave me the name of someone."

Wells promptly leaned over, holding tightly to Brinley so she didn't fall off his lap, and took his cell phone from his back pocket and handed it to her. "Here, call them and set up an appointment. Explain what happened to you and let them know you need to get in as soon as possible."

"But…I…"

"No buts. We'll head back later today so try for tomorrow."

Hearing the resolve in his voice, Brinley got up from his lap and went to her purse where she had the referral. Taking the slip out she quickly punched in the number and waited until the call was answered. Brinley explained the situation and was relieved when they told her she could be seen the next day at two o'clock.

"Done," she said as Wells put his arms around her from behind.

"Good. Now, we have a few things more to discuss."

"Like what?" she asked.

"Just about everything but for now let's stick to the most important. I want you with me. I don't want to ever be away from you!"

Turning in his arms, Brinley looked up at his face. They'd practically been living together as it was but that was due to the situation in her life. Now, the concerned, inquiring look on his face made her realize that he truly thought she might argue with his statement. But today, for the first time in so long, there were no shadows across her heart. She knew this man was her happily-ever-after and there was no way she was going to let that slip through her fingers.

"I agree," she announced.

As Wells fixed them something to eat from the almost bare cabinets, Brinley sat at the table as they discussed the future. First and foremost, she was moving forward with selling her house. She didn't really feel comfortable at Wells's condo—bad memories of being abducted from there—so they made the decision to look for a house together. Besides, as Wells pointed out, they were going to need more room to raise a family.

The rest of the day they worked together on packing up both the cabins they'd been staying in, loading what needed to go in the back of his truck. After returning Brinley's rental car to the local dealer, they notified Mr. McKinley that they were departing and cleared any balances that were due. It was hard to leave Green River because this was where it all started, but Brinley found comfort when Wells promised they'd be back for family vacations whenever possible.

The thought of coming back with their child to vacation here brought a smile to Brinley's face. This was where she had found herself again…this was where she found the love of her life.

Chapter Twenty-Seven

LATER THAT NIGHT as they pulled into the parking lot of the condo, Brinley had a momentary reaction of panic. Wells quickly grabbed her hand to settle her down.

"It's okay," he insisted. "I'm right here. Nothing is going to happen. Remember, this is only temporary, just until we find our new place."

"Sorry, you're right, I know that."

Together they unloaded things from the back of his truck and carried them into the condo. After stacking everything against one wall, Wells made Brinley sit on the couch with her feet up while he went out to grab them something to eat. By the time they went to bed the only thought on Brinley's mind was Wells. She desperately wanted to make love, but he kept refusing her advances, insisting she was too injured to even think about doing that. It wasn't until he mentioned his worry about the baby and wanting to make sure everything was okay before they had sex that she understood his reticence.

Smiling to herself, Brinley lifted the covers and shimmied down Wells's side. Zeroing in on her target, she reached out and grasped him firmly in her hand. She couldn't suppress her pleasure as he instantly got hard. The fact that he slept naked made her seduction that much easier.

"Brin..." he exhaled abruptly, trying to pull her back up onto the pillow.

"I understand why you want to wait," she said, brushing his hands aside. "But there's no reason why I can't pleasure you. Right?"

It took a few seconds for it to dawn on Wells that this wasn't just about the sex for Brinley. This was about her need to feel connected to him. After the ordeal that she had endured, she needed the security of knowing that they were okay. "Be careful of your injuries," he admonished softly.

Happy to get her way, Brinley carefully maneuvered so she could sit just below his knees. Leaning in she took him in her mouth, sighing in pleasure as he shivered at her touch. It was a definite turn-on to know that she could affect him like this.

"God, you feel good," he said with a significant lifting of his brows. His smile had a spark of eroticism that merely encouraged her to push him further.

As she continued to pleasure him, Brinley couldn't help but run her hands over his stomach and down his legs. Being able to touch him was as reassuring to her as breathing air. When she caressed the back of his knee, he let out a soft chuckle and moved to get out of her reach.

The warmth of his laugh sent shivers down her spine. "Ticklish?" she paused to ask.

"Yes," he answered as she moved her hand from his leg and grasped his penis, working up and down. Wells knew he wasn't going to last much longer so he tried to pull her up. Brinley, however, had other ideas. Seeing her determination, he closed his eyes and let the overwhelming sensations signaling his release take over his body.

When he could finally catch his breath, he glanced down to see Brinley looking at him with an air of pleasure about her. She was smiling and radiant and it thrilled him to see some of the shadows gone from her eyes.

The next morning she woke to Wells standing on her side of the bed grinning down at her as he held a tray of food. He seemed so pleased with himself that she felt bad when she had to rush out of bed, practically pushing him aside as she raced for the bathroom, arriving just in time. He'd gone to so much trouble for her, but the smell of the eggs turned her stomach.

Instead of getting upset, he simply followed her into the bathroom and held her hair back as she threw up. When she was through, he handed her a warm washcloth and put toothpaste on her toothbrush for her.

"I'll make you some tea and see if there are any saltines in the cupboard," he said worriedly.

"I'm okay, Wells."

"You're still recovering from what happened. You hardly ate anything while you…you know. If you can't eat now, how can that be good for the baby?"

"I ate well last night and managed to keep it down. Don't worry. It's going to be fine."

Wells was skeptical about that but the fact that they were seeing the doctor today calmed him to a small degree.

When two o'clock rolled around, Wells had never been so relieved. He insisted on going to the appointment and sat quietly as the doctor spoke to Brinley getting her history, past pregnancy, and what had happened the past week and why their concerns. Wells liked the doctor and her no-nonsense attitude. She took everything in stride and didn't seem rattled at the most recent events. She ordered blood to be drawn to run a few tests and had Brinley lay back as they wheeled an ultrasound machine into the room.

Wells sat at Brinley's head, holding her hand as they both watched the screen as the technician moved a wand over her abdomen. When a whooshing sound echoed in the room, he looked over in a panic.

"That's your baby's heartbeat," the doctor informed him from the foot of the bed. "Nice and strong," she smiled. "You're about six weeks along I would say. You're lucky because this early sometimes you can't pick up the heartbeat."

Before the technician left, she handed them a small black and white picture, then wheeled the machine out. Wells looked down at it confused by what he was seeing. The doctor went over and pointed out a small round image.

"That's your baby. It's early to see much but he or she is definitely there and doing well. I'll get the results of the blood work but right now I don't see anything that concerns me. Because of the situation, I want to see you again in a few weeks."

"Should we hold off on having sex?" Wells asked.

Brinley looked away as her face began to redden. "Wells," she whispered.

"It's a good question," the doctor informed him. "And yes…it's safe to have sex," she smiled.

By the time they left the doctor's office they were armed with pamphlets of information, a list of vitamins Brinley was to take, and a card with their next appointment on it. To Wells it was all so overwhelming but Brinley, having been through it before, took everything in stride.

On the way back from the doctor's office, Wells and Brinley stopped by to see his mom. They both decided not to wait to tell Ruby but would keep it between the three of them. While there was no indication so far that anything was wrong, you never knew what might happen so they felt it best to keep it quiet for a while.

When they walked in the house, Ruby jumped up and made a beeline for Brinley. She held her in her arms for several minutes before letting her go. "I was so worried about you, honey. How are you?"

Brinley let her fuss over her for a while. Before she knew it Ruby had them seated on the back patio with a cheese and cracker tray in front of them and her homemade lemonade. Wells sat beside Brinley, holding her hand as they chatted with his mom and nibbled on the treats. Fortunately, her stomach had settled so she was able to eat.

"Mom," Wells began. "We have something to tell you."

"Oh, Lord. What's wrong?"

"Nothing," he assured her. "It's good news. I mean, I think you might like being a grandma, unless of course you think you're too young, in which case it might be bad news," he joked. He knew very well that his mother wanted nothing more than for him to give her grandchildren.

"Grandma," she squeaked.

"Yes, we've adopted a puppy," he beamed.

Brinley swatted him on the arm. "Stop torturing your mother," she admonished. "I'm pregnant, Mrs. Kennedy."

"Oh, my stars," Ruby exclaimed, getting up from her chair and enveloping Brinley in a hug. "A grandma…I'm going to be a grandma," she cried. "And stop calling me Mrs. Kennedy. It's Mom or Ruby if you prefer. I can't believe this. Finally, I'm going to be a grandma. Let's celebrate. I have a bottle of sparkling cider. I'll go get it." Before she left Ruby hugged her son, kissed his forehead, and headed into the house.

"I think she's happy," Brinley smiled.

"Want to know what will make me happy?" Wells asked.

"I thought you *were* happy," Brinley frowned.

"Deliriously. But I need one more thing."

"And that would be?"

Wells got out of his chair and knelt in front of Brinley. "For you to marry me," he answered, producing a ring from his pocket.

"Wells," she whispered.

"Say yes," he encouraged. "I promise I'll make you the happiest woman on earth. Let's raise our family together, grow old together, and promise to never leave each other's side. I love you so much, Brinley. I can't imagine my life without you."

"On one condition," she smiled.

"Name it," he grinned.

"I don't want a big wedding, just a few friends and your mom. And I don't want to wait."

"Just what I was thinking," he said, slipping the ring on her finger and kissing her knuckles.

Just then Ruby came back out and set the tray with the cider and glasses on the table.

"Mom," he asked. "Do you think Brinley and I could get married next weekend here in your backyard?" he inquired, knowing full well that there would have been nothing better for his mom than to have her only son get married at her home.

Brinley glanced out the window of Ruby's bedroom into the backyard. It was already a magical place, but Wells and JP had worked hard the day before to make it even more beautiful. Toward the back of the property, they built an arch that Ruby had draped in sheer, gauzy material. A string of fairy lights wrapped around the wood shone through the material, setting off the pale blue roses and baby's breath that had been lovingly attached around the fixture. On either side of the arch a pedestal stood, adorned with vases of Verena blue hydrangea flowers with white roses interspersed throughout. The look was stunning and more than she could have hoped for in the short amount of time they had to plan.

It was easy to organize a small catered dinner for the reception and the music was quickly handled by JP and Conrad. Ruby insisted on making them a cake, so the only issue became her dress. Wells planned on wearing a navy suit he had in his closet so he was set, but she was at a loss.

It was only when Ruby intervened and insisted they go out shopping together that her nerves calmed. They ended up going to the local David's Bridal Shop and spent almost an entire afternoon trying dresses on. Brinley was starting to get discouraged until Ruby, handing her a dress and asking her to not judge and try it on, found what she wanted. The second she put it on and looked at herself in the mirror she knew she had found the one.

The dress was clean and modern with a V-neckline, side pockets, and a tea-length skirt that twirled when she walked. The sleeveless dress had an empire waist that showed off her figure, which made her grateful that it was still early in her pregnancy. The ivory satin color shimmered as light bounced off it, making her feel like a princess. Opting not to wear a veil, she curled her hair, pulled back a little on each side and used a diamond-studded bridal clip to hold it in place in the back. When she stepped back to look at the full effect, she was pleased with what she saw and hoped that Wells would be too.

"Oh, honey, you look beautiful," Ruby said as she entered the room. "Wells is a lucky man," she added.

With tears in her eyes, Brinley hugged the older woman. This past week Ruby had been nothing but loving and supportive, which meant more to her than she could ever explain to the woman. "Thanks, Mom," she said simply, knowing how much that word would mean to her.

Dabbing the tears in her eyes, Ruby patted Brinley's shoulder. "Ready, love? Wells is getting impatient."

"I am," she answered.

"Then let's do this. When you hear the music, that's your cue," Ruby explained as she kissed Brinley's cheek and went out to find her seat.

Brinley walked down the steps, making sure to stay hidden from view until she heard the music to *Over And Over Again* by Nathan Sykes start to play. As instructed, she waited until the first verse was sung then started out the back door. Pausing on the deck, she looked to where Wells was standing in front of the arch and inhaled sharply. He was so gorgeous it nearly took her breath away. And he was hers.

Aside from the beautiful flowers all around them, Brinley took in the incredible colorful fall leaves dotting the backyard that added to the joy of the occasion. The cool October day dawned with bright sunshine and a gentle breeze wafted around allowing those in attendance to be more comfortable.

Sitting on chairs sprinkled around the yard were just a few invited guests. Among them were, of course, JP and Conrad as well of several other members of Wells's former Seal team who had been instrumental in saving her. Ruby was sitting beside Chief Kenneth Dubois—too close, Wells thought—and next to them was Detective Bob Morris and his wife. Ten in all, the perfect number for a small wedding.

As Brinley approached the makeshift altar, she realized that Wells had tears in his eyes. It humbled her that he was as moved by the importance of the ceremony as she was. As they spoke their vows, not once did he look away or let go of her hand. When they were instructed to turn to the audience and were introduced as man and wife, there wasn't a dry eye among them.

The simple dinner was served on long tables set up in front of the deck. Soft music played in the background as servers set plates of filet mignon with hollandaise sauce, fresh asparagus, and mashed potatoes in front of each guest. When dinner was completed, Wells and Brinley cut the cake and had their first dance as husband and wife. As the sun began to set, they bid their guests goodbye, thanked them for coming, and made their way to the airport.

They arrived in Aruba the next day. They could have found some place closer off the coast of California for their honeymoon, but the warm sandy beaches of Aruba appealed to them both. When they finally checked in to their hotel, the first thing they did was to change into their swimsuits and lie on the beach outside their private bungalow. They played in the water, napped on the beach, and fed each other snacks they'd bought at a local store.

When the sun began to sink behind the clouds, Wells held out his hand and helped Brinley to her feet. He showered quickly, then when it was her turn, he put together a supper of steaks and vegetables. They ate on the outside deck, taking in the wonderful views of the ocean. With dinner finished, they sat and watched as the stars came out, admiring them as they twinkled in the sky.

After a bit Wells insisted on doing the dishes so while he was doing that, Brinley disappeared into the bedroom to change into the surprise outfit she'd picked up before the wedding. She'd spent far too much money on it, but she was hoping the suggestiveness of it would bolster her confidence. Besides, she needed to ensure there would be no possible way that Wells could refuse her overtures, and this bridal nightgown might just do the trick. Even though her doctor had given them the okay to make love, Wells was still hesitant in an effort to give her time to heal.

When Wells finished the dishes, he called out to Brinley that he would meet her on the deck when she was through. Grabbing the sparkling cider and two glasses, he stepped out onto the deck enjoying the sound of the ocean as the waves washed ashore. He deftly opened the bottle and had just poured their drinks when he heard a noise and looked up. What he saw nearly made him drop the bottle. Brinley was stunning!

"This okay?" she asked with a smile when Wells couldn't seem to get his tongue to work. Stepping out onto the deck she felt like a Roman goddess, especially with the way Wells was staring at her.

The champagne satin material of the nightgown flowed down her body, clinging in all the right places. The gown had a V-neckline in both the front and back and was embroidered with Versailles lace with scalloped lace-trimmed edges. The see-through lace offered tiny glimpses of her smooth skin and beaded nipples. The satin skirt flowed to the floor and was trimmed in the same lace at the bottom. It was sexy and yet classically subtle.

"You're incredible," Wells whispered as he moved toward her and leaned in for a kiss.

"Thank you," she whispered almost shyly.

It seemed strange that not ten days ago she was scared that she was going to die. Now here she was, blissfully happy and married to an amazing man. Life certainly took some strange twists and turns.

Brinley was content for a little while to stand looking out at the water with Wells's arms around her. She tried to ignore the obvious bulge nudging her lower back, but it was getting more difficult. It was clear that he wanted her as desperately as she wanted him, but he seemed insistent on protecting her. Against what she wasn't sure. She knew that the sight of her fading bruises bothered him; in fact, she saw him frown when she stepped to the altar and he noticed them. She'd tried to hide as much as she could with makeup but some of them were just too dark a color to accomplish that. She worked at her facial expressions as well, not wanting a momentary hitch of pain from her ribs to upset him.

But this was their honeymoon, damnit, and she wasn't going to allow him to get away with using her wounds as an excuse.

Turning in his arms, she leaned up, grasped his face between her hands, and planted a kiss on his mouth. When she felt him relax, she pushed her tongue between his lips and nearly did a jig when he matched her move for move. Within minutes they were both gasping for air and rubbing their bodies against each other. She was just starting to revel in it when she felt his body stiffen and he started to pull away.

"Don't you dare," she nearly growled.

"But your inj…"

"If you rob me of my honeymoon, Wells, so help me, I'll never let you forget it. I appreciate that you want to be careful with me but I'm fine. And the doctors have cleared me so you can't use that as an excuse."

"But I…"

Wells stopped short when Brinley grasped him over the material of his shorts. She rubbed gently, then gracefully went to her knees, taking his shorts and boxers as she went down. Within seconds she was cradling him intimately, looking at him as if he was the sweetest treat. What man can possibly resist that?

"You know we're outside, right?" he grinned.

"I'm sure you'll tell me if someone comes along," she answered before taking him into her mouth. They were pretty secluded at the end of the beach so she was fairly certain they were alone.

The feel of her warm mouth on his skin was sheer heaven. Closing his eyes, he inhaled and exhaled slowly, enjoying her ministrations. This woman…his wife…was a wonder to him.

Not wanting for it to end too soon—and knowing it would if she didn't stop—he pulled back until she released him with a soft pop. She frowned at him until he helped her up and kissed her deeply. Before Brinley knew it, Wells turned her to face the ocean and moved her to the railing of the deck and gently pushed on her back until she was leaning over it. He moved her hips until her backside was jutting out and lifted her gown, sweeping the thong panties down her legs. She was a sight to behold, the pale skin of her rounded buttocks shimmering in the moonlight, begging for him to take her.

When he was sure she was braced, he took himself in hand and slowly entered her from behind, watching and listening for any signs of duress from her. When he was fully seated, he sighed in pleasure. It felt amazing to finally be inside her. He'd missed their connection!

"Are you okay?" he asked, kissing the side of her neck.

"More," she begged.

Pushing the material from her shoulders, Wells moved the top part of the nightgown down to her waist, baring her breasts. He played with them as they came to sharp peaks, loving the fullness of them. When she was gasping for air, he began a slow rhythm of pumping in and out, massaging her breasts as he moved. The bliss of being inside her, knowing she was his, and the erotic feeling of being out in the open, hearing the waves and smelling the ocean, it wasn't long before Wells felt himself let go. To his great relief, Brinley was with him, nearly yelling out her release.

They stayed like that for several minutes, catching their breath while looking for any interlopers that might be in the area. When they had calmed and were certain no one else was around, Wells pulled out, sheltering Brinley's body with his.

"Let's go inside. We're not done yet. Not even close," he informed her as a grinning Brinley made for the door.

Chapter Twenty-Eight

Brinley grasped her lower back, massaging the ache as she moved to the next room that needed cleaning. Two more weeks and she and Wells would be able to hold their bundle of joy. Finally! She was tired of waddling around, tired of constantly getting up in the night to go to the bathroom, and tired of the worry she saw in Wells's eyes. No matter how many times she or the doctor told him things were fine, he still worried and still hovered.

They'd been in their new home for six months and Brinley still—much to Wells's dismay—had a tendency to rearrange things. Each time he would go out to his woodworking shop behind the house to work on one of the many orders he'd garnered, he'd come in for lunch and there she'd be, scooting a chair or a coffee table to a different location. It drove him nuts that she couldn't seem to settle on an arrangement. Not that he cared where she put things; he'd just prefer if she would tell him so he could do the moving.

It hadn't taken long for them to find their new home. Within weeks of looking, Brinley came home excited, exclaiming to Wells that she found it. When he went with her to look, he had to admit that she had in fact found the perfect home. It was within two miles of where his mother lived, at the end of a cul-de-sac, with a wooded area next to it and other young families living close. It was perfect, except for the offer that was already pending. On the advice of their realtor, they put an offer in anyway, in case something fell through, and waited to see what would happen. In the meantime, Brinley put her house up for sale and had an offer in just a few days, which she accepted. Wells listed his condo and that too went quickly but they needed to delay the sale until they heard on the new house. As it happened, the financing fell through for the couple who originally offered on the house so Wells and Brinley found themselves moving faster than even they had anticipated.

The picturesque home was a two-story house with four bedrooms and three and a half baths—plenty of room to grow a family. Brinley fell in love with the open-floor plan and state-of-the-art kitchen. She especially loved the detached mini bungalow in the backyard that they made into a woodworking shop, so Wells had space to do what he loved the most and yet still be close.

The month of May brought some unusual, yet necessary, changes to Brinley's life. It had been bothering her that a stranger was buried next to her daughter's ashes. When she spoke with the people who ran the cemetery about the situation, at first they weren't very helpful. Then one day out of the blue they contacted her and mentioned that they learned from the police who the stranger was and although the family had lost contact with him because of his illegal tendencies, they still wanted to retrieve his remains and have them brought back to be buried at their family plot. Brinley was so grateful she nearly wept with relief. A week later she was contacted by the county morgue asking her what she wanted done with Dean's ashes. It had been a while since she had even thought of him, so it was a shock to find out this hadn't been dealt with. Brinley didn't even need to consult with Wells about it; she told the coroner to let the state decide. He'd caused her so much pain that she could care less what became of his ashes.

Wells walked in from the back door to find Brinley with a dust rag in her hand, awkwardly bending over the bookcase to reach the bottom shelf. "What are you doing?" he inquired with a smile. He'd read in one of her pregnancy books about how women "nested" during the late stages of pregnancy. He found her utterly adorable but worried because he felt she should be resting instead of cleaning. He eventually gave up, deciding it was better to just keep an eye on her and not argue.

"I'm almost done," Brinley assured him. "I just have to dust your dad's desk and then everything is complete.

"Until tomorrow," he joked as he walked over to her, kissed her soundly on the lips, and rubbed his hand over her stomach. "Tell your mama to rest," he said conspiratorially to the baby. "I'm going to take a shower. I'll be right out, then you're going to sit while I fix us dinner."

"Fine," she harrumphed. "But stop using the baby to sway me. It won't work now and it won't work when this little tyke is born."

Grinning, Wells headed upstairs to the master bathroom. He took a quick shower then headed back down, knowing full well that if he didn't get a start on dinner that Brinley would do it herself and he really wanted her to rest. Rounding the corner he saw her on the floor by the desk—how she got down there he'd never know—and pulling on the cloth she'd been using to dust.

"What's wrong?" he asked.

"My rag is snagged on something. I can't get it lose. Can you grab me a flashlight?"

Wells took his cell phone out of his pocket, turned the flashlight on, and handed it down to her. "Do you see anything?" he asked after a few seconds.

"It's snagged on a latch of some sort."

"Honey, there's no latch down there. It's probably a loose piece of wood. Leave it for now. I'll take care of it after dinner."

"Oh my God," Brinley exclaimed. "Wells, it is a latch. I just pushed on it and a small drawer opened."

Wells knelt beside Brinley and looked under the desk. To his surprise, Brinley had been correct. A small compartment stood open toward the back of the desk on the right-hand side. The secret latch was so beautifully incorporated into the grain of the wood that he'd never noticed it before. Leave it to his father to make something that intricate and secretive.

He watched as Brinley put her fingers inside the drawer to see if anything was there. He held his breath as she lifted out a small USB drive.

"I don't believe it," she said as she handed it over to Wells. "What do you think it is?"

"Let's find out," he said as he got up and held his hands out to Brinley. "You okay?" he asked when she swayed a little on her feet.

"I'm fine. Let's check it out," she said, taking his hand and pulling him toward the office.

With Brinley sitting on his lap, Wells booted up his computer and waited for the screen to come to life. Inserting the USB, he opened the thumb drive and watched as a series of folders appeared on the screen. Clicking on the first document, he and Brinley sat silently as they read the incriminating words on the display.

"Oh, dear God," Brinley whispered.

Wells remained silent, stunned at the implication of what he was reading. His father had been right all along. And this was the proof. Each document he opened was more damning than the one before it. Spreadsheets of where and to whom money had been disbursed, orders placed and charged for but never received. Kickbacks received and whom they were sent to along with bank account numbers where money was hidden. His father had it all. Every last detail of the horrible men, their deeds, and the people hurt by them. Both James and Dean McGill had been up to their necks in the entire mess.

The final document was a letter to Wells from his dad, explaining how he'd found out about what was happening and the steps he took to collect the evidence he needed to bring the McGills down. Jeremy Kennedy apologized to his son for leaving him so early—for if Wells was reading this letter, he surely had been silenced—and told him how proud he was of him. Jeremy's final request was for Wells to look after his mother, to take care of the woman who had been the love of his life.

"He was killed for trying to do the right thing," Wells said sadly.

Brinley wrapped her arms around Wells and held him close. She knew he had a good idea why his father died—not as a heart attack as was stated—but to have confirmation was something entirely different.

They sat like that for a while until Wells heard her stomach grumble. "Let's get dinner," he murmured as he lifted Brinley off his lap.

"What are we going to do about the thumb drive?" she asked, following him into the kitchen. He was being far too stoic and it was starting to worry her.

"After dinner I'm going to call Chief Dubois and ask for an appointment tomorrow morning. We'll hand over the information to him then."

"You want to wait?" she asked surprised.

"I want to have a nice quiet meal with my wife," Wells informed her. "Tomorrow will come soon enough."

Chapter Twenty-Nine

Today was an important day for Wells so Brinley wanted nothing to distract him from what needed to be done. Not even the labor pains she started having the night before. At first, she'd assumed that it was Braxton Hicks contractions but as the night went on and the pains became stronger and closer together, she knew it wasn't the case. At this point her goal was to get through the appointment this morning at the police department, then she would let Wells know what was happening.

She was still a few weeks out, but it seemed this baby was insistent on making an appearance early. The only saving grace for her was that Wells was so distracted by the upcoming appointment that he hadn't picked up on her distress. She was getting pretty good at racing around a corner when a contraction hit so at this point, he was still clueless. If she estimated correctly, she had plenty of time to be with him during the appointment, make the drive home, grab her bag, and perhaps casually mention to him that they should head to the hospital.

Once they arrived at the police station they were led back to Chief Dubois's office. Detective Morris was there as well and greeted them warmly. Brinley took a step behind Wells as he shook hands with the chief and grabbed her stomach as she inhaled a sharp breath. When Bob Morris noticed her actions and started to speak, she merely shook her head, hoping the man would take the hint and not say anything. Nodding his head with a smile, he stepped back and shook Wells's hand.

"You seemed anxious to speak with us, Wells. What's this all about?" the chief asked.

"You both might want to have a look at this," Wells said, handing the device over to them.

He and Brinley took a seat as Bob joined the chief behind the desk and read the contents as they came up on the screen.

"Holy hell," the chief exclaimed. "Where did you find this?"

"Actually, Brinley found it when she was dusting my father's desk. There was a secret compartment he put in when he built it. I had no idea it was there until she found it."

"This doesn't really change your circumstance, Wells, but at least now we know the truth of how your father died. Your instinct was right on, I'm sorry to say."

"I know," Wells answered.

"The really great news is that now we know the identity of the councilman involved and, I'm sorry to say, a few other people in the city offices. The corruption went a little deeper than I had originally suspected," Detective Morris stated.

"Now, Wells, I have to advise you not to mention this new evidence to anyone for the time being. It could put you and Brinley in the crosshairs of some pretty nasty people. I need you to give us time to get some warrants issued and arrests made," Chief Dubois inserted.

Wells stood up and took Brinley's hand helping her to rise. "You have my word, Chief. Besides, I have more important things to worry about right now. I'm just relieved to leave it in your hands."

"Good thinking," he laughed. "Now, why don't you take this pretty lady out for a bite to eat. I think she deserves a treat for finding the evidence we needed."

Brinley let out a yelp and grabbed on to Wells's hand, panting to relieve the pain of the contraction. "I think I'd rather go to the hospital," she groaned from her bent position.

"Jesus, Brinley, what's wrong?" Wells nearly yelled, panicked that she seemed in so much pain. It was too early!

"She's in labor," Bob said mildly. "For a while now would be my guess."

"Brinley?" Wells questioned as he helped her to her full height. When he saw the admission in his wife's eyes, he wanted to throttle her. "For how long? Why didn't you tell me?"

"You've been worried about that USB thingy, and I wanted to be with you when you brought it in. You know…for support."

"How long?" Wells stressed.

"Last night sometime."

"Christ," Wells exploded. Seeing tears form in her eyes he felt bad for yelling. "No, no…it's okay. We're okay," he immediately placated.

"No, it's not," she cried. "My water just broke."

Seeing that Wells was slightly unhinged, both the chief and Bob ushered them out of the office and to the front door.

In a calm voice Bob told Wells to get Brinley in the car. "Are you okay to drive to the hospital?" he asked. When Wells nodded yes, he continued. "Wait right here with the car running. I'm going to get my car and pull in front of you. I'll turn the lights and siren on, and you just follow me, okay?"

"We're fine," Wells hesitated as he reclaimed his senses and helped Brinley into the passenger seat. "I got this."

"Take the escort," the chief laughed. "It's the least we can do," he insisted waving them off.

Chapter Thirty

WELLS SAT IN the chair by Brinley's bed and watched as his wife slept peacefully. His son lay in his arms, wrapped in a pale blue blanket, a little knit cap on his head. The beauty of the moment brought tears to his eyes. In a million years he would have never thought that when his military career ended he would have something else in his life that meant even more to him.

Brinley's labor had been hard. Many times he begged her to give up and let them do a C-section but she adamantly refused, insisting that they let her try as long as the baby was okay. She'd been in active labor for nearly twelve hours before finally, she was able to give birth naturally. From the beginning they both had insisted on not knowing the baby's gender so it was unadulterated joy when the doctor announced that it was a boy. He had a son. He was humbled beyond belief to be able to witness his child being born. Brinley had insisted that his mom also share in this experience, simply adding to the moment. He wasn't sure that life could get any better.

Watching Brinley struggle to give birth had been hard. He was still reeling from everything they'd gone through and how close he'd come to losing her. Wells worked at making sure that Brinley never saw how scared he felt sometimes. When something so amazing comes into your life, it's more terrifying to imagine losing it.

"Okay to visit?" a voice whispered from the door.

Wells turned and nodded when he saw that it was JP. Motioning him in Wells had to grin when he saw the bouquet of balloons he was carrying as well as a four-foot, blue, stuffed teddy bear. "These are from Conrad and me," JP said as he set the bear down and arranged the balloons before going over to grasp Wells's shoulder and peek at the baby. "Congratulations, man," he whispered so as not to wake Brinley or the baby. "He's a handsome one."

"Thanks," Wells answered.

"How's she doing? Your mom said it was a struggle for a while."

"It was, but you know Brinley. She's strong," Wells said proudly.

"That she is. So, have you decided on a name yet? We can't keep calling him Lil' Tyke, you know," JP informed him as he reached over and touched the baby's tiny hand.

"Not yet."

"JP's a good name. Strong…trustworthy…handsome."

"I'll throw it in the ring," Wells grinned. "Want to hold him?"

"Naw, not this time. He's too new. I'll let you break him in first. Look, I'm going to head out. I just wanted to say hello and congratulations. Give Brinley my love. Conrad and I will stop back in later."

"Thanks, JP. For everything," Wells said sincerely.

"Always," JP said as he fist bumped Wells's free hand and quietly left.

Wells had just sat down and settled the baby in his arms when he heard another sound from the doorway. Thinking it was one of the nurses coming in to check on Brinley and the baby, he was surprised to see his mother. "Mom, what are you doing back? I thought you were going to try and get some rest. You were here until late last night."

Ruby took in the sight of her only child holding his son. With tears in her eyes, she walked over and kissed two cheeks, one rough with whiskers and one soft and smooth. Glancing at the bed she merely smiled. "I know. I tried but I couldn't stay away knowing my grandson was here and I wasn't. How's Brinley? Poor thing had such a hard time of it."

"I'm fine, Mom," Brinley said sleepily from the bed. "You don't have to worry."

"I'm allowed to worry," Ruby smiled as she went over to the side of the bed and kissed her daughter-in-law. "Can I get you anything, honey?"

"No, I'm good." Looking over to see her husband holding their son she smiled. "Really good."

While Wells beamed at the two women staring at him, Brinley shook her head. "Wells," she said softly. "Give the baby to your mom." She knew Ruby was too polite to ask to hold him but by the look in her eyes it was clear she couldn't wait to get her hands on her grandson.

"Oh, sorry, Mom. I guess I should share him."

When Ruby had her grandson in her arms. she looked at Wells standing next to the bed holding Brinley's hand and asked, "Have you decided on a name yet?"

The hospital had been asking that same question since the moment the baby had been born. With everything going on, Wells didn't feel it was necessary to push Brinley. They had discussed a lot of names, both male and female, but hadn't really decided on any one in particular.

"We're not really sure yet…" he began.

"I have one," Brinley spoke up.

"What were you thinking?" Wells asked curiously. He really wasn't all that picky, as long as it wasn't anything like Butch or Alastor.

"Ian Jeremy Kennedy," she announced softly.

"Ian Jeremy," Ruby repeated with tears spilling from her eyes as she nuzzled the baby's head.

Wells couldn't speak beyond the knot in his throat. He was amazed and touched that this beautiful, courageous woman—his wife and the mother of his son—who had the gentlest of souls, wanted to honor both their fathers in the naming of their son. It was perfect!

About the Author

P. L. Byers is the author of a dozen novels and counting, including her Out of the Darkness Series and Sister's of the Heart Trilogy. She is a member of RWA (Romance Writers of America), NERW (New England Romance Writers), and PAN (Published Authors Network).

Her love for creating her characters and the stories behind them has been an all-consuming ambition.

"If any of my readers get a tenth of the enjoyment in reading my books as I do in writing them, then all the time and effort put into this dream will make it all worthwhile," she writes.

P. L. Byers lives in Franklin, Massachusetts with her kind and patient husband and two incredibly spoiled cats.

You can contact P. L. Byers through her website at www.plbyers.com or e-mail her at paula@plbyers.com. You can also follow her on Facebook at www.facebook.com/PLByers.

Lightning Source UK Ltd.
Milton Keynes UK
UKHW011841060921
390144UK00008B/554/J

9 781665 535779